FACES OF FEAR

Further Titles by Graham Masterton from Severn House

BLACK ANGEL
DEATH TRANCE
MANITOU
MIRROR
NIGHT PLAGUE
NIGHT WARRIORS
THE SWEETMAN CURVE

Also in this series
FORTNIGHT OF FEAR
FLIGHTS OF FEAR
FACES OF FEAR

FACES OF FEAR

Graham Masterton

SEVERN SH HOUSE

This first world edition published in Great Britain 1996 by
SEVERN HOUSE PUBLISHERS LTD of
9–15 High Street, Sutton, Surrey SM1 1DF.
First published in the USA 1996 by
SEVERN HOUSE PUBLISHERS INC of
595 Madison Avenue, New York, NY 10022.

Copyright © Graham Masterton 1996

British Library Cataloguing in Publication Data
Graham Masterton
  Faces of Fear
  I. Title
  823.914 [FS]

  ISBN 0-7278-4854-2

Typeset by Hewer Text Composition Services, Edinburgh.
Printed and bound in Great Britain by
Hartnolls Ltd, Bodmin, Cornwall.

INTRODUCTION

Fear comes in many guises. It can wear the face of a stranger, watching you with unnatural interest. It can wear the face of a long-lost friend. Sometimes its face can be imaginary – a glowering beast who appears in your wallpaper, or in the whorls of woodwork in your closet, when you're trying to sleep. At other times, it can press itself pale and horrified right against your window.

In this new collection of stories. I have brought together many different faces of fear, from many different parts of the world. Some of the faces are subtle. Some are erotic. Others are out-and-out horrific.

I wanted to show that life always has more than one face to it – that there are other existences and other realities some of them terrifying, but some of them magical and irresistibly alluring. I wanted to show how people from all kinds of different cultures share the same fundamental fear – the fear of parallel worlds where the dead still walk, and any kind of horror is conceivable.

I wanted to show that not everything in life is what it appears to be, and that we should always be wary of taking things on face value. Very wary indeed.

In *Faces of Fear*, you will find stories of Celtic terrors – sinister strangers who can entrap you with guile and charm, and by offering you your heart's desire. Fathers and brothers from Wales – long dead, but walking through the foggy valleys.

You will find stories set in rural England, where the face that pursues you through the woods is too terrible to look at. You will visit France, too, where even the face that you adore will frighten you to death.

In America, you will meet the faces of hideous greed and the faces of terrible self-destruction. You will also confront one of the most malevolent faces of Native American magic.

Even in Scotland, you will come across a miraculous face that embodies the greatest fear of all – the fear of God.

Before you read these stories, take a long look at your own face in the mirror. This, too, will become a face of fear.

And when you've finished, take another look – not just to see how much you've changed, but also to make sure that there is no other face beside you . . . that you're really alone.

The danger is not so much that you will forget the faces of fear. The danger is that they will never forget *you*.

Graham Masterton.

CONTENTS

Evidence of Angels   1
The Hungry Moon   29
Grief   55
The Secret Shih-Tan   103
Men of Maes   139
Fairy Story   163
Suffer Kate   225
Spirit-Jump   257

Evidence of Angels

Edinburgh, Scotland

Edinburgh is my family birthplace, so of course I always feel a great affinity for it, quite apart from the fact that it is one of the finest and most ancient cities in Europe. The rock of Edinburgh has been a fortress since Roman times, and its imposing castle is still an essential tourist attraction, especially for its wide views over Leith, the Firth of Forth and the hills of Fife.

The backbone of old Edinburgh is the street which runs along the steep ridge from the castle to Holyrood Palace – variously called Canongate. Netherbow, High Street, Lawnmarket and Castle Hill – but together known as the 'Royal Mile'. The houses along this street are very old and lofty, arranged in a series of closes. A close which is wide enough to admit a carriage (2 m) is called a 'wynd'.

Apart from its political and social history as Scotland's capital, Edinburgh is also the seat of Scotland's presbyterian religion. And it is religion – with all of its glory, and all of its awesome trappings – that brings us into confrontation with our first face of fear.

EVIDENCE OF ANGELS

Before he was born she loved him with a fierce and sisterly love, and called him Alice. Her mother let her rest her head against her stomach to hear his heart beating inside her, and sometimes she felt the strong fleshy ripple of his kicking. With some of the money that her parents had given her for her thirteenth birthday, she went to Jenner's and bought him a little lace-collared dress in the Stewart tartan, and kept it hidden to surprise him on the day that he was due to be born.

She was so sure that he was going to be a girl that she played out imaginary scenes in her head, in which she taught Alice her first ballet steps; and in which they danced the opening scenes of *La Fille Mal Gardée* to amuse their mother and father. And she imagined taking her for walks on winter mornings up to the Castle Mound, where strangers would stop and coo at Alice and think that Gillie was Alice's mother, instead of her older sister.

But one January morning she heard her mother crying out; and there was a lot of running up and downstairs. And father drove mother off to the Morningside Clinic, while the snow swarmed around them like white bees, and eventually swallowed them up.

She spent the day with Mrs McPhail, who was their cleaner, in her neat cold house in Rankeillor Street, with its ticking clocks and its strong smell of lavender-polish. Mrs

McPhail was tiny and disagreeable, and kept twitching her head like a chicken. She gave Gillie a bowl of greyish stew for lunch, with onions in it, and watched and twitched while Gillie miserably pushed it around and around, and the snow on the kitchen windowsill heaped higher and higher.

Mrs McPhail's rotary washing-line stood at an angle in the centre of her back-yard, and that was clogged up with snow, too. It looked to Gillie like a seraph, with its wings spread; and as she looked, the sun suddenly broke out from behind the clouds, and the seraph shone, dazzling and stately, yet tragic, too, because it was earthbound now, and now could never hope to return to heaven.

"Do you no care for your dinner?" asked Mrs McPhail. She wore a beige sweater covered with pills of worn wool, and a brown beret, even indoors. Her face made Gillie think of a plate of lukewarm porage, with skin on, into which somebody had dropped two raisins for eyes, and drawn a downward curve with the edge of their spoon, for a mouth.

"I'm sorry Mrs McPhail. I suppose I'm not very hungry."

"Good food going to waste. That's best lamb, and barley."

"I'm sorry," she said.

But then, unexpectedly, the disagreeable Mrs McPhail smiled at her, and said, "Don't fash yourself, darling. It's not every day that you get a new baby, now, is it? Now what do you think it'll be? A boy or a girl?"

The thought of it being a boy had never entered Gillie's head. "We're going to call her Alice," she said.

"But what if she's a he?"

Gillie put down her fork. The surface of her stew was floating with small globules of fat. But it wasn't the stew that made her feel nauseous. It was the unexpected idea that her mother might have been harbouring a brother, instead of a sister. A brother! A son and heir! Wasn't that what grandma had always complained about, every time that they visited her? "Such a pity you never had a son and heir, Donald, to carry on your father's name."

A son and heir wouldn't want to learn ballet-steps. A son and heir wouldn't want to play with her doll's house, which she had carefully brought down from the attic, and fitted with new carpets, and a dining table, and three plates of tiny plaster cast meals with sausages and fried eggs.

She had saved for so long for that tartan dress. Supposing the baby was a boy? She flushed at her own stupidity.

"You look feverish, pet," said Mrs McPhail. "Don't eat your dinner if you don't feel like it. I'll warm it up for later. How about some nice pandowdie?"

Gillie shook her head. "No, thank you," she whispered, and tried to smile. In the backyard, the sun had vanished, and the sky was growing grim; but the rotary clothes-line looked more like a wrecked angel than ever. She could hardly bear to think of it standing there, throughout the night, unloved, and abandoned, and unable to fly.

"Let's watch telly," said Mrs McPhail. "I can't miss *Take The High Road*. I wouldnie have a thing to talk about tomorrow, doon the bingo."

They sat on the clumpy brown sofa and watched television on Mrs McPhail's blurry ex-rental television set. But every now and then, Gillie would look over her shoulder at the seraph in the backyard, watching his wings grow larger and thicker as the snow fell faster still. Perhaps he would fly, after all.

Mrs McPhail was noisily sucking a humbug. "What do you keep keekin' at, pet?"

Gillie was embarrassed at first. But somehow she felt that she could tell Mrs McPhail almost anything, and it wouldn't matter. It wouldn't get 'reported back', the way that her grandma had once reported her comments about school back to her mother and father.

"It's your clothesline. It looks like an angel."

Mrs McPhail twisted herself around and stared at it. "With wings, you mean?"

"It's only the snow."

"But you're right, pet. That's just what it looks like. An angel. Seraphim and cherubim. But they always arrive, don't you know, when a baby arrives. It's their duty to take good care of them, those little ones, until they can stand on their own two feet."

Gillie smiled and shook her head. She didn't understand what Mrs McPhail was talking about, although she didn't like to say so.

"Every child has a guardian angel. You have yours; your new baby has hers. Or his. Whatever it's turned to be."

It has to be Alice, thought Gillie, desperately. *It can't be a son and heir.*

"Would you like a sweetie?" asked Mrs McPhail, and offered her the sticky, crumpled bag.

Gillie shook her head. She was trying to give up sweeties. If she couldn't make the grade as a ballerina, she wanted to be a supermodel.

By four o'clock it was dark. Her father came at five o'clock and stood in the porch of Mrs McPhail's house with snow on his shoulders and whisky on his breath. He was very tall and thin, with a tiny sandy mustache and bright grey eyes like the shells you could find on Portobello Beach before they went dry. His hair was thinning on top and it was all sprigged up.

6

"I've come to take you home," he said. "Your mum's well and the baby's well and everything's fine."

"You've been celebrating, Mr Drummond," said Mrs McPhail, with mock disapproval. "But you've every right. Now tell us what it was and how much it weighed."

Dad laid both his hands on Gillie's shoulders and looked right into her eyes. "You've a baby brother, Gillie. He weighed seven pounds six ounces and we're going to call him Toby."

Gillie opened her mouth but she couldn't speak. Toby? Who was Toby? And what had happened to Alice? She felt as if Alice had been secretly spirited away, and her warm place in her mother's womb given to some strange and awful boy-baby whom she didn't know at all, the human equivalent of a cuckoo.

"That's grand!" said Mrs McPhail. "No wonder you've been taking the malt, Mr Drummond! And a cigar, too, I shouldn't be surprised!"

"Well, Gillie?" asked her father. "Isn't it exciting! Think of all the fun you'll be able to have, with a baby brother!"

Gillie was shaking with a genuine feeling of grief. Her eyes filled with tears and they ran down her cheeks into her tartan scarf. *Alice! They've taken you away! They never let you live!* She had thought of Alice so often that she even knew what she looked like, and what they were going to play together, and what they would talk about. But now there was no Alice, and there never would be.

"Gillie, what's the matter?" her father asked her. "Are you feeling all right?"

Gillie's throat felt as if she'd swallowed one of Mrs McPhail's humbugs without sucking it. "I bought—" she began, and then she had to stop because her lungs hurt and every breath was a painful sob. "I bought – I bought her a dress! I spent my birthday money on it!"

Her father laughed and gave her a hug. "There now, don't you go worrying your wee head about that! We'll go back to the shop and swap it for a romper-suit, or maybe some trews! How about that? Come on now, this is such a happy day! No more greeting now, you promise?"

Gillie sniffed and sniffed again and wiped her eyes with her woolly gloves.

"Girls of that age," said Mrs McPhail, sagely. "She's been good today, though. She didn't eat much of her lunch, but she's an angel."

They crossed Clerk Street in the whirling snow. Her father had parked outside the Odeon Cinema and already the car was beginning to look like an igloo on wheels. The Odeon was showing *Alice In Wonderland* and Gillie could almost believe that it wasn't a coincidence at all, but that the cinema management had arranged it with her parents in order to mock her.

They drove back toward the centre of the city. Above Princes Street, the castle rock was scarcely visible through the blizzard, and last-minute shoppers trudged along the gritty, salted pavements like lost souls struggling through a dream from which they could never wake up.

A year passed and it was winter again. She sat in front of her dressing table mirror with a tablecloth on her head and wondered what it would be like to be a nun. She liked the look of herself as a nun. She was very thin, very small-boned for fourteen, with a pale complexion and large dark eyes – eyes that were rather soulful and droopy the way that some Scottish eyes are. She could work among the sick and homeless, selflessly bandaging their sores and giving them drinks of water.

The only trouble was, nuns had to give up men and she was very keen on John McLeod in the lower sixth, even though he had never noticed her (as far as she knew, anyway.) John McLeod was very tall with raging red hair and he was the captain of curling. She had gone to watch him play and once she had given him a winter-warmer. He had popped it in his mouth and said, "Ta."

The other trouble was that becoming a nun was a very Roman Catholic sort of thing to do and the Drummond family were Church of Scotland through and through.

She stood up and went to the window. The sky was the colour of pale gum, and the gardens of Charlotte Square were filled with snow.

"What do you think, Alice?" she asked. Alice was still alive, somewhere in the back of Gillie's mind somewhere dark and well-protected. She knew that if she ever forgot about Alice, then Alice would cease to exist, completely, as if she had never been thought of.

You want to become a nun? Alice replied. *Do it secretly. Take your holy orders without telling anybody.*

"But what's the point of that? What's the point of becoming a nun if nobody else knows?"

God will know. Devote your life to serving God and honouring the Virgin Mary, and to helping your fellow human-beings even if they're drunk in doorways, and you will be rewarded in heaven.

"But what if John McCleod asks me to the pictures?"

In that case you may renounce your nunly vow, at least for one night.

She was still looking out of the window with the tablecloth on her head when her father unexpectedly came into her bedroom. "What's up with you?" he asked. "Are you playing at ghosts?"

Gillie dragged off the tablecloth and blushed.

9

"Your mother wants you to feed Toby his lunch while she gets the washing done."

"Do I have to? I'm supposing to be finishing my homework."

"Where? What homework? I don't see any homework. Come on, Gillie, mum's awful busy with the house to keep and Toby to take care of. I do expect you to lend a hand."

Gillie reluctantly followed her father downstairs. They lived in a large four-storey house in Charlotte Square which they had inherited from mum's parents when they died and which they could barely afford to keep up. Most of the decorations were still unchanged from granny and grandfather's day: brown floral wallpaper and brown velvet curtains, and large gloomy paintings of stags at bay. About the most cheerful picture was a view of Ben Buie in a thunderstorm.

Her mother was in the large, yellow-tiled kitchen, strapping Toby into his highchair. She was slender and slight, like Gillie, but she was fair-haired rather than dark, with very sharp blue eyes. Toby had inherited her fairness and her eyes, and he had a mop of curly blond hair as fine as cornsilk, which her mother refused to have cut. Daddy didn't like it much because he thought it made Toby look like a girl; but Gillie knew better. Alice would have been gentle and dark, like her, and they would have spoken together in giggles and whispers.

"His hotpot's ready," said mum, and gave Gillie the open jar, wrapped in a cloth because it was hot. Gillie drew up a chair at the large pine kitchen table and stirred the jar with a teaspoon. Toby smacked his fat little hands together and bounced up and down on his bottom. He was always trying to attract Gillie's attention but Gillie knew who he was and she didn't take any notice. He was a cuckoo. Dear dark Alice had never been allowed to see the light of day, and here was this fat curly *thing* sitting in her place. He even slept in Alice's crib.

Gillie spooned up pureed hotpot and put it up against Toby's lips. The instant Toby tasted it he turned his head away. Gillie tried again, and managed to push a little bit into his mouth, but he promptly spat it out again, all down his clean bib.

"Mum, he doesn't like it."

"Well, he has to eat it. There's nothing else."

"Come on, cuckoo," Gillie cajoled him, trying another spoonful. She held his head so that he wouldn't turn away, and squeezed his fat little cheeks together so that he *had* to open his mouth. Then she pushed the whole spoonful onto his tongue.

There was a long moment of indignant spluttering, while Toby grew redder and redder in the face. Then he let out a scream of protest, and hotpot poured out of his mouth and sprayed all over the sleeve of Gillie's jumper.

Gillie threw down the spoon in fury. "You cuckoo!" she screamed at him. "You horrible fat cuckoo! You're disgusting and I hate you!"

"*Gillie!*" her mother protested.

"I don't care! I hate him and I'm not feeding him! He can die of starvation for all I care! I don't know why you ever wanted him!"

"Gillie, don't you dare say such a thing!"

"I dare and I don't care!"

Mum unbuckled Toby from his highchair, picked him up and shushed him. "If you don't care you'd better get to your room and stay there for the rest of the day with no tea. Let's see how *you* like a bit of starvation!"

It started to snow again. Thick, tumbling flakes from the Firth of Forth.

"They really believe that I don't know what they did to you, Alice."

You must forgive them, for they know not what they do.

"I don't want to forgive them. I hate them. Most of all I hate them for what they did to you."

But you're a nun now. You've taken holy vows. You must forgive them in the name of the Father, and of the Son and of the Holy Spirit amen.

Gillie spent the afternoon lying on her bed reading *Little Faith* which was a novel about a nun who started a mission in the South Seas and fell in love with a gun-runner. She had read it twice already, but she still loved the scene where the nun, who has fasted for five days and five nights as a penance for her passionate feelings, is witness to a miraculous vision of St Theresa, "incandescent as the sun", who forgives her for feeling like a woman.

At five o'clock she heard her mother carrying Toby upstairs for his bath. At half-past five she heard mummy singing to him in his bedroom, across the corridor. She sang him the same lullaby that she always used to sing for Gillie, when she was small, and the sound of it made Gillie feel even more depressed and left out. She turned her face to the wall and stared miserably at the wallpaper. It was supposed to be roses, but it seemed to have a sly hooded face in it, medieval-looking and misshapen, like a leper.

"Dance to your daddy, my little babby. Dance to your daddy, my little lamb. You shall have a fishy, in a little dishy. You shall have a fishy when the boat comes in . . ."

Not long after her father opened her door. "Are you ready to say that you're sorry?" he asked her.

Gillie didn't answer. Her father waited at the door for a while, and then came in and sat on the side of the bed. He laid his hand gently on her arm, and said, "This is not like you, Gillie. You're not jealous of Toby, are you? You don't have to be. We love you just as much as ever. I know that mummy's busy with Toby a lot of the time, but she still cares for you, and so do I."

But what about me? said Alice.

"How about saying you're sorry, and coming down for some tea? There's fish fingers tonight."

You never cared about me.

"Come on, Gillie, what do you say?"

"*You never cared about me! You wanted me dead!*"

Her father stared at her in disbelief. "Wanted you dead? What put such a thought into your head? We love you; we wouldn't have had you otherwise; and if you want to know the truth you would have stayed our only child, and we would have been glad of it, if only Toby hadn't been conceived by accident. We didn't mean to have him, but we did, and now he's here, and we love him. Just the same way that we love you."

Gillie sat up in bed with reddened eyes. "Accident?" she said. "Accident? Try telling Alice that Toby was an accident!"

"Alice? Who's Alice?"

"*You killed her!*" Gillie screamed. "*You murdered her! You murdered her and she never lived!*"

Alarmed, angry, her father stood up. "Now, come on, Gillie. I want you to calm down. Let me call mummy and we'll have a wee chat."

"I don't want to talk to either of you! You're horrible! I hate you! Go away!"

Her father hesitated for a moment. Then he said, "The best thing for you to do, my girl, is to have your bath and get yourself to bed. We'll talk some more in the morning."

"I don't want your stupid bath."

"Then go to sleep dirty. It makes no difference to me."

She lay on her bed listening to the noises in the house. She could hear her mother and father talking; and then the bath running. The cistern roared and whistled just above her room. She heard doors opening and closing, and the burbling of the television in her parents' bedroom. Then the door was closed and all the lights were switched off.

Outside the window, the city was so thickly-felted in snow that it was totally silent, from Davidson's Mains to Morningside, and Gillie could almost have believed that everyone was dead, except for her.

She was woken by a bright light dancing on the wallpaper. She opened her eyes and frowned at it for a while, not quite sure where she was, or whether she was sleeping or waking. The light quivered and trembled and danced from side to side. Sometimes it was like a wide squiggly line and then it would suddenly tie a knot in itself, so that it formed the shape of a butterfly.

Gillie sat up. She was still fully dressed and her leg had gone dead because she had been sleeping in a funny position. The light was coming from under her door. First of all it was dazzling and then it was dim. It danced and skipped and changed direction. Then it retreated for a while, so that all she could see was a faint reflected glow.

Oh, no! she thought. The house is on fire!

She climbed off her bed and limped dead-legged to the door. She felt the doorknob to see if it was hot. The Fire Brigade had come to the school to give them all a lecture on do's and don'ts, and she knew that she wasn't to open the door if it was hot. Fire feeds on oxygen like a babby feeds on milk.

But the doorknob was cold, and the door-panels were cold. Cautiously, Gillie turned the knob, and opened the door, and eased herself into the corridor. Toby's room was directly opposite; and the light was shining from all around Toby's door. At times it was so intense that she could scarcely look at it, and it shone through every crevice, and even through the keyhole.

She sniffed. The odd thing was that she couldn't smell smoke. And there was none of that crackling sound that you normally get with a fire.

She approached Toby's door and dabbed the doorknob with her fingertip. That, too, was quite cold. There was no fire burning in Toby's room. For a moment, she became dreadfully frightened. She had a cold, sliding feeling in her stomach as if she had swallowed something really disgusting and knew that she was going to sick it up again. If it wasn't a fire in Toby's room, what was it?

She was just about to run to her parents' room when she heard an extraordinary noise. A thick, soft, rustling noise; and then the sound of Toby gurgling and giggling.

He's laughing, said Alice. He must be all right.

"I wish it had been a fire. I wish he was dead."

No you don't; and neither do I. You're a nun now; you're in holy orders. Nuns forgive everything. Nuns understand everything. Nuns are the brides of Christ.

She opened Toby's door.

And *Holy Mary*! cried Alice.

The sight that met her eyes was so dramatic and so dazzling that she fell to her knees on the carpet, her mouth wide open in disbelief.

In the centre of Toby's nursery stood a tall white

15

figure. It was so blindingly bright that Gillie had to shield her eyes with the back of her hand. It was so tall that it almost touched the ceiling, and it was dressed in swathes of brilliant white linen, and it seemed to have huge folded wings on its back. It was impossible for Gillie to tell if it were a man or a woman. It was so bright that she couldn't clearly see its face, but she could vaguely distinguish two eyes. floating in the brilliance like chicken embryos floating in egg-white; and the curve of a smile.

But what made Gillie tremble more than anything else was the fact that Toby was out of his crib, and standing on his cribside rug, *standing*, with this tall, dazzling creature holding his little hands for him.

"Toby," she whispered. "Oh God, Toby."

But all Toby did was turn toward her and smile his cheekiest smile, and take two unsteady steps across the rug, while the dazzling creature helped him to balance.

Gillie slowly rose to her feet. The creature looked at her. Although it was so bright, she could see that it wasn't staring at her aggressively. In fact there was something in its eyes that seemed to be appealing for understanding; or at least for calm. But then it lifted Toby up in its arms, right up in the air in its brilliant, flaring arms, and Gillie's composure fell apart like a jigsaw falling out of its box.

"*Mum!*" she screamed, running up the corridor and beating on her parents' bedroom door. "Mummy there's an angel in Toby's room! Mum, mum, mum, come quick! There's an angel in Toby's room!'

Her father and mother came bursting out of the bedroom ruffled and bleary and hardly knowing where they were going. They ran to Toby's nursery and Gillie ran after them.

And there he was, tucked up in his blue-and-yellow

16

blanket, sucking his thumb. Content, curly, and right on the edge of falling to sleep.

Dad turned and looked at Gillie with a serious face.

"I saw an angel," she said. "I'm not making it up, I promise you. It was teaching Toby to walk."

Dr Vaudrey laced his fingers together and swung himself from side to side in his black leather armchair. Outside his window there was a view of a grey brick wall, streaked with snow. He had a dry pot plant on his desk and a photograph of three plain-looking children in sweaters that were too small for them. He was half-Indian, and he wore very thick black-framed glasses and his black hair was brushed back straight from his forehead. Gillie thought that his nose looked like an aubergine. Same colour. Same shape.

"You know something, Gillie, at your age religious delusions are very common. To find a faith and to believe in its manifestations is a very strong desire for adolescent young women."

"I saw an angel," said Gillie. "It was teaching Toby to walk."

"How did you know it was an angel, what you saw? Did it say to you, 'Hallo, excuse me, I am an angel and I have just popped in to make sure that your baby brother doesn't have to scurry about on his hands and knees for the rest of his life?'"

"It didn't say anything. But I knew what it was."

"You say you knew – but how? This is the point that I am trying to make to you."

Gillie lowered her eyes. Her hands were resting in her lap and somehow they didn't even look like hers. "The fact is I'm a nun."

Dr Vaudrey swung around to face her. "Did I hear what you said correctly? You are a *nun*?"

17

"In secret, yes."

"An undercover nun, is that what you're saying?"

Gillie nodded.

"May I ask to which order you belong?"

"It doesn't have a name. It's my own order. But I've given my life to God and the Blessed Virgin and to suffering humanity even if they're drunk in doorways."

Dr Vaudrey slowly took off his spectacles and looked across his desk at her with infinite sympathy, even though her head was lowered and she couldn't see him. "My dear young lady," he said, "you have the most laudable aims in life; and it is not for me to say what you saw or what you didn't see."

"I saw an angel."

Dr Vaudrey swung himself around in the opposite direction. "Yes, my dear. I believe that you probably did."

The young minister was waiting for her in the library. He was stocky, with thinning hair and fleshy ears, but she thought he was really quite good-looking for a minister. He wore a horrible sweater with reindeer leaping all round it and brown corduroy trousers.

"Sit down," he said, indicating a dilapidated sofa covered with cracked red leather. "Would you care for some coffee? Or maybe some Irn Bru? Mind you I'm fairly sure the Irn Bru's flat. They bought it in two Christmasses ago, and it's been sitting in the sideboard ever since."

Gillie sat pale and demure at the very far end of the sofa and gave the minister nothing more than a quick negative shake of her head.

He sat astride a wheelback chair and propped his arms across the top of it. "I can't say that I blame you. The coffee's no good, either."

There was a long silence between them. The library

18

clock ticked so wearily that Gillie kept expecting it to stop, although it didn't.

"I suppose I ought to introduce myself," said the young minister. "I'm Duncan Callander, but you can call me Duncan if you want. Most of my friends called me Doughnuts. You know – Duncan Doughnuts?"

Another long silence. Then Duncan said, "You've seen an angel, then? In the flesh so to speak?" Gillie nodded.

"This Doctor Vaudrey . . . this psychiatrist . . . he thinks that you've been suffering some stress. It's partly due to your age, you see. Your mind and your body are going through some tremendous changes. It's only natural to look for something more to believe in than your parents and your schoolteachers. With some girls it's a pop group; with other girls it's God. But Doctor Vaudrey thought your case was very interesting. He's had girls with religious visions before. But none like yours. He said he could almost believe that you really saw what you said you saw."

He took out his handkerchief and made an elaborate ritual out of wiping his nose. "That's why he passed you onto your own minister, and why your own minister passed you onto me. I'm a bit of specialist when it comes to visions."

"I saw an angel," Gillie repeated. She felt that she had to keep on saying it until they believed her. She would go on saying it for the rest of her life, if necessary. "It was helping Toby to walk."

Duncan said, "It was six-and-a-half to seven feet tall, dazzling white, and you could just about make out its eyes and its mouth. It may have had wings but you're not at all sure about that."

Gillie turned around and stared at him. "How did you know that? I haven't told that to anybody."

"You didn't have to. Yours is the twenty-eighth sighting since 1973, and every single one sounds exactly like yours."

Gillie could hardly believe what she was hearing. "You mean – *other* people have seen them – as well as me?"

Duncan reached out and took hold of her hand and squeezed it. "Many other people, apart from you. It's not at all uncommon. The only uncommon thing about *your* seeing an angel is that you're just an ordinary girl, if you can forgive me for saying so. Most of the other manifestations have come to deeply religious people, ministers and missionaries and such, people who have devoted all of their life to their church."

"I have, too," Gillie whispered.

Duncan gave her an encouraging smile. "You have, too?"

"I took holy orders."

"Where did you do this? At St Agnes?"

Gillie shook her head. "In my bedroom."

Duncan laid his hand on her shoulder. "Then you're a very exceptional novice indeed. And you must be pure of heart, and filled with love, or else you couldn't have seen what you saw."

"Are angels dangerous?" asked Gillie. "Toby won't get hurt, will he?"

"Quite the opposite, as far as I know. In all of the sightings of angels that I've read about, they've been protecting people, particularly children. We don't really know for sure whether they come from heaven, or whether they're some kind of visible energy that comes out of the human mind. All kinds of people have been trying to prove their existence for years. Physicists, bishops, spiritualists . . . you name them. Just think what a spectacular boost it would be if the church could prove that they were real, and that they had been sent by God!"

He reached across his desk and picked up a book with several marked pages in it. "You see these pictures? This is the closest that anybody has ever come to proving that angels exist. For forty years, pediatric studies of babies taking their first steps have proved beyond a shadow of doubt that they are technically in defiance of all the laws of physics when they begin to toddle. They don't have the physical strength, they don't have the balance. And yet – miraculously – they do it.

"In 1973 a team of doctors set up an experiment at Brigham & Women's Hospital in Boston, in America, using children who were just on the verge of walking. They took ultra-violet and infra-red photographs . . . and here, you can see the results. In at least five of these pictures, there's a tall shadowy shape which appears to be holding the toddler's hands."

Gillie studied them closely, with a prickling feeling down her back, as if centipedes were crawling inside her jumper. The shapes were very dim, and their eyes were barely visible. But they were just the same as the dazzling figure who had visited Toby's bedroom.

"Why hasn't anybody said anything about this before?" she asked. "If there have been twenty-seven other sightings, apart from mine, why hasn't anybody said so?"

Duncan closed the book. "Church politics. The Roman Catholics didn't want the sightings mentioned in case they prove not to be angels, after all, but simply some sort of human aura. And the Church of Scotland didn't want them mentioned because they frown on miracles and superstition and hocus-pocus. Nobody said anything because they were all monks or nuns or ordained

21

clergy, and they were under strict instructions from their superiors to keep their visions to themselves."

"But I'm not a real nun! I could say something about it, and nobody could stop me!"

Duncan said, "First of all I have to speak to the kirk elders, to see what they think about it. After all, if a statement is made to the effect that one of our parishioners has witnessed an angel, then the church is going to be closely involved in all of the publicity that's bound to follow."

"You do believe me, though, don't you?" said Gillie. "I'm not mad or anything. I really saw it and it was really there."

"I believe you," smiled Duncan. "I'll talk to the elders tomorrow, and then I'll come around to your house and tell you what they've decided to do."

That evening, while they were having supper at the kitchen table, lamb chops and mashed neeps, little Toby came wobble-staggering across the floor and clung to the edge of Gillie's chair. He looked up at her and cooed.

"Go away, cuckoo," she told him. "You'll have your Marmitey fingers all over my skirt." For a split-second, she thought she saw his eyes flash – actually *flash* – like somebody taking a photograph.

You'd better watch what you say, Alice warned her. Toby's got a guardian angel, and you don't want to go upsetting him.

A weak sun was shining through the dishrag clouds when Duncan Callander came to call the next afternoon. He sat in the best room and mum gave him a cup of tea and a plateful of petticoat tails.

"I talked to the kirk elders this morning. We had a

special meeting, in fact. I want to tell you that they all extend their warmest best wishes to young Gillie here, and that they very much appreciate her bringing such a delightful story to their attention."

"But it's not a story!" Gillie interrupted.

Duncan raised his hand to silence her. He didn't look her in the eye. He looked instead at the pattern on the carpet and spoke as if he had learned his words from a typewritten sheet of paper.

"As I say, they were very appreciative, and very amused. But they find that there is no evidence at all that what Gillie saw was anything more than an optical illusion; or a delusion brought on by the stress of having a new baby in the household. In other words, the most likely explanation is a little show of harmless attention seeking by an older sister who feels jealous and displaced."

Gillie stared at him. "You said you believed me," she whispered. "You said you believed me."

"Well, yes, I'm afraid that I did, but it was wrong of me. I have a rather mystical turn of mind, I'm afraid, and it's always getting me into hot water. The kirk elders – well, the kirk elders pointed out that nobody has ever produced any conclusive proof that angels actually exist, and until that happens the kirk's official line is that they do not." He took a breath. "I apologize if I misled you."

"And that's all?" Gillie demanded. "That's all that's going to happen? I saw an angel and you're going to say that I was making it up because I was jealous of Toby?"

"If you want to put it that way, yes," Duncan told her, although he spoke so soft and ashamed that she could hardly hear him.

Mum took hold of Gillie's hand and squeezed it. "Come on, sweetie. You can forget it all now; put it behind you. Why don't I bake you your favourite cake tonight?"

Where are you going to sleep? asked Alice.
"I don't know. I'll find somewhere. Tramps have to."
You're not going to sleep in a doorway on a freezing-cold night like this?
"I'll find a squat. Anywhere's better than home."
Your supper's waiting on you. Mum baked that rich thick chocolate cake. Your warm bed's all turned down.
"I don't care. What's the point of cakes and warm beds if people say you're a liar. Even that minister said I was liar, and who was the one who was doing the lying?"

She had trudged the whole length of Rose Street, between brightly-lit pubs and Indian restaurants, jostled by rowdy teenagers and cackling drunks. Maybe Mrs McPhail would have her for the night. Mrs McPhail believed in angels.

By the time she had crossed Prince's Street and started the long walk up Waverley Bridge, it had started to snow again. Sir Walter Scott watched her from his Gothic monument as if he understood her predicament. His head, too, had been full of fancies. She was wearing her red duffelcoat and her white woolly hat, but all the same she was beginning to feel freezing cold, and her toes had already turned numb.

At the top of the hill the streets were almost deserted. She crossed North Bridge Street but she decided to walk down the backstreets to Mrs McPhail's in case dad was out looking for her in the car.

She had never felt so desolate in her life. She had known that people would find it difficult to believe her. She hadn't minded that. What had hurt so much was Duncan's betrayal. She couldn't believe that adults

24

could be so cynical – especially an adult whose chosen calling was to uphold truth and righteousness and protect the weak.

She was half-way down Blackfriars Street when she saw a young man walking very quickly toward her. He was wearing a tam and an anorak and a long Rangers scarf. He was coming toward her so fast that she wondered if somebody were chasing him. His face was wreathed in clouds of cold breath.

She tried to step to one side, but instead of passing her he knocked her with his shoulder, so that she fell back against a garden wall.

"What did you do that for?" she squealed at him; but immediately he seized hold of the toggles of her duffel coat and dragged her close to him. In the streetlight she could see that he was foxy-faced and unshaven, with a gold hoop earring in each ear, and skin the colour of candlewax.

"Give us your purse!" he demanded.

"I can't!"

"What d'you mean you can't? You have to."

"I'm running away. I've only got six pounds."

"Six pound'll do me. You can always run away again tomorrow. I don't even have anywhere to run away from."

"No!" screamed Gillie, and tried to twist away from him. But he clung onto her duffel coat and wrenched her from side to side.

"Out with your purse or it'll be the worse for you, bonny lass!"

"Please," she swallowed. "Please let me go."

"Then let's have your purse and let's have it quick."

His face was so close to hers that she could smell the stale tobacco on his breath. His eyes were glassy and staring. She reached into her pocket, took out her furry Scottie-dog purse and handed it to him. He glanced down at it in disdain.

"What's this? A dead rat?"

"It's my p-p-p—"

He thrust the purse into his pocket. "Trying to make me look stupid, is it? Well, how about a little souvenir to make *you* look even stupider?"

He dragged off her woolly hat, seized hold of her hair, and wrenched her from side to side. She couldn't scream. She couldn't struggle. All she could do was gag with fear.

But it was then that she felt the pavement vibrating beneath her feet. Vibrating, as if a heavy road-roller were driving past. She heard a deep rumbling noise, that rapidly grew louder and louder, until she was almost deafened. The young man let go of her hair and looked around in alarm.

"What in the name of—" he began. But his words were drowned out by a thunderous blast of sound, and then a dazzling burst of white light. Right in front of them, a tall incandescent figure appeared, crackling with power, a figure with a crown of sizzling static and immense widespread wings.

It was so bright that the entire street was lit up, as if it were daylight. The falling snow fizzed and evaporated against its wings. Gillie stayed with her back to the garden wall, staring at it in disbelief. The young man stood staring at it, too, paralysed with fear.

The wings flared even wider, and then the figure reached out with one long arm, and laid its hand on top of the young man's hand, as if it were blessing him, or confirming him.

There was a sharp crack which echoed from one side

of the street to the other. The young man screamed once; and then smoke started to pour out of his mouth and his nose; and he exploded. Fragments of tattered anorak were strewn all over the pavement, along with smoking ashes and dismembered shoes.

Almost immediately, the figure began to dim. It folded its wings, turned, and vanished into the snow, as quickly and completely as if it walked through a door. Gillie was left with nothing but the young man's scattered remains and an empty street, although she could see that curtains were being pulled back, and people were starting to look out of their windows to see what had happened.

She picked up her purse. Next to it, there were six or seven white feathers – huge and soft and fluffy as snow, although some of them were slightly scorched. She picked those up, too, and started to walk quickly back toward North Bridge Street, and then to run. By the time she heard the fire engines she was well on her way home.

She pushed Toby through the kirkyard gate and up between the snow-topped gravestones. Duncan was standing in the porch, pinning up some notices. He gave her an odd look as she approached, although he didn't turn away.

"What have you come for?" he asked her. "An explanation, or an apology? You can have both if you like."

"I don't need either," she said. "I know what I saw was true and I don't need to tell anybody else about it. I know something else, too. Everybody has a guardian angel of their own, especially the young, because everybody has to do something impossible, now and again, like learning to walk, or learning that your parents do care about you, after all."

"You seem to be getting on better with your little brother," Duncan remarked.

Gillie smiled. "God must have wanted him, mustn't he, or else he wouldn't have sent him an angel. And God must have wanted me, too."

Duncan gave her a questioning look. "There's something you're not telling me. You haven't seen another angel, have you?"

"Did you hear about the lad who was struck by lightning last night, in Blackfriars Street?"

"Of course. It was on the news."

"Well, I was there, and it wasn't lightning. Whoever heard of lightning in a snowstorm?"

"If it wasn't lightning, then what?"

Gillie reached into her pocket and took out a handful of scorched feathers, which she placed in Duncan's open hand. "There," she said. "Evidence of angels."

He stood in the porch for a long time, watching her push Toby away down the street. The wintry breeze stirred the feathers in his hand and blew them one by one across the kirkyard. Then he turned around and went inside, and closed the door.

The Hungry Moon

Lewes, Sussex

Lewes is the county town of East Sussex, set on the River Ouse with idyllic views of downland toward Glynde and Eastbourne. I lived here many years ago, next to the fifteenth-century residence of Anne of Cleves, and I always enjoyed its steep cobbled streets and its characteristic tile-hung houses. It was at Lewes in 1264 that Simon de Montfort defeated King Henry III; and the town's strategic importance is remembered in its castle, with a Norman inner gate.

Other significant ruins include a Cluniac Priory dating from 1078, where I often used to walk. There were shadows here, and whispers, as if the monks were still going about their business.

Lewes has changed dramatically since I knew it. A new bypass cuts across the water-meadows by the Priory. The old chandlers and butchers and haberdashers have all vanished. Two fine Lewes institutions remain intact, however: Harveys Brewery, with its fine range of Sussex ales; and the annual Lewes Bonfire celebrations, when bonfire societies parade in the streets and blazing tar barrels are thrown into the River Ouse.

Some older traditions have survived in the area, however – traditions that are alien to Sussex. Come and see if you can face up to them now.

THE HUNGRY MOON

Marcus sat at the breakfast table and stared at the hungry moon. The hungry moon winked back at him, the way it always did, mouth crammed full of farmhouses and hayricks and trees and black-and-white Friesian cows. There was something lewd and knowing about the way that the hungry moon winked at him, although he was only nine and he didn't know what 'lewd' meant. All he knew was that the hungry moon didn't look like the kind of hungry moon from which you should accept gobstoppers outside the school playground.

Not that you would ever meet the hungry moon outside the school playground. The hungry moon existed only on the side of Moon Brand Wheat Flakes – a rather tasteless, old-fashioned breakfast cereal which Marcus's father insisted they bought, because it reminded him of the time when *he* was a boy, and the *Dandy* was only tuppence, and the funniest programme on television was Mr Pastry, and you could walk all the way to Waddon Ponds to look for tiddlers without any fear of being molested. Besides, Moon Brand Wheat Flakes were 'ideal for growing children,' even though they tasted like dried butcher's paper.

It was Moon Brand's 'hungry moon' trademark that fascinated Marcus. It floated just above a wheatfield, with a huge spoon in its hand, shovelling up the countryside

31

and devouring it. It was drawn with immense attention to detail: it had craters all over its face, and it wore button-up gloves. In the background, there were high, windswept downs and a church spire, with rooks circling around it.

Marcus liked to play a kind of Kim's game with the hungry moon, memorizing all the different things that it was swallowing. Tractor, fence, pig, gate, swill bucket.

"Aren't you finished yet?" asked Marcus's mother, coming into the dining-room with flour on her hands. "I know you're on holiday now, but it'll be lunchtime before you've eaten your breakfast."

Marcus's father came in too, his hair brushed and brilliantined, his moustache neatly clipped. Marcus's mother said, "Here, wait," and started to pick hairs from his navy-blue blazer, but he flapped her away.

"I don't have time," he told her. "I have to be in Hemel Hempstead by three."

He opened out his RAC road map on the other side of the table. "Here, I've got it. Bovingdon Road. But where's Bovingdon Close? I wish they wouldn't print these names so damn small."

"French!" scolded Marcus's mother, which was what she always did when he swore. She opened the top drawer of the sideboard and took out a magnifying glass. "There – try this. Perhaps you need glasses."

"I do not need glasses!" Marcus's father retorted, but all the same he took the magnifying glass and peered through it like a detective looking for clues. "Ah, yes. Here it is. That's stupid, they've abbreviated it to Bvngdn Cl. How on earth is anybody supposed to know that means Bovingdon Close?"

"Perhaps the RAC credits its members with a little intelligence," smiled Marcus's mother.

Marcus's father ruffled Marcus's hair, kissed Marcus's mother, and then he left. Marcus was left alone in the dining-room, laboriously finishing his toast. He always ate slowly because he had a plate in his mouth to straighten his top teeth.

He picked up the magnifying glass and angled it into the diagonal shaft of sunlight that came through the dining-room window. He focused the sun's rays on his discarded crusts, seeing if he could make them burn. Then he examined the writing on the Moon Brand Wheat Flakes packet, and eventually his attention focused on the drawing of the hungry moon.

The curved lens gave the hungry moon an almost three-dimensional quality, as if it were floating off the side of the packet. Marcus was amazed to discover scores of tiny details that he had never noticed before. There was a hare standing upright in the grass at the edge of the field. There were cornflowers and butterflies and sheep grazing on the distant downs.

But then he saw something that made him frown, and squint at the drawing even more closely. Tucked in the left-hand corner of the hungry moon's mouth was a small boy, his mouth an 'O' of horror and desperation, one arm raised as if he were desperately waving.

Marcus stared at the boy for almost a minute. He could understand why he had never noticed him before: without a magnifying glass, he looked just like part of the dug-up wheatfield that the hungry moon was eating. Marcus wondered if the people who made Moon Brand Wheat Flakes knew that the boy was there; or if the artist had cunningly slipped him in so that people wouldn't notice. But why would anybody want to do that? It didn't seem like a very good idea to have a picture of a child being eaten on the side of a packet of cereal meant for children.

33

The other odd thing was, the boy didn't seem to have a hand. His arm was upraised, but it only went as far as his cuff.

Marcus's mother came back in. "Oh, Marcus, haven't you finished *yet*? You really are a snail sometimes."

"Look," he said, holding up the cereal packet. "There's something I never noticed before. The hungry moon's eating a boy."

Marcus's mother glanced at it without really looking. "Poor chap," she said, gathering up the breakfast plates.

"But look – he's eating a boy and the boy's really screaming."

"I'm not surprised. Can you go down to the shop for me, and get me some suet?"

"Can I have a shilling for going?"

"A shilling! Do you think I'm made of money?"

Marcus bicycled down to the shop on the corner. It was a warm, pale day. As he pedalled, he kept thinking about the boy that the hungry moon was eating. He wondered what it would be like, to be spooned up with farmhouses and screaming livestock, and then ground up alive between giant molars. He wondered why the boy had no hand. Perhaps the hungry moon had bitten it off already. It all seemed so odd.

Behind the pollarded plane trees, the faintest of daylight moons kept pace with him, as if it were watching him, just to make sure that he didn't give its secret away.

His old school friend Roger Fielding invited him down to Sussex for the weekend. He didn't really want to go, because he hated reunions. Too many years had passed to make his schooldays topical, and not enough years had passed to gild them with a nostalgic glow. But he had put Roger off three times already, and he knew that he couldn't postpone his visit any longer. Besides, Roger was something in the Department of the Environment, and there was a remote possibility that he could be helpful when it came to seeking planning permission for historic or ecologically sensitive sites.

It rained most of the weekend, in miserable misty curtains, so they spent their time playing backgammon and drinking Roger's home-brewed beer. Roger had three damp, lolling Labradors and a small, birdlike wife called Philippa. Philippa was what Roger called "a dab hand" at anything artsy-craftsy. She upholstered furniture and restored paintings and did brass rubbings, which were framed and hung up everywhere. She had redecorated almost all of their eighteenth-century house herself, and Marcus had to admit to himself that she had done it rather well. It was a plain but elegant house with a long sloping garden and a view toward Glynde and Eastbourne.

"This has always been such a *creative* house," Philippa enthused. "Turner stayed here once, and of course Duncan Greenleaf used to live here, you know, before us."

Marcus raised his hand to decline a third gooseberry tart. "Duncan Greenleaf?" he asked. "Can't say that I've heard of him."

"One of the great illustrators of the 1930s," Roger explained.

"One of the great, *great* illustrators of the 1930s," added Philippa. "He's still alive, as a matter of fact, but the house got too much for him. He must be – ooh – eighty or ninety by now."

After tea, the rain suddenly cleared, and the house filled up with silvery sunlight. Roger and Marcus took the dogs out for a run – Marcus wearing a pair of borrowed wellingtons that made a loud wobbling noise when he walked.

They left the house by the garden gate and walked down a narrow lane. Water was still trickling down the stones and the trees kept dripping down Marcus's neck.

"I love Sussex," said Roger. "I just wish I could live down here all the time."

Marcus gave him a tight smile. He couldn't wait to take off these wobbling wellies and take the first train back to London. The dogs didn't help, either. They kept running through the fields and the ditches and then hurtling back again to shake themselves all over Marcus's overcoat.

As they approached a dense stand of trees, however, Roger whistled sharply to the dogs and called them to heel. They came trotting around him, and he fixed them all to the leash.

"Got to be careful around here," Roger explained. "The ground on the other side of those trees is pretty boggy. Brambly, too. Quite a few people have lost dogs in there. Caught up in the thorns, drowned, who knows what, and once they're in there, you've no chance of getting them out."

"Can't you get the council to clear it?" asked Marcus.

Roger pointed up at a small white sign. It read, 'Strictly Private: No Trespassing'.

"This is the back of Hastings House. All this land belongs to the Vane family. They've been here for two hundred years. Very reclusive lot. Big in shipping, mainly. Sometimes you see one or other of them at a charity dinner or something like that, but most of the time they like to keep themselves to themselves."

"Not the sort of neighbours you can ask for a cup of sugar, then?"

"You could try, but you'd probably get your bum

filled with buckshot the moment you stepped through the front gate."

They passed the trees, and the lane turned into open countryside again. The wind had risen, and the sky was being hurriedly emptied of clouds. In the distance Marcus could see the long backs of the South Downs, a farm, and a small village with a church spire.

"Beautiful, isn't it?" said Roger, taking a noisy snort of fresh air. High above the downs, the last of the clouds unraveled and fled away, revealing a wan, cream-coloured moon. And it was then, almost at the same time, that the church bell chimed five, and a flock of rooks circled around it, cawing and complaining.

Marcus stopped in astonishment. "It's *here*," he said.

"What's here?"

"This is the actual place. I can't believe it."

Roger smiled and shook his head like one of his Labradors. "Sorry, old chap. Don't follow."

"There was this cereal we used to have when I was a boy . . . and it had picture on the side, a sort of a trademark. A moon, and a farm, and a village with a church spire. I used to spend hours looking at that picture . . . and here it is. Whoever drew it must have used this place for reference."

"Well, well," said Roger. "There's a coincidence for you." He picked up a stick and threw it for the dogs, who went streaming off through the long grass with only their black flapping ears visible. "Wonders will never cease, eh?"

"The moon had a spoon and it was eating everything . . . the farm, the cattle, the fences. And it was eating a small boy, too. That's what used to disturb me about it. You had to use a magnifying glass to see him, but— "

Marcus suddenly realized that Roger wasn't in the

slightest bit interested. "Well," he finished lamely, "you wouldn't have noticed him if you weren't looking for him."

They walked as far as the farm and then Roger looked at his watch. "What train do you want to catch?" he asked. "There's a good one at 6:50, or we can go and have a last drink in the pub and you can catch the 7:45."

Marcus said, "That's all right. I'll catch the early one." It was obvious that Roger was beginning to think what he had thought from the very beginning: that school reunions have an awkward emptiness all of their own. The feeling of conspiracy has gone: the intense closeness of twenty or thirty young minds, all trying to learn about the world together. Also gone has the blithe belief that life will last for ever.

They walked back to the house. Philippa gave Marcus a bag of gooseberry tarts to eat on the train. A few miles past Haywards Heath station, he opened the window and threw them into the darkness.

He found out from Companies House that Moon Brand Ltd, used to have a factory in Hemel Hempstead, Herts, but they were absorbed in 1961 by Anglo-Amalgamated Foods, and over half of their products were discontinued, including Moon Brand Wheat Flakes. There were no surviving records to show who might have drawn the hungry moon, although Marcus managed to make a photostat of it.

Back in his flat near Wandsworth Bridge, he pinned a hugely-enlarged copy of it on his living-room wall, and sat staring at it evening after evening. During his lunch hours, he went from one library to another, looking up reference books on trademarks, logos and packaging design.

Eventually, in Putney Library, he came across a huge

coffee-table book called *Advertising & Packaging Art* – and there, to his surprise, he found a *colour* reproduction of the hungry moon. He had never realized that it had originally been painted in colour – on the cereal box, it had always been black-and-white. The painting was unsigned, and neither the caption, the text or the index gave him any clue as to who the artist might have been.

All it said was 'trademark used by Moon Brand Ltd for their Wheat Flakes, ca. 1937.'

He borrowed the book and took it to his local copy-shop so that he could make a colour copy. It was there, on a wet Thursday afternoon, that he discovered who had painted the hungry moon, and the answer was so obvious that it almost made him slap his forehead like a cartoon character.

The girl who was operating the copier pulled out a sample and said, "Is the colour all right? That leaf doesn't look very green."

Leaf, green. Green, leaf. And right next to the leaf was a rusty-coloured watering-can. Dun can. The hungry moon *had* been signed, after a fashion, by Duncan Greenleaf.

The girl stared at him. "Are you okay?" she asked. "You don't look very well."

He was so old and frail that he was almost transparent. He sat by the window, staring out over the gardens, wrapped in a camel-coloured dressing-gown with braided edges, the sort of dressing-gown that only children wear. His nose was large and well-sculptured, and his hair rose from the top of his head in a fine silver flame. He held his wire-rimmed spectacles in his lap as if he no longer cared to see anything very distinctly.

"Duncan, you've got a visitor," said the plump nurse with the pink cheeks.

Duncan Greenleaf raised his head. His eyes must have been startlingly blue once, but now they were faded and glutinous, and Marcus wasn't sure whether he could see him or not.

"Mr Greenleaf? My name's Marcus. I'm an admirer of yours."

"Admirer? You're not a homosexual, are you?"

"I meant that I admire your work."

"I haven't worked for fifteen years, dear boy. A few sketches, that's all. The eye can see and the brain can understand, but the hand won't do what I want it to do."

Marcus sat down opposite him. "I've come about the hungry moon. Well, I've always called it the hungry moon. The trademark you painted for Moon Brand Wheat Flakes."

Duncan Greenleaf gave a querulous sniff. "What of it? I painted scores of trademarks."

"I know. But the hungry moon was the only one with a little boy in it. A little boy with only one hand."

There was a very long silence. To begin with, Marcus wasn't sure if Duncan Greenleaf had heard him. But then the old man unfolded his spectacles, put them on, and looked at Marcus with an expression that was close to sadness. "Yes. A little boy with only one hand. I'm surprised you discovered him – he was very tiny, wasn't he? Very tiny indeed."

"I used a magnifying glass."

"Yes, you would have had to. I used a magnifying glass to paint it."

"The background – that's the view from the back of your house, wasn't it? The chap who bought it from you is an old school friend of mine."

"Yes, you're right. Looking westward, toward Glynde."

40

There was another silence. Then Marcus said, "Who was he? The boy being eaten by the hungry moon?"

Duncan Greenleaf slowly shook his head. "It's an old story, Marcus. One that's best forgotten."

"But why did he have only one hand?"

"The other . . . he lost."

"Can't you just tell me what it means? I've been thinking about it on and off for years. Now I've met you – now I've seen where you used to live . . . the whole thing's come alive again. Please."

Duncan Greenleaf shrugged. "They didn't believe me then. There's no reason why you should believe me now."

"Why don't you try me? Please. I seriously think I'll go crackers if I don't find out."

The plump nurse brought them two cups of weak tea and a plate of soft digestive biscuits. When she had gone, Duncan Greenleaf said, in the lowest of voices, "The boy was my younger brother Miles. When I was fourteen and he was twelve, we both wanted to be artists and we both wanted to be adventurers. We decided to go exploring at the back of Hastings House. I presume you saw the back of Hastings House?

"Miles and I had heard all kinds of stories about the family who lived there, the Vanes. Some of our friends said they were only half-human. They looked quite normal by day, but by night they turned into some kind of dreadful beast. Of course, being boys, we went by night, so that we could see them at their worst.

"We crawled through all of that appalling undergrowth. I lost count of the times I scratched my face and ripped my clothing. It was a bright moonlit night, you know, but parts of those woods were so dense that we lost sight of

41

each other, and we had to keep in touch with our famous owl noises.

"We found ourselves descending into a very swampy part of the wood. The ground was so muddy that I thought that I was going to sink right up to my waist. There were brambles, too – worse than barbed wire. We stopped and decided to turn back; but just as we did so we heard a whimpering noise not far away. It sounded like an animal in pain, so we made our way towards it. After a long search we found a golden retriever lying on the ground. Both of its front legs were caught in a man-trap. Not a gin-trap, mark you, but an actual man-trap with metal teeth. One of its paws was almost completely severed, and the other leg was almost certainly broken.

"Miles and I tried to open the trap with a stick, but we couldn't find anything strong enough. In the end Miles said that he would run for help if I stayed behind and tried to comfort this unfortunate dog."

Duncan Greenleaf stopped for a moment. He sipped a little tea, and then he said, "You are only the third person to whom I have told this story. On the night that it happened, I told an inspector of Lewes Police. I told my father. Neither of them believed me, and for that reason I decided that I would never tell it again. The only way in which I could commemorate the events of that night was to include them in my work ... and even now, of course, Moon Brand Wheat Flakes have gone by the board. All these sugary cereals they have these days ... and the packaging – so lurid!"

"The hungry moon is a work of art," said Marcus.

"The hungry moon, as you call it, is a work of explanation, and of love."

Duncan Greenleaf appeared to be losing the thread, so

42

Marcus asked, "What happened then, when Miles went for help?"

"I waited. The poor dog was in such a state that I was sure it was going to die. I stroked it and tried to reassure it. I was appalled that anybody could have sprung such a trap and left it in the woods where any animal could have walked into it. I was still waiting when I heard the noise of somebody coming through the woods – not from the direction by which Miles and I had entered them, but from the direction of Hastings House. At first I thought I ought to call out 'help!' But then something deterred me. It was the *heaviness* of the person who was approaching. It was the way that they came crashing through the bog and the brambles as if they weren't even worried about being scratched.

"I regret to say that I abandoned the dog and ran to hide between some nearby trees.

"I didn't have long to wait. The undergrowth seemed literally to *burst* apart, a whirlwind of leaves and branches and brambles flailing around like spiky whips; and out of this whirlwind came the most appalling apparition that I had ever seen, or ever *will* see. It was a human figure, of sorts, dressed in a black cowl and billowing black robes. It was immensely tall, but I could see its eyes glittering inside its cowl, and I could see that it had a huge downturned mouth like a shark's. I was so frightened that I couldn't move a muscle.

"This terrible creature seized that poor dog and ripped it out of the man-trap without even opening it. It had long clawlike fingers. The dog screamed, but the creature took hold of its ribcage and pulled it apart, as easily as you might pull a chicken's ribcage apart. The dog's innards dropped to the ground and the creature fell on them and started to cram them into its mouth

43

indiscriminately, strings of fat and liver and shredded intestine.

"After a while, the creature left its feast and slowly made its way back through the undergrowth, toward the house. I was shivering and sick to my stomach, as you can imagine, and I turned immediately for home. I had only gone a few yards, however, when I heard another scream up ahead of me – and this time, it wasn't a dog. I ran as fast as I could. I nearly tore out my eye on one bramble – here, you can still see the scar.

"I didn't have to go far before I found Miles, with his hand caught at the wrist in another man-trap. His face was grey with shock. He must have tripped, and put out his hand to save himself. The steel teeth had gone right through skin and flesh, and his hand was dangling by not much more than few shreds of skin.

"I tried to open the trap, but it was just as strong as the first one. While I was trying, Miles kept begging me to set him free, but I simply couldn't. And it was then that I heard that *rushing* sound again, those fearful crashing footsteps, and I realized that the creature in black was coming for Miles.

Duncan Greenleaf took out his handkerchief and wiped his eyes. "There was nothing else I could do. I couldn't have left him there for the creature to tear apart."

"So what did you do?" asked Marcus, although he could easily guess.

"I took out my penknife, and I cut off my brother's hand."

"Oh, God," said Marcus.

"Oh, God, indeed," said Duncan Greenleaf.

"So that's him . . . with just one hand, being eaten up by the hungry moon."

Duncan Greenleaf said, "Somehow I dragged him out

44

of the woods. I took off my belt and used it as a tourniquet to try to stop the bleeding, but he just went on pumping out more and more. By the time my father could call for the ambulance, he was unconscious; and by the time they got him to hospital, he was dead."

"But your father didn't believe what had happened? And neither did the police?"

"Grown-ups don't believe in black monsters with mouths like sharks, Marcus. Especially when they searched the woods and found nothing at all – no man-traps, no dog. And the Vanes, of course, denied all knowledge of such things, as you would expect them to.

"I don't expect *you* to believe me, either. Why should you? But let me tell you this: I looked into the history of the Vane family when I was older. In fact it became something of an obsession of mine, and I expect you can understand why. The Vanes made all of their fortune in shipping, in the Mediterranean, and especially Greece. But in 1856 they were financially ruined: they lost several valuable cargoes and made some bad investments in America. However, only two years went by before the Vane's main competitors suffered some catastrophic shipwrecks, while the Vanes themselves suddenly appeared to have more money than they knew what to do with."

"I don't understand what you're getting at," said Marcus.

"Simply this: that John Vane, who was the head of the family at the time, went to Thessaly on the borders of Macedonia, and was publicly said to have 'consulted with business experts', who assisted him to rebuild the family fortunes. But what 'business experts' could he have possibly found in a Godforsaken place like that?"

"I'm sorry. I have no idea."

"Ah! Thessaly, as you probably don't know, has always been notorious for its black magic and its sorcery, and for its witches."

"He went to see *witches*?"

"Who else, in Thessaly? The Greeks say that these women have the power to 'draw down the moon' – to use all the evil aspects of lunar forces to bring poverty and confusion to anybody they want. All they ask in return is a regular supply of living flesh, human or animal. It said in the *Illustrated London News* that after his return from Greece, John Vane was seen in the company of a tall woman dressed entirely in black, her identity unknown."

"You surely don't think that— "

"*They're cloaked in black, Marcus*! That's what it says in the books! Cloaked in black, with teeth like razors, and they live for ever, if you keep on feeding them!"

He stared at Marcus desperately, gripping the arms of his chair. He appeared to be incapable of saying any more.

After a long, rigid silence, the plump nurse came up and touched Marcus's shoulder. "I think it's time to go now. He does get rather tired, when he talks about the old days, don't you, Duncan?"

Marcus walked across the thickly-shingled driveway and climbed the steps to the front door. Hastings House was huge, with crenellated battlements, and turrets, and spires. Its west wall was overgrown with ivy, as though somebody had casually thrown a huge green blanket over it. Marcus pulled the doorbell and waited.

After a very long time, a thirtyish man in a mustard-coloured tweed waistcoat and brown corduroys appeared from around the side of the house, accompanied by two slavering bull terriers. He was very pale, with an almond-shaped head and slicked-back hair.

"Can I help?" he asked, briskly, as if he wasn't at all interested in doing any such thing.

"I don't know," said Marcus. "I'm looking for Mr Gordon Vane."

"I'm Gordon Vane. You don't have any kind of appointment, do you?"

"No, I don't. But I'm afraid that I've lost my dog."

"I can't see what that has to do with me."

"It ran into your woods, I'm afraid. I was wondering if you'd seen it. It's a Sealyham cross."

Gordon Vane shook his head. "If it's gone into *those* woods, I doubt if you'll ever see it again."

"I was wondering, if you hadn't seen it, whether I could go and look for it."

"Out of the question, I'm afraid."

"I wouldn't do any damage."

"That's not the point. Those woods are very marshy in places, and really quite dangerous."

"They don't *look* dangerous," Marcus persisted.

"Well, I'm afraid they are, and if anything were to happen to you, we're not insured. If you leave me your telephone number, I'll let you know if your dog turns up."

"I saw somebody else in the woods," said Marcus.

Gordon Vane had been patting his dogs, but now he sharply looked up. "You saw somebody? Who?"

"I don't know . . . somebody very tall. Enormously tall, and all dressed in black."

Gordon Vane stared at Marcus as if he could see right through his eyes into his brain. Then, without a word, he took a gold mechanical pencil out of his waistcoat pocket, along with a visiting-card, and said, "Here. Your telephone number."

47

He stood and watched as Marcus walked away, his feet scrunching on the shingle. Marcus wasn't sure if he had done the right thing by pretending to have lost a dog. Maybe he shouldn't have alerted the Vanes at all. But he couldn't think of any other way of flushing out Duncan Greenleaf's "terrible black creature". If the Vanes thought that there was a stray dog wandering in the woods, and that there was the strong possibility that its owner might be wandering in the woods, too, looking for it, then they might let the creature out.

What was more, if the Vanes were concerned that Marcus had actually seen the creature, and might report it, they might let it out to silence him.

Except, of course, that Marcus was ready for it. He had brought a camera, and a large scouting knife, and a baseball bat. He had tried to persuade Roger to lend him his shotgun, on the pretext that he wanted to go clay-pigeon shooting, but he didn't have a licence and Roger was a stickler for things like that.

More than anything else, though, Marcus wanted to go back to Duncan Greenleaf and show him that he hadn't imagined the creature in black, and that he had done his very best for the tiny boy in the mouth of the hungry moon.

He waited until well past midnight before he walked past Roger's house and along the lane that led to the woods. The night was clear and still and the moon shone like a lamp. He left the lane just where the sign said 'Strictly Private' and began to crunch and rustle his way through the dry leaves and the blackberry bushes. He was tense, and a little jumpy, especially when a bird suddenly fluttered out of the undergrowth right in front of him, but he wasn't especially afraid. It seemed as if he had been destined to do this, ever since he had first seen the hungry moon on the cereal packet. It seemed as if he had been chosen all those years ago to right an outstanding wrong.

He had looked up more about the witches of Thessaly, and Duncan Greenleaf was quite right about their appearance, and what they could do. Apparently they could also transform themselves into birds and animals, and they had an intimate knowledge of aphrodisiacs and poisonous herbs. A Thessalonian witch's den would be filled with incense, and strange engravings, and the beaks and claws of birds of prey, as well as pieces of human flesh and small vials of blood taken from the witch's victims. They particularly relished the noses of executed men.

Duncan Greenleaf was quite right about the woods, too: the brambles were worse than barbed wire. Marcus hadn't ventured more than a hundred feet into the woods before his hands and his face were scratched, and he had torn the shoulder of his jacket. It seemed almost as if the undergrowth were viciously alive, cutting and tearing and catching at him.

He kept criss-crossing the undergrowth in front of him with his torch, in case of man-traps. It might be absurd to suspect that they were still set here, after more than sixty years, but it was no more absurd than suspecting that a Thessalonian witch-creature was lying in wait for him in the half-darkness, with glittering eyes and teeth like a shark.

After ten minutes of struggling forward, he began to reach the edges of the boggy ground. He heard an owl hooting, and then a quick, loping rustle through the bushes. His heart beating, he pointed the torch up ahead of him, and it reflected two luminous yellow eyes. He said, "*Ah!*" aloud, and almost turned and ran, but then

49

the creature loped off in the opposite direction, and he glimpsed the heavy swinging brush of a large fox.

He hefted his baseball bat and continued to edge slowly forward over the soft, muddy ground. He wondered how far the bog extended, and how deep it was. He tried to walk quietly, but his boots made a thick, sucking sound with every step.

He took one more step, and the mud began to drag him in, right up to his knees. He tried to pull his left foot out, but he overbalanced, and fell forward, dropping his baseball bat and stretching out his hands to save himself.

He heard it before he felt it. A ringing, metallic *chunk!* Then suddenly his left hand was ablaze with pain, as if he had thrust it directly into an open fire. He tried to pull his hand out, but the steel trap had caught him by the wrist, half-chopping his hand off. By the light of his fallen torch, he could see tendons and bone and bright red muscle. The man-trap was splattered with blood, and he could actually feel his arteries pumping it out onto the mud.

Don't panic don't panic. It's bad, but it's not terminal. These days they can do wonders with microsurgery. That policeman's hand, they sewed that back on. That woman who lost her hands in a wallpaper trimmer, they sewed hers on too. *Don't panic, think.*

With his free left hand, he reached out for his baseball bat. Aluminium, make a good lever, pry this fucking thing apart. But the bat had bounced too far away, and he couldn't get anywhere near it without causing himself so much pain that he bit right through the end of his tongue.

Tourniquet. First thing to do is to stop the bleeding. With his left hand, he unbuckled his belt and tugged it off. After three tries, he managed to flip it over his wrist, and then buckle it up. He gripped the end of it in his teeth

50

and pulled it and pulled it until his veins bulged out. The flow of blood seemed to slow to a steady drip. He pulled even tighter, and it stopped altogether.

Now, *think*. Try to attract attention. He picked up his torch and waved it wildly from side to side, but he couldn't shout out because that would have meant releasing his grip on the tourniquet.

Think. What can I do now?

But it was then that he heard a rustling sound, somewhere in the woods. A fast, relentless rustling, like something coming through the undergrowth with blood on its mind. Oh Jesus it's the witch. It's the witch and I'm trapped here the same way young Miles Greenleaf was trapped.

The rustling sounded heavier and quicker, and Marcus could hear branches breaking and bushes shaking.

There was nothing else for it. He scrabbled into his pocket and took out his scouting knife. He could bite his belt, that would stop him from screaming and from biting his tongue any more. He just hoped that he could cut himself free before the black-cowled creature came exploding out of the woods and tore him to pieces.

He placed the blade of the knife against the teeth of the man-trap. Then he began to cut into his wrist. The first cut felt freezing cold, and hurt so much that he started to sob. But he could hear the witch roaming through the woods, nearer and nearer, and even this was better than a violent death.

He cut through skin and nerves and muscle, but when he reached the wristbone he couldn't cut any further. He closed his eyes, took a deep breath, and rolled himself over in the mud, so that his bones were twisted apart, and he was free.

Whimpering, holding up the stump of his hand, he

started to struggle out of the woods. Without his torch he couldn't see where he was going, and every time the brambles caught him they put him off course. He staggered around and around, falling, climbing up onto his feet again, staggering, falling.

He knelt on the ground, shocked and exhausted. A dark shape approached him through the bushes. It seemed to stand in front of him for so long that he thought that time must have stopped.

Then a dazzling light shone in his eyes, and a voice said, "He's here! Gordon, he's here!"

More footsteps; more lights. Then, "Oh my God, he's lost his hand. Barker, call for an ambulance, would you, and tell them to bloody well step on it."

He was sitting in the waiting room at Roehampton Hospital to have his new hand adjusted when he thought he saw somebody he knew. An elderly, white-haired man, with a large distinctive nose. He was sitting at the opposite end of the waiting room, reading a copy of *Country Life*. His right hand was covered by a leather glove.

Marcus frowned at him for a long time, but he couldn't place him. It was only when the nurse came out and called "Mr Greenleaf, please!" that he realized who he was.

He waited for him and met him outside the hospital. The traffic was so noisy that they had to shout.

"Mr Greenleaf? Mr *Miles* Greenleaf?" he asked him.

The old man looked surprised. "I'm sorry. Do I know you?"

"No, you don't. But I know your brother, Duncan."

"Well, well. How is he these days?"

"Don't you ever see him?"

Miles Greenleaf pursed his lips. "He writes, but I

52

don't write back. He wouldn't understand my letters anyway."

"He told me you were dead."

"Hmph! Most of the time he thinks that I am. He has his good moments and his bad moments. Mostly bad moments, these days."

"He told me about your hand. How you lost it, I mean."

"Did he now? And which story was it this time? Not the Thessalonian witches, I trust?"

Marcus nodded, and lifted his own hand. "I went looking for it, to prove him right. Exactly the same thing happened to me."

Miles Greenleaf looked bemused. "My dear fellow, I don't think you *know* what happened to me. My brother and I were both naturally talented artists. The truth was, even though I was younger, and even though I say it myself, I was very much better. That was why, when I won the school prize for art and Duncan didn't, he took me into the woods, knocked me semi-conscious with a hammer, tied me up, and deliberately cut off my right hand with a carpentry saw. It was in all the local papers."

Marcus felt himself trembling. "No man-traps? No dog?"

Miles Greenleaf shook his head. "Just all-consuming jealousy, I'm afraid to say. And a mind that wasn't altogether balanced."

"But there were man-traps. I was caught by one myself. The Vanes told the police that it was just a Victorian relic, left undetected in the woods. But it didn't *work* like a Victorian relic."

Miles Greenleaf held out his left hand and shook Marcus's left hand. "As far as the Vanes are concerned,

I think it's wiser to remain ignorant. You never know. I might not be telling you the truth, and there might be a Thessalonian witch there, after all."

That night the moon came out and turned the woods to white, the colour of bones and claws. One of Roger's dogs snuffled through the undergrowth, searching for voles or mice.

Roger, at his back gate, was whistling and calling, but the dog didn't pay him any attention, and Roger was too far away to hear the biting mechanical *snap!*

Neither did he hear the heavy rushing of something black and cloaked, with glittering eyes, hurrying through the brambles with all the terrible greed of a hungry moon.

Grief

Mont St-Michel, France

Mont St-Michel is a granite islet in the bay of St-Michel, near the mouth of the River Couesnon, in the department of Manche. It is connected to the mainland by a causeway 2 km long, which frequently floods at high tide. The island is 73 m high, and is crowned by a Benedictine Abbey, established in the tenth century, and built by extraordinary effort and loss of life.

Although it has been featured on thousands of postcards and tourist guides, Mont St-Michel still presents an eerie and uplifting spectacle as you approach it. There is a village on the south-east side protected by ramparts, and these withstood the English in the Hundred Years' War and the Huguenots in the religious wars. After the French Revolution, the abbey was used as a political prison.

Close to the peak of Mont St-Michel, you can see the island and the sea-washed sands around it through a *camera obscura*. It gives you an unparalleled view of a quiet and rural land where almost anything could happen.

GRIEF

Behind Mont St-Michel, the sky had grown thunderously dark, and lightning was already flickering at the spire of the Benedictine Abbey. Yet here on the water-meadows of the Couesnon, less than three miles away, the sun was still shining through the broken clouds, so that the fields and trees were turned into a jigsaw of light and shade.

All the same, Gerry was never sure why he didn't see her. He wasn't even driving particularly fast. One moment the narrow roadway seemed to be completely deserted in both directions. The next she was cycling across it, right in front of him.

There was a deep thump, followed by the clatter of her falling bicycle. He saw a primrose-yellow dress billow, one arm flapped up, with a wrist-watch on it. He didn't see her face. He braked so hard that the rented Citroën slewed sideways, with its two front wheels on the opposite verge. Its engine stopped.

"Oh Christ," he said, out loud. "Oh Jesus Christ."

His chest was rising and falling and he was trembling so much he could hardly open the door-handle. He climbed out of the car and looked back along the road. The bicycle was lying on its side, its old-fashioned handlebars raised like the horns of a skeletal cow. The girl was lying further away, on her side, an impressionistic splash of yellow in the French countryside.

Gerry walked toward her. He felt as if he were wading knee-deep in clear molasses. Behind him, he could hear the thunder rumbling, and all around him the grass began to quicken and stir.

He was less than half-way toward her when he stopped. There were no other vehicles in sight for as far as he could see. The only witnesses to what had happened were a herd of Friesians, who stared at him dispassionately, their lower lips rotating as they chewed.

He thought for a second: supposing she's still alive? Supposing she's still alive, and I leave her here to die?

But he could see the dark-red tributaries of blood that were flowing from the side of her head, and he knew for certain that he had killed her. It was then that he turned around, and walked back to the Citroën, and climbed into the driver's seat.

He was appalled by what he was doing. How could he knock a girl down, and simply drive away? But what was the logic of staying here? He hadn't intended to kill her. He hadn't been speeding, or driving carelessly. He had drunk a bottle of St Estephe with lunch, but he was sure that he wasn't drunk. It had been an accident, pure and simple. I mean, why had she cycled across the road like that? Why hadn't she looked? She must have seen him coming. It was just as much her fault as his.

He started the engine, and backed the Citroën onto the road again. He glanced up at his rearview mirror and the girl was still lying in the same position. The wind lifted her dress, so that he could see a thin, pale thigh. No doubt about it, she was dead. Even if he went to the French police and gave himself up, that couldn't bring her back to life.

He hesitated for one moment more, giving himself a last chance to decide what he was going to do. Then

58

he released the handbrake, and drove very slowly away from the girl, no more than fifteen kph, watching her all the time in his mirror. Two hundred feet away, he stopped. The girl's dress rose and fell like a windblown daffodil. The sky was darker now, and fat spots of rain began to speckle the Citroën's windshield.

"God forgive me," he said, and drove away.

That evening, in his flock-wallpapered hotel bedroom in St Malo, he called his sister Freddie in Connecticut.

"Freddie? It's Gerry. Just called to say hi."

"Gerry? Are you back in the States? You sound so clear!"

"No, no. I'm calling from France. I probably won't be back till September or October, the way things are going. We've already found three really excellent hotels, and we're negotiating with a fourth."

"That's wonderful. How are you? I was just saying to Larry that we hadn't heard from you in a coon's age."

"I'm great, really great. It's really beautiful here. I love it."

He carried the phone over to the window and looked down into the Rue St Xerxes. It was shadowed and angular, like the street outside Joseph Cotten's hotel in *The Third Man*, where Orson Welles was waiting in the doorway. Beyond the rooftops, the harbour lights dipped and sparkled in the dark.

Freddie said, all of a sudden, "You sound strange."

"Strange? In what way? I'm fine!"

"Gerry – is something wrong? I mean, really? You don't sound like yourself at all. And, well, I don't mean to be rude, but when do you ever call?"

"Everything's great. Couldn't be better. How are the kids? And that big stupid dog of yours?"

59

"Petey and Nancy are fine. We lost poor old George, though. He was run over by a mail truck. He didn't die right away but we had to have him put down."

"Hey, I'm sorry. I liked George."

Freddie went on chatting about the summerhouse they were building, but Gerry couldn't help thinking about the girl lying in the road, her yellow dress rising and falling in the wind, and her blood trickling across the asphalt, into the grass.

In the end, he said, "I have to go now. I'll call you again real soon. I'll send the kids some postcards, too."

"Are you sure you're not in any kind of trouble?"

"What trouble? I'm great."

"You're not in love, are you?"

He put down the phone, very quietly. In the street below two men were talking. He could see the glow of their cigarettes. He saw them turn their heads, toward the shadows, and almost at once a young girl appeared, in a spotted yellow dress, riding a bicycle. And just as an upstairs window in Joseph Cotten's hotel had opened and spotlighted the upturned face of Orson Welles, an upstairs window in Gerry's hotel was noisily flung wide. The girl looked up, photographed, and for a split-second she caught Gerry's eye. Pretty girl, he thought. Then she was gone.

He went over to his bureau and poured himself a miniature vodka. In the brown-measled mirror he saw a thin young man with an angular face and brush-cut hair. Red-and-white striped shirt, red braces. At twenty-five years old, the youngest vice-president in charge of overseas property acquisitions that TransWestern Hotels had ever had. This was his dream job. He loved the hotel business, and he loved France. More than anything, he loved the French people. Now he had killed one of them, and driven away without stopping.

That night, as he lay in bed, not sleeping, he listened to the doleful clanking of ships' rigging from the harbour, and the wind that made his shutters quake, and he tried to think rationally about what he had done at Mont St-Michel, as if by thinking about it he could give himself some kind of absolution. He heard the thump of the girl's body hitting his car. He saw her skirt billowing, and her thin wrist raised, with a watch on it. A cheap gold-plated watch, with a thin red-leather strap. It had imprinted itself so much on his consciousness that he was sure that he could visualize the brand name, if he concentrated hard enough.

I left her there, lying in the road. She might have been alive. Maybe I could have saved her, if I had driven her to a hospital. Maybe somebody *did* find her, and resuscitated her. He would never know; and it would be far too risky to try to find out.

He whispered a clumsy, almost childish prayer. He hoped that the girl in the primrose-yellow dress had died instantly, without pain, not knowing what had happened to her. He hoped that she had been discovered by people who loved her, and that they had given her the kind of funeral she deserved. With flowers, and hymns, and tears of grief.

In the middle of the night, he was sure that he heard the *tick-tick-tick* of somebody riding a bicycle along the Rue St Xerxes outside.

He was sitting at an outside table at the Moulin du Vey when he noticed the girl looking at him. She had glanced at him once when he first sat down, but now she kept staring at him all the time, and making no attempt to conceal her interest in him. He gave her a brief smile and Carl said, "What? What is it?"

"Nothing. I was just admiring the view, that's all."

Carl made an issue of turning around in his white plastic chair. "Yes, see what you mean. Very scenic. Two trees, the side of a building, and a girl to make your hair stand on end."

"She's just been smiling at me, is all."

Carl laughed, and sat back, and took out a cigar. "You should go for it. You know what the girls call you, at the office? Gerry the Cherry. I mean, you're not really a virgin, are you?"

"Get out of here. I was engaged once, when I was in college. And don't you remember Francoise?"

"Oh yes, Francoise. Who could forget her? Legs like the Eiffel Tower."

Gerry shook his head and devoted himself to his pork in mustard sauce. The Moulin du Vey was one of his favourite restaurants in Normandy: an old ivy-covered mill on the banks of the Orne, with a huge barnlike dining-room and a pretty gravelled verandah overlooking the river. It was a warm, lazy day, and he and Carl had driven out here to look for new country hotels to add to TransWestern's inventory. Butterflies blew around them, and geraniums nodded in the breeze.

It was the girl, however, who had completely caught his attention, and he found that he could hardly taste what he was eating or understand what Carl was talking about. She was sitting with a very smart middle-aged couple who could have been her mother and her father. Her hair was long and blonde and it shone in the sunlight like the gilded thistledown that blew across the surface of the river. She had one of those disturbing French faces that attracted Gerry because of one imperfect feature. Her eyes were wide; her cheekbones were high; her nose was short and straight; but she had a slight overbite, which gave her a look of vulnerability. She wore a white sleeveless blouse with embroidered lapels, and Gerry could see from where he was sitting that she was very full-breasted.

In a strange way, she reminded him of somebody, but he couldn't think who it was.

Carl was saying, "When you take over a place like this, there's always a problem with rationalizing the menus."

"Yes. I know."

"You have to find frogs with sixteen legs; otherwise you'll never meet the demand. The trouble is, if they have sixteen legs, you can never jump up high enough to catch them."

"Absolutely. You're right."

Carl tapped his knife on his wineglass. "Hallo in there? Have you heard a single word I've been saying?"

"What?" asked Gerry. Then, "Hey, I'm sorry. I don't know what the hell's the matter with me."

Carl turned around again, just in time to catch the girl giving Gerry a fleeting, secretive smile. "I know what the hell's the matter with you. You're in lust."

After lunch, Carl had to drive down to Falaise to see a man about a franchise, so Gerry took the opportunity to go up to his room and finish his report. He sat at a faded rococo desk in front of the open window, tapping away at his laptop, but it wasn't long before he stopped tapping and sat back, listening to the endless sliding of the river over the weir, and the rustle of the ivy leaves against the open shutters.

He wondered if the girl were still out on the verandah, talking to her parents. He stood up, and peered outside. The parents were there, talking and drinking coffee, but

63

the girl had gone. Gerry was just about to return to his report when he glimpsed a flicker of white, further up the river bank. The girl was walking through the apple orchard that had been planted almost down to the water's edge, trailing her hands through the long feathery grass.

Gerry watched her for a while, Then, decisively, he switched off his laptop and closed it. He hurried down the steep stairs to the Moulin's reception desk, and out into the brilliant sunlight. He crossed the gravel and went down the steps into the orchard.

He found the girl leaning against a tree, chewing a long stem of grass. He tried to approach her as if he had simply decided to go for a stroll, and found her here by accident. Small bees bobbed and droned around the ripening apples, and the sunlight made dancing patterns on the girl's face. For some reason, that reminded Gerry of something, but he couldn't think what.

He stood a little way away from her, looking at the river.

"Are you American?" she asked him, after a while.

"How did you know?"

"I heard you talking to your friend. Besides, you look American."

"I thought I was beginning to look quite French."

"No, no. A Frenchman would never wear a suit like that. And you never use your hands when you talk."

"Maybe I should take some gesticulation lessons."

She smiled. "You shouldn't. I like men who are very restrained."

He came closer. He guessed from the smoothness of her skin and the firmness of her breasts that she wasn't much older than nineteen or twenty. The vulnerability of her slightly-parted lips was contradicted by the

64

look in her eyes. It was challenging, watchful, provocative.

Her eyes were really the most remarkable colour. They were steely grey, almost silver, like the surface of a lake just before a heavy storm. Close up, Gerry could smell a light floral perfume, and an underlying biscuity fragrance. It was a combination that he hadn't smelled for years: the smell of warm young girl.

"It's very peaceful here, isn't it?" he remarked.

"It's too peaceful for me," she replied. "I hate the countryside. I always dream of living in a big city in America."

"You'd hate it. All that noise, all that pollution. All that crime."

"Do you hate it?"

"Why do you think I wanted to work in France?"

She stood against the tree watching him and watching him, and flicking the stem of grass across her lips. "Would you hate it if I was with you?"

This could have been the simplest of questions. Yet the way she put it, it was like a clock mechanism, full of complicated levers and springs and secret movements.

"I guess that could make a difference," Gerry replied. "I never liked Paris too much; but then I've never been there with anybody I loved."

"There you are, then," she said.

She started to walk through the orchard and he followed her. Beneath her blouse she wore a pale yellow linen skirt, through which the sunlight cast tantalizing shadows of her legs. She wore sandals made of twisted leather thongs, which laced around her ankles.

"My name is Marianne," she said, without turning around. "I've lived in the country all my life. My father wants me to be a famous cellist."

"But what do *you* want to be?"

She caught hold of the branch of one of the apple trees, and swung around, laughing. "I want to be the greatest prostitute that ever lived."

He laughed, too. "That's some ambition."

"You think I'm joking?"

"I think you're teasing me."

She reached up and plucked one of the apples from the tree. She held it up in her hand. "You see this apple? We use them for making calvados." She bit into it, so that its juice smothered her lips. She chewed and swallowed the fragment of apple, and then she reached out and took hold of his hand, and drew him toward her.

At first he couldn't think what she was doing, but then she lifted her face to him, and kissed him. He tasted sharp, sticky apple and saliva. He felt her tongue-tip, probing between his lips. He felt her full breasts pressing against his shirt.

He kissed her more urgently. They smothered each other's faces in kisses and apple juice. She bit his tongue, bit his lips, and dug her fingernails into his back. They were both panting, as if they run all the way here.

Abruptly, she stopped kissing him and held him away. Her eyes were dark and excited. "You know what we did?" she asked him. "We were like Adam and Eve, in the Garden of Eden. Now we don't have to pretend to be innocent any longer."

She took two or three paces back. She twirled around, so that her yellow skirt billowed up. Then she stood facing him, and the expression on her face was almost triumphant. Without a word, she lifted up her skirt and bunched it around her waist, revealing long suntanned legs and the fact that she was wearing nothing underneath. Her thighs were so slender that they formed a triangle of empty space between them. Her pubic hair was as golden as the hair on her head, and shone just as brightly.

"There," she said, walking away from him, her skirt still lifted. "The greatest prostitute who ever lived. How much will you pay me?"

He couldn't think what to say. Was she serious? Would she really have sex with him for money? Or was she simply making a monkey out of him?

He glanced around the orchard. Maybe this was some kind of elaborate practical joke that Carl had set up, to show that 'Gerry the Cherry' wasn't so virginal after all. Maybe he was being filmed by a hidden camcorder. But all that he could see were trees and long grass, and they had now walked so far into the orchard that they couldn't be seen from the hotel.

"Marianne—" he began.

"How much do you think I'm worth?" she challenged him. "A thousand francs? Two thousand francs?"

"I can't put a price on it."

She let her skirt fall back a little way, although her vulva was still exposed. "You don't want me?"

He hesitated for a moment. Then he reached into his back pants pocket and took out his billfold. He took out all that he was carrying – over 7,500 francs – and he held it out to her.

She didn't even look at it, and for a moment he was afraid that she had been subjecting him to some obscure test of character, and that he had lost. But then she unfastened her waistband and let her skirt drop into the long grass. She unbuttoned her blouse, and let that fall, too. Finally, without hesitation, she reached behind her and unclipped her bra. Her breasts were bared with a soft double-bounce – huge creamy-pale breasts with nipples as pink as sugar mice.

67

She came up to him, completely naked except for her sandals, and kissed him. By now he thought that he was delirious, that this couldn't be true. Her fine hair floated against his face, and her fragrance almost overwhelmed him. The orchard was so quiet that he could actually hear her stiffened nipples brushing against his shirt. Still she didn't look at the money. She opened his shirt, and caressed his bare chest. She unbuckled his belt, tugged down his pants, and then lifted his tusk-hard penis out of his shorts. She rubbed it up and down a few times, his huge penis in her small long-fingered hand, the glans leaving glistening moisture on the inside of her wrist.

"Now then," she whispered, and lay back in the grass, her thighs apart, her knees raised, her arms stretched out for him. He dropped the money and it fluttered and flicked across the orchard. All Gerry could see was that dreamy, girlish smile, and those rounded breasts, and that glistening pale-pink opening with its wavelike lips.

He knelt down between her legs. She took hold of him and guided him up against her. The feeling of her warm, wet flesh was such a pleasure that he wasn't sure that he was going to be able to bear it. He pushed into her, and she gripped hold of his buttocks and pulled him as deep as he could go. When he drew out of her again, he felt the gentle breeze cooling the juices that anointed him, and the feathery grass tickling his thighs.

They made love for over an hour, while the thick white clouds floated over their heads, and the afternoon moved as slowly as a dream. At last she sat up, and drew back her hair with her hand. There was semen sparkling in her eyelashes.

"I have to go," she said. "My parents will be wondering where I am."

"When can I see you again?" he asked her.

She started to collect up the money that he had dropped – naked, crouching in the grass. "You want to see me again? A prostitute like me?"

"You're not a prostitute."

"Well, no." She smiled. She picked up the last 1000 F bill and handed all of the money back to him. "I just like to play games."

She dressed. He sat on the ground watching her.

"I'd still like to see you again."

"Then you shall."

They walked back to the Moulin du Vey. Marianne's parents were still on the verandah, talking to *madame la patronne*.

"Come and meet them," Marianne urged.

"Do I have to? Your father looks as if he can drill a hole in six-inch steel just by looking at it."

"Oh, don't worry about papa. He's a darling."

Very reluctantly, Gerry followed Marianne up to their table.

"Papa, maman, I wish you to meet my new friend," said Marianne.

Marianne's father was silver-haired, with a silver summer suit and a clipped white goatee beard. He reached into his breast pocket, took out a stainless steel spectacle case, opened it up, and put on a pair of rimless glasses.

"How do you do?" he said, grimly.

"I'm fine, thank you, sir. Enjoying this wonderful afternoon."

"God blesses us," her father replied.

Marianne's mother was silver-haired, too, but even in her mid-fifties she was just as attractive as her daughter. She wore a summer dress of clinging dove-grey wool and a wide-brimmed black straw hat.

"What kind of a man are you?" she asked him.

69

"Well, I'm in the vacation business. Hotels, restaurants, you name it."

"I didn't ask you what you did. I asked you what kind of man you were."

Gerry frowned at Marianne. "I'm sorry, madame, I'm not sure I understand the question."

"It's really very simple," she persisted. "Are you, for instance, the kind of man who would give his life for the woman he loved?"

Gerry glanced back at Marianne, looking for clues. Did her mother really expect him to answer a question like that? What the hell did it mean? But Marianne continued to smile at him, and her papa continued to stare at him through those rimless spectacles as if he couldn't decide whether to hit him or bite him, and maman waited unflinchingly for the answer to her question.

"I, uh . . ." Gerry wiped his sweaty forehead with the back of his hand. "I think that's kind of hypothetical. It all depends on the circumstances, if you know what I mean. Not only that, it all depends on being in love."

"Are you in love?" asked Marianne's mother.

"We only just met each other."

"My wife didn't ask when you met," Marianne's father interrupted. "She asked if you were in love."

"I can't say that I am, no sir."

Marianne's father snapped shut his spectacle case. "If that's how you feel, then perhaps your acquaintanceship with my daughter should go no further. I am not a prudish man, but I believe in honour."

"Sir?"

"Are you also deaf? I said you should stay away from her."

"Don't you think that rather depends on her?"

Marianne's father looked up at Gerry for a very long

70

time, his face marked with some deep, unspoken pain. "Unfortunately, yes. But I have the right to make my feelings plain."

"Nice to have met you," said Gerry. He nodded to Marianne's mother, turned on his heel and walked away. Marianne started to go after him, but her father gripped her wrist, and gave her a quick, imperious shake of his head.

The next day was warm but heavily overcast, and when Gerry woke up the rain was pattering through his open window onto his freshly-printed report. Outside, the ivy was glistening with wet and there were puddles in the gravel verandah. All of the plastic chairs had little pools in their seats, too.

He hadn't seen Marianne again after that encounter with her parents. At about six o'clock he had seen all three of them leaving in a big silver Renault. As the car crossed the stone bridge over the Orne, Marianne had glanced back once, but that was all.

He dressed and went across to the *salle à manger* for coffee and croissants and boiled eggs. The rain trickled hesitantly down the windows. He had brought his notepad with him to list his appointments, but he found that he kept doodling the name *Marianne* over and over again, and drawing pictures of apples with bites taken out of them, and wavelike designs that could have been orchids or could have been Marianne's slightly-parted lips.

After breakfast, Gerry went back to his room, took out his travel-bag and started to pack. He rang the office in Paris, and told his secretary Alexis to arrange a meeting with TransWestern's lawyers, so that they could discuss terms with *madame la patronne* at the Moulin du Vey and two other hotels he was interested in. She took an age on the other line, and Gerry sat drumming his fingers impatiently on the desk. But the moment she got back to him, Gerry saw a figure in a yellow waterproof crossing the verandah below. It was a girl, and she was walking toward the hotel. He couldn't see her face, but something made him lower the receiver and lean out of the window to make sure that she was coming up the steps.

"Hallo?" Alexis demanded. "Monsieur Philips, are you there? I said, hallo!"

Gerry replaced the receiver on its cradle without answering. He stood waiting, and he could feel his heart beating like a man punching a cushion. He heard footsteps outside his room, the rustling of a waterproof coat coming up the stairs. There was a moment's pause, and then a knock.

He went to the door and opened it. Marianne was standing outside, still wearing her dripping yellow waterproof, her hair stuck wetly to her forehead, but smiling.

"You didn't think you would see me again?"

"No, I didn't." Why was he so breathless? He was suddenly conscious of his notepad, lying on his desk, covered in dozens of illuminated versions of her name. "Listen . . . why don't you come in, and take off that coat? I was just packing."

She stepped into his room and he closed the door. She looked around, admiring the grey silky fabric on the walls, and the chateau-style furniture. "It's very comfortable," she said. "Personally I prefer modern things. Modern music, modern art, modern furniture. I like everything to be new and exciting."

"Take off your coat," he suggested. "It won't take me five minutes to pack. Then we can go share a bottle of champagne together, or something." He smiled ruefully. "A little wet for walks in the orchard, I'm afraid."

He was clearing his brushes and his aftershave from the dressing-table when he heard her taking off her coat. He glanced in the mirror and what he saw made him drop everything with a clatter. In the pale, silvery glass, he could see that she was completely nude, except for black stockings and a black garter belt. He saw her walk toward him, and hold him from behind, her breasts squashed against his back.

"How could I let you go?" she said, and he could feel the warmth of her breath through his shirt. "Whatever we begin, we have to finish, don't we?"

Gerry turned around, and took her into his arms. She was goosebumpy because of the rain, and her nipples were knurled and stiff. He kissed her wet face. He kissed her wet hair. He kissed her wet mouth. He squeezed and caressed her breasts and rolled her nipples between finger and thumb. He slipped one finger between her thighs and she was warm and juicy as an overripe apricot.

She unbuttoned his shirt and unfastened his belt, and they climbed onto the bed together with even more eagerness than they had yesterday, in the orchard. Marianne pushed him gently onto his back, and sat astride him, her slippery stockinged thighs gripping his sides, her breasts dancing a complicated dance, her face flushed with secretive pleasure. Outside the open window, the rain continued to whisper in the ivy leaves, and the river slid endlessly over the weir.

Afterward, they lay side by side and talked. She told him that she was twenty years old, and that her father was a magistrate in the Manche district. They had come to Clecy to visit her aunt and uncle. They came every summer. She told him that she was studying cello in

Caen, and that she hoped to go to Paris eventually, and then to America. Unselfconsciously, she sat on the end of the bed, her thighs apart, playing an imaginary cello concerto for him. He watched her, and the way the grey Norman light turned her skin to pearly white and strained all the colour out of her hair, and he began to think that he might have begun to fall in love with her. Not just a matter of honour, but of love.

She sang for him, a ridiculous falsetto song about a cat that fell in love with its own shadow. They lay back on the bed and laughed, and it never occurred to him *why* this had happened; or that it could ever end.

She had borrowed her aunt's bicycle to ride here – a large ungainly machine with a wide leather saddle and a basket in front. He walked with her to the end of the bridge, his coat-collar turned up against the rain. A tethered goat watched them with yellow eyes.

"Will I see you later?" he asked her.

She kissed him. Her lips were wet with rainwater. "I will come when you least expect it."

He held the bicycle for her while she climbed onto it. He glimpsed her plump furry vulva pressed against the saddle, pink flesh squashed against leather. Then she drew the skirts of her waterproof around herself, and cycled off slowly across the bridge. In the middle, she turned and waved. He waved back, and then he started to walk along the driveway toward the Moulin du Vey, filled with such elation that he could have skipped. Ever since he had graduated from Hartford, he had worked seven days a week to build his career, and it had never actually occurred to him that he might fall in love. He had dated Francoise, who had been superior and distant, and treated lovemaking as if it were a slightly messy

74

minor hobby, like pottery; and Alexandra, a handsome but horsey blonde who had a poster of Giscard d'Estaing pinned over her bed.

But Marianne was something completely different. Marianne was magical. She was pretty and she was funny and she would do anything he wanted in bed. *Anything*, lovingly and enthusiastically and without complaint, even when (once) he had brought tears to her eyes.

He had almost reached the hotel when he heard the sound of a truck speeding down the hill from Vey. He didn't know why, but he stopped, and half-turned, and listened.

He heard the truck braking, with a huge echoing groan, like a rhinoceros in pain. He heard a dull echoing thump. Then a terribly familiar clatter.

He said, "*No,*" out loud, and started to run back to the bridge. He reached it just in time to see the truck driving away – a greasy green farm truck loaded with wet hay.

He ran across the bridge, his feet slapping on the wet stone. He saw her when he was halfway across. She was lying face-down in the road, her yellow waterproof flapping, one pale arm at an awkward angle, her cheap wristwatch smashed. Her aunt's bicycle was over fifty feet away, its front wheel bent double.

He knelt down beside her in the roadway. Her black stockings were torn and there was blood and mud on her legs. Blood ran into the gutter from the side of her head, and mingled with the rainwater in the gutter.

"Marianne," he whimpered. He knew she was dead. Her blonde hair was thick with blood and clotted with something beige and jellyish which he realized with absolute horror were brains. The truck had knocked her off her bicycle and driven straight over her head.

He stood up. He had to hold onto the road-sign beside

the bridge to stop himself from toppling over. He felt as if his entire being had been gripped in a clamp of utter misery, as if he would never be able to breathe, or speak, or think, or even take one step in front of the other – as if he would have to stay here, in the summer rain, beside this spot for the rest of his life.

A watery sun came out. A 2CV stopped nearby, and a farmworker in a flat cap climbed out, the burned-down butt of a cigarette between his lips. He came over and laid his hand on Gerry's shoulder.

Gerry looked at him with tears running down his cheeks.

"Why her?" he asked. "Why did it have to be her?"

The farmworker shook his head. "*Je ne comprends pas, monsieur.*"

A month later he was in Rouen, sitting in a cafè opposite the cathedral, waiting for Carl to arrive. He had already eaten a ham baguette and drunk three cups of coffee and there was still no sign of him. The Gothic facade of the cathedral changed in the sunlight from austere grey to warm gold, in the same way it had in Monet's paintings of the same facade.

A woman sitting close to him was making a studied, pouting performance of painting her lips. On the radio, Vanessa Paradis was singing *Joe Le Taxi*. Gerry had a newspaper on the table next to him but he wasn't reading it.

At last Carl came bursting in through the cafè door with an overnight bag, a briefcase, a raincoat, and a shopping bag from Elegance. "My meeting overran," he gasped. "Then I couldn't find a cab. Jesus, what a morning! How about a beer?"

"I'm fine, thanks."

Carl crammed all his bags onto the chair next to him. "You don't look fine. You look worse than the last time I saw you."

"I'm fine, for Christ's sake."

"Have you eaten already? You've lost weight. Henry thinks you're overworking. You should take a few weeks' vacation, go to Nice, or Menton maybe. A friend of mine has an apartment in Menton. Hey, monsieur, *deux bieres, s'il vous plait.*"

"I don't want a beer," Gerry told him.

"You'll have a beer and shut up. Listen your uncle Carl. Everybody thinks you're doing a great job, but don't let them see you cracking under the strain. Once you've cracked, there's no way back."

"The work's fine, I can handle the work."

"Oh, really?" Carl took a deep gulp of beer and ended up with a foam moustache. "You look like shit."

Gerry looked into his empty coffee-cup. "The truth is, Carl, I'm grieving."

"Grieving? You mean somebody died?"

Gerry pressed his hand over his mouth. His eyes filled with tears and he could hardly speak.

"Hey, come on, man," said Carl, and took hold of his arm. "I didn't realize. I'm sorry. Why didn't you tell me? It wasn't your old man, was it?"

"No," said Gerry, at last. "It was just somebody I met, that's all."

"Somebody you met here in France?"

"I didn't even know them very well. It's just that – well, there could have been a lot of possibilities. A whole lifetime of possibilities."

"We're talking about a woman here, yes?"

Gerry nodded.

77

"Not Francoise? I didn't really mean that, you know, about the legs."

"No, not Francoise."

"You can't tell me who?"

Gerry shrugged. "It doesn't matter who. Not now."

They finished their beers in silence. At last Carl looked at his watch. "We'd better get across to Lapautre's for that next meeting. Are you ready?"

Gerry went up to the counter to pay. There was a large mirror behind it, stuck with advertisements for Maes Pils and Orangina and Citron Pressé. While the waitress was ringing up the register, Gerry looked into the mirror at the sunny street outside, the passing traffic and the front of the cathedral and the postcard stands.

Just as the waitress said, "*Merci, monsieur*," and started to count his change into the palm of his hand, a red and cream bus drew up outside. Gerry glanced at it only casually at first, but then a movement of a hand caught his eye, and he looked again, and a dreadful creeping feeling went down his back. Sitting in the fifth or sixth window along was a pale, blonde girl in a yellow cotton anorak. She seemed to be staring directly at him, in the mirror.

It was Marianne. He was sure it was Marianne.

"Monsieur!"

He scattered his change as he ran out of the café, colliding with the table where the lipstick woman was sitting, tipping over the chair on which Carl had crammed all his bags. He ran across the wide sidewalk, right up to the bus, and stared directly into the girl's face. She stared back at him – not afraid, as a stranger might have been – but calm and composed and even faintly amused. But she was so pale she could have been dead.

"*Marianne!*" he shouted at her. "*Marianne, it's me!*"

People turned in the street. The girl kept on staring at him for a while, but then she turned away. He slammed his hands on the side of the bus and yelled, "Marianne! For Christ's sake, Marianne! It's me, Gerry! Moulin du Vey! Don't you remember?"

He ran along to the front of the bus; but just as he reached the doors, they closed with a soft pneumatic hiss, and the bus began to pull away.

Gerry hit the side of the bus again, and shouted, "Stop! *Arretez!*" But the driver ignored him and the bus continued to gather speed.

He looked up and glimpsed the girl one more time. She was smiling at him. He stepped back, baffled, both hands bruised. He was about to turn away when he saw who was sitting in the very rear of the bus. A silver-haired man in rimless spectacles and a woman in a black hat with a bow. They were both grey-faced, like the girl, and their expressions were grim. Marianne's parents. Or at least they looked like Marianne's parents. Then, in a blue cloud of diesel, the bus was gone.

Carl put his arm around his shoulder and led him back to the café.

"What the hell was all that about?"

Gerry sat down. Everybody in the café was staring at him unblinkingly. "I thought it was her. The girl who died."

"How could it have been, if she died? You're right. You're grieving. Grief plays funny tricks with your brain. Have another beer. It'll do you good. Or how about a calvados?"

"It was so much like her. I even thought I saw her parents, too."

"Anybody I know, pardon me for being so intrusive?"

"I don't know whether you'd remember her. It was that girl who kept flirting with me when we were having lunch at the Moulin du Vey."

"*Her*? How come you got to know her so well?"

"I didn't. I never knew much more than her name. But she was – well, she was very special."

"Maybe you thought she was dead and she wasn't dead. What was she, ill or something?"

"Road accident. I saw it myself. They took her in an ambulance and they covered her face up. She was dead."

Carl swallowed more beer. "That couldn't have been her, then, on the bus?"

"No. Logically, I guess it couldn't."

"And, let's put it this way, if it really *was* her, you wouldn't be tempted to renew your acquaintanceship, would you?"

"I don't know. Do people come back from the dead, if you miss them badly enough?"

Carl slapped him on the back. "Come on, old buddy. We've got hotels to buy."

That night, back in his apartment in Paris, he dreamed about the thunder clamouring all around the Mont St-Michel. He dreamed of a thin wrist with a cheap gold wristwatch on it, flailing in the air. A girl in a yellow dress was lying on the road with blood streaming from her. It began to rain, and the rain washed the blood away, but it washed the girl's dress away, too, like sodden tissue, and then her white body began to melt, and run into the ditch.

He could clearly read the brand name on the wristwatch. It was *Pity me*.

Close to his ear, he heard a voice whisper the same thing, "Pity me."

80

He shouted out loud, and sat up in bed, knocking his glass of water across the carpet.

Carl was right. He was still grieving, and his grief was giving him nightmares and hallucinations.

Marianne was dead; and even if she *had* found a way of coming back to him – well, that was one embrace that he didn't want to think about.

He was crossing the courtyard in front of the Louvre when he saw a girl in a wide-brimmed straw hat pushing a bicycle. It was a hot, bright morning, and the reflection from the dusty white surface of the courtyard was dazzling, so that he could scarcely see her. She disappeared behind the glass pyramid, and for a moment he was tempted to forget about her, and carry on walking; but there had been something about the way she walked and the way she was dressed that gave him an unsettling feeling.

He circled around the pyramid and there she was. Her bicycle was lying on its side on the ground, and she was kneeling down to lace up the thongs of one of her sandals. She wore a yellow blouse and a very short white pleated skirt. Her knees were brown, and the sun shone on the fine blonde hair which flowed out from underneath her hat.

His shadow fell across her foot. She looked up at him, and her eyes were so grey that it looked as if his shadow had fallen into her eyes, too.

"It's you," he said; and inside he felt as if he were sliding down a wall of melting ice. He had never been so frightened in his life, and it took all of his self-control to prevent himself from urinating.

"*Pardon, monsieur?*" she frowned.

"It's you. I saw you in St Malo. I saw you in Rouen. It's you."

81

Slowly, she smiled. "I've never been to St Malo. And I haven't been to Rouen since I was at school."

"I don't understand this," he said. "How can it not be you?"

She stood up, still smiling. "Are you disappointed that I'm someone else? Who did you want me to be?"

"You're Marianne. You must be."

The girl shook her head. "My name is Stephanie. I live in the 6 arrondissement with my father and my mother and a big fat cat."

Gerry looked at her more closely. He simply couldn't believe that it wasn't Marianne. Yet, seriously, how could it be?

"You know that it's rude to stare," Stephanie told him. Underneath her yellow blouse she had the same full breasts as Marianne.

"I'm sorry. I made a stupid mistake, that's all."

"Well, perhaps you could make up for it by buying me an ice-cream. I cycled all the way here and I forgot it was Tuesday, and that the Louvre is closed on Tuesdays."

He actually opened his mouth to form the word "yes". But then something warned him; something disturbed him. It wasn't just the fact that Stephanie looked so much like Marianne. There seemed to be something wrong the whole day. The light was odd. The shadow of the bicycle didn't seem to fall where he would have expected it to fall. He was attracted to her. He wanted her. He thought of Marianne, lying back in the orchard, with her thighs wide apart. But for some reason he turned around and they were standing not far away, the silver-haired man and his wife in black.

"I'm sorry," he said. "I'm late. I have to go."

"Well, you're mean, as well as rude," she pouted.

"I have to go. I'm sorry."

He began walking away as fast as he could. Stephanie stayed where she was, beside the pyramid, watching him. The silver-haired man and the woman in black watched him, too.

That night he fell asleep as soon as he went to bed and dreamed of Marianne, and the orchard. He could almost feel his penis sliding in and out of her warm vagina. He woke up, sweating, with a painful erection, and the deepest sense of loss that he had ever experienced.

It was still only eight o'clock in Connecticut, so he phoned Freddie.

"Freddie, what would you do if Larry died, but then you found somebody exactly the same?"

"What kind of a question is that?"

"It's just a question. What would you do?"

"When you say exactly the same, how exactly?"

"Exactly exactly. Right down to the last mole."

"I don't know. I guess I couldn't help finding him attractive. I mean, since Larry is my type, then this guy who was *exactly* the same would have to be my type, too."

Gerry looked across at his empty, crumpled bed, and said, "Yes, of course."

They stepped out of the comfortable warmth of the Huitre d'Or and straight into a brisk, face-slapping wind from the Channel. Carl gripped his arm, his hair flying, and said, "How about going back for another marc?"

"No, I'm sorry. I have to get back to Paris this evening. Marketing conference eight thirty sharp."

"Oh, well, another time. At least you're looking a damned sight better than you did before."

"You can't grieve for ever. And maybe somebody

else will come along, just when I'm least expecting it."

They were walking along the promenade at Arromanches, which had once been Gold Beach, where the Allies landed on D-Day. The dark hulking remains of the Mulberry harbour still lay in the shallows, and a Sherman tank still perched on top of a nearby hill. Gerry was here to evaluate the possibilities of TransWestern opening a hotel/restaurant to cater for 'living history' package tours.

The Channel was the colour of pale gum. The wind was thick with salt and grit, and they had to shield their faces with their hands.

"I'll say goodbye," Carl told him, and clasped his hand. "Take more care of yourself, will you? And if that right person comes along – well, grab her with both hands."

He watched Carl drive away, and then he walked a little further along the front, and down to the beach. He was crying, but only because of the wind. Two spaniels were scampering around and around on the sand, and a small boy was huddled against the promenade wall with his trousers round his ankles, trying unsuccessfully to pee against the wind.

Gerry walked out to the water's edge, even though he was wearing Oxfords. A little way away, a young woman was standing on her own, a woman with a yellow headscarf and a long cream coat. He wondered what she was doing out here, all by herself, staring at the rusting remains of a war that must have been over twenty years before she was born.

He walked up to her. She didn't turn around, but stood with one hand clasping the knot of her scarf, quite still, oblivious to the single strand of blonde hair which waved in front of her face.

"Kind of spooky, isn't it?" he asked her.

At first he thought she wasn't going to answer, but then she said, "I don't think so. I think it's sad. So many lives lost. So many lovers, husbands and sons. So much grief."

"Do you know how they built the Mulberry harbour? They towed the damn thing all the way from England."

She turned and faced him. "I'm not very interested in old things. I like only new things."

He stared at her and he felt as if centipedes were crawling down his back. She was so much like Marianne that it could have been her. The same complexion, the same cheekbones, the same faint overbite. Most of all, she had the same colour eyes; like a reflection on a winter lake.

He knew that it couldn't be Marianne, any more than the girl on the bus in Rouen had been Marianne, or Stephanie, outside the Louvre. But she was so much alike that he couldn't speak. He just stood looking at her, his arms by his sides, while the wind flapped his collar against his cheek.

"Is something wrong?" she asked him.

"I'm sorry. I'm really sorry. You remind me of somebody, that's all."

"I hope it was somebody you were fond of."

He gave her a tight smile. He didn't know that he could answer that question without a catch in his throat.

"Well," she said, "I have to be going now. My parents are expecting me."

"I was just going for a cup of coffee. Why don't you join me? We could have it the Norman way – you know, with a dash of calvados in it. Just the thing to warm you up."

She hesitated, and then she said, "All right. But not for too long. My father gets impatient."

They walked back across the beach.

"Do you live nearby?" he asked her.

"I live in St Martin de Fontenay. It's a little town near Caen. I keep telling myself that I must get out and see the world, but I don't know. Something always conspires to stop me."

They went into a small café with a tiled floor and tables covered with red checkered cloths. The ceiling was hung with fishing nets and plaster lobsters. They sat by the window and ordered two cups of black coffee and two small glasses of calvados. It was too cold to take off their coats.

"You're American, aren't you?" the woman said. "Do you come from a big city in America?"

"I was born in a place called New Milford. That wasn't exactly your throbbing metropolis. But since then I've spent a lot of time in New York, and London, England."

"I'd love to live in a big city."

"Believe me, it's no great shakes."

"I don't care. I'd love to be famous all over the world, and live in a big city."

He tipped his calvados into his coffee and stirred it. "What do you want to be famous for? Or do you just want to be famous?"

"I play the cello. Well, I'm learning to play the cello. It's very demanding for a woman."

Gerry lowered his cup and stared at her intently. The woman stared back, quite unabashed. Neither of them said anything for almost a minute.

"You're her," he whispered.

Her eyes flickered for the first time. "I don't know what you mean. My name isn't Marianne. It's Chloe."

"And your father isn't a magistrate?"

"Of course not. He's retired. He used to be the head-teacher at the lycee."

Gerry cleared his throat. "I know this is really a stupid thing to ask you, and I won't be offended if you don't want to answer, but do you know me at all? Have you ever met me before, anywhere?"

Chloe shook her head. "I would have remembered, don't you think?"

Gerry said, "It's incredible. The resemblance is incredible. You're just like her."

There was another long pause, during which they simply sat and looked at each other. Even though Chloe wasn't Marianne, there seemed to be the same affinity between them, the same erotic magnetism. When they started talking, they talked as if they were continuing a conversation which they had broken off only yesterday, and as the afternoon began to darken they leaned closer and closer together across the table, until Gerry's hand was resting on hers, and they could smell the coffee and the cider spirit on each other's breath.

At 4:30, Chloe looked at her watch and said, "Oh, no! It's so late! Father will be furious!"

"Can I see you tonight?" asked Gerry.

"I thought you were supposed to be going back to Paris."

"I've changed my mind."

"Not just because of me?"

"What other reason could there be to stay in Arromanches?"

He walked her back along the windy, twilit promenade until they reached her hotel, Le Duc Guillaume. They pushed their way through the revolving doors into the empty, overheated lobby, which smelled of polish and French cigarettes. Unexpectedly, Chloe took hold of both of Gerry's hands and kissed him.

"Meet me at eight," she smiled.

"I'll bring some champagne."

"No, no. Just bring money."

"Money?"

"You want to make love to me, don't you?"

"For money?"

"Why not? All women are prostitutes, in one way or another. If I can't be the greatest cellist of all time, perhaps I could be the greatest prostitute of all time."

He looked at her for a moment, trying to read her expression. "This is a game, isn't it?"

"A game? Only if you want it to be."

They ate in the hotel restaurant. It was off-season, of course, and they were the only diners, apart from a very old couple who scarcely spoke, and a single bald man who read a book while he ate and kept clearing his throat. The waiter's shoes squeaked monotonously as he brought them moules marinieres, demoiselle lobsters and stuffed Seine shad. Their eyes glittered in the lamplight.

"Do you think it's possible for two people to be exactly alike?" asked Gerry.

"Of course not. There will always be differences. Even one person isn't exactly alike to all of the different people who know them."

Under the table, Chloe dropped off her shoe and began to massage the side of Gerry's calf with her stockinged foot. It was so gentle and so familiar that he could almost believe that she was doing it absent-mindedly, but all the same he felt his penis stiffen, and he knew that he wanted her very much.

He didn't care whether it was impossible that she looked so much like Marianne. It just seemed to him that Marianne had been trying to get back to him, in one form or another, ever since her death. Why should he deny her any longer – especially when he wanted her so much. Blurred pictures of the orchard flickered through his mind; and the waiter's squeaking shoes became the squeaking of a yellow waterproof on a rumpled bed.

After their meal, they sat in the hotel lounge and finished their wine. The clock by the fireplace sonorously struck twelve.

"I'd better go," said Gerry. "At midnight, I turn into a langoustine."

"Don't tell me you forgot your money?"

He had already half-risen from his chair. He sat down again, and took hold of her hand. "Listen, don't get me wrong. I think you're fabulous. I want to make love to you. But before we get into anything serious, I have to be sure about the way I feel."

"Who said anything about anything serious? This is commerce."

Her words sounded cold but she said them with such a teasing smile that Gerry gave in. He took out his billfold and said, "How about 7,500F?"

She took the money and tucked it into the front of her dress. "Come on," she said, and led the way to the elevator.

Her room was high-ceilinged, very warm, lit only by a bedside lamp with a dim pink shade. She drew back the bedcover as if she were unveiling a painting. Then she turned to him and kissed him again. Her tongue licked and teased at his lips, and then deeply penetrated his mouth. All the time she kept her eyes open, staring at him unblinkingly. Her eyes were as grey as thunderstorms, and ball-bearings, and empty country roads.

She unbuttoned her long black woollen dress, and as it fell to the floor it exhaled female warmth and Chanel

89

No.5. Underneath she wore a lacy black bra and a black lace thong, and black hold-up stockings with lace-edged tops. She took off her bra, and her breasts were just like Marianne's, full and rounded and pale as milk. He touched her nipples with his fingertips, and she kissed him again, her head uptilted, eager for the taste of his mouth.

He stripped off his clothes. His penis stood up at an acute angle and cast a shadow on the wallpaper. She kissed him and laughed and said, "Look," so that he could see her stroking it in silhouette. She rubbed the shaft slowly up and down, so slowly that it was almost frustrating.

"Now . . . you've paid for me, you can take me," she whispered. She turned and lay face-down on the bed, her breasts pressed against the sheet. She raised her bottom and reached behind her with both hands to part the cheeks of her bottom, although she was still wearing her thong.

Gerry, naked, mounted the bed behind her. He pulled the thong aside, so that her vulva was exposed. It was already moist, and slightly gaping. The curves of her inner lips were pink and wavelike.

He took hold of his penis in his fist, and buried it inside her, as deep as he could, until he was pressing her into the bed. With one hand she reached between his legs and began to stroke his scrotum with his fingernails, very lightly at first, but then harder and harder, until she was digging her nails into his skin and forcibly tugging it. His thighs quaked, and he felt as if his whole soul was concentrated between his legs.

At the instant he climaxed, Chloe deliberately pulled him out of her, and rolled over, so that his semen sprayed all over her leg. She held him and scratched him and nuzzled him and bit him, thrashing from side to side on the bedcover, until he felt that he was being attacked by wild animals.

Afterward, she lay back on the bed and stared at the ceiling. He rested on one elbow and watched her, tracing a pattern on her bare stomach with his fingertip, occasionally sliding it down far enough to entwine it with her pubic hair.

"Where did you first make love to your Marianne? Tell me."

"An apple orchard, near Clecy."

Chloe smiled at him. "Did you know that whenever they brought apples anywhere near to Duchesne, the secretary to Francois I, blood poured from his nose?"

"No, I didn't know that. But blood didn't pour from *my* nose."

"Just from your heart?"

He nodded. He still felt grief for Marianne, but it was difficult to grieve quite so sorely while another Marianne was lying next to him: a woman of the same erotic appetites, a woman of the same game-playing flirtatiousness, a woman who would do anything to please him.

They made love twice more before dawn. The third time, Chloe insisted that he tie her wrists and ankles with silk scarves, and cover her eyes with a blindfold. As the first grey light began to fill the room, he knelt between her thighs, his fingers deep inside her, while she gasped, and gasped, and called out his name.

Just before he fell asleep, he heard her watch ticking on the nightstand, and he was sure that when she breathed out she whispered, "*Pity me.*"

When he dressed he found that his money was back in his billfold. He took it out and went to the bathroom where she was standing in front of the mirror brushing her teeth.

"What's this?" he asked her.

Her reflection grinned at him. "You didn't think that I was really a prostitute, did you? I want to be a great cellist."

"Marry me," he told her.

"*Marry* you? You don't even know me. I might be the worst cellist in the world."

"I don't have to know you. I feel like we were fated to meet each other, that's all. I mean, did you ever make love with any other man before?"

"That's none of your business."

"But did you?"

She brushed past him, naked. He caught her arm. They stared intensely into each other's eyes. He could smell the peppermint of her toothpaste, as well as the smell of sex.

"Marry me," he repeated.

"Why should I? Because I remind you so much of your Marianne?"

"Because you've allowed me to forget her."

She didn't say yes and she didn't say no. But she kissed her own fingertip, and placed it on his lips, and he knew that what she had done was both a seal and a sign, and that one day soon they *would* be married.

She took him to meet her parents, in a large grey house just outside the village of Ossuaire, on the flat water-meadows that led to Mont St-Michel. Gerry parked in the curving shingled driveway, and climbed out. It was always windy here, so close to the sea, and the grey house fluttered with pale wisteria. In the distance, the 200-foot peak of Mont St-Michel stood dark in a sun-dazzling sea, but somehow the heart seemed to have gone out of it. It had withstood the English in the Hundred Years' War and the Huguenots in the religious wars, but it had fallen, in the end, to tourists.

Her father was waiting for them in the dim, uncarpeted sitting-room, his back to the light. He wore a grey suit and a grey silk necktie, and a grey cat sat on his lap, its eyes squeezed shut in self-satisfaction. Gerry approached him and held out his hand. The old man kept on stroking the cat, and made no attempt to take it. "Chloe tells me that you wish to marry her," he said, in the dryest of voices.

"Yes, sir. I do."

"Well . . . she is old enough to make up her own mind, I suppose."

Gerry found it difficult to see his face. "You don't sound very enthusiastic, sir, if you don't mind my saying so."

"Why should I mind your saying so? I'm not."

"Sir – I love Chloe with all my heart. Nobody could take care of her the way that I'm going to take care of her."

"That's what I'm afraid of."

Gerry looked toward Chloe, perplexed. Chloe was rearranging sweet peas in a large glass vase. She said nothing, but smiled to herself.

"Won't you give us your blessing, then?" asked Gerry.

"I'll pray for you."

Just then, Chloe's mother came in from the garden, carrying a basket full of lettuce and chives.

"It's so windy out there today," she complained. She set down her basket, and took off her veiled gardening-hat, and it was then that Gerry saw that she looked almost exactly like Marianne's mother – the woman in the black woollen dress to whom she had introduced him at the

Moulin du Vey. He stared at her, and then he stared at Chloe. He felt as if the day were folding in on itself, like origami.

Chloe came across and possessively took hold of his arm. "Maman, this is my husband-to-be."

Her mother stared back at Gerry with undisguised dislike. "So, it has come to this, has it?"

Gerry said, "I'm sorry . . . I'm not too sure what this is all about. All I want to do is to marry Chloe and make her as happy as I can."

Chloe's mother picked up her basket of lettuces and walked past him toward the kitchen. At the doorway, she paused. "You will never make anyone happy, Chloe least of all."

"Take no notice," Chloe smiled, and kissed Gerry's cheek. "Mother doesn't approve of anybody."

They were married in September at the hotel de ville in Beauvoir. Chloe seemed to have hundreds of relatives, stocky matrons in black suits with hair like scouring-pads, and thin uncles in camphorated pinstripes who chainsmoked and talked racing. A reception was held at the large grey house at Ossuaire, with roast hams and galantines and pickled herring. The sun shone, but it rained, and the wind blew the rain against the garden in golden curtains.

Gerry found Chloe sitting upstairs in her old room. He sat down on the bed next to her and kissed her.

"Are you all right?" he asked her. "You're looking pale."

"I'm fine. A little queasy, that's all."

"Do you know how much I love you?" he breathed, very close to her ear.

94

She nodded, and smiled. "That's why I'm here. That's why I married you."

She paused for a moment, and then she said, "That's why I'm having your child."

"You're not—?"

"Pregnant, yes. The doctor confirmed it yesterday."

"You're kidding me! Why didn't you tell me as soon as you knew?"

"Perhaps you would have changed your mind. Perhaps you wouldn't have married me."

"Are you crazy? I'm over the moon!"

"Really?"

"Of course really. I've just married the most beautiful woman in the world and the most beautiful woman in the world has just told me that she's carrying my child. Hey, come on downstairs, we have to tell everybody. We have to break open some more champagne!"

She clasped his hand. "No, Gerry, don't tell everybody. Not on our wedding day. Wait till we come back from Nice."

He kissed her, and she kissed him back. Before he knew it, she had pushed him back onto the bed and straddled him, hitching up her cream linen skirt to reveal cream stockings with lacy suspenders.

"Chloe—" he protested, but she almost suffocated him with kisses. At the same time, she reached down and yanked open the zipper of his formal black pants.

"Chloe, supposing somebody—" he panted, but there was no stopping her now, even if he'd wanted to stop her. She twisted her skirt up around her waist, and he saw then that she wasn't wearing any panties.

She grasped his crimson-headed penis and nestled it up between her legs. Then, with a long sigh, she sat down on it, so that it slid right up inside her.

"You're pregnant," he gasped. "What about the baby?"

"Don't worry." She smiled, as she lifted herself up, and then eased herself down again. "There's plenty of room for both of you."

He had never in his life felt so ridiculously happy. His secretary Alexis renamed him "Gerry the Merry" and Carl thought he was on Prozac; but his only stimulus was Chloe, and their new life together, and the prospect of having a child. They flew to Nice for two weeks on honeymoon, and when they came back he started to look for apartments around Caen.

In the second week of October he found a huge newly-decorated apartment overlooking a park on the south-west side of the city. He called Chloe from the realtor's office, while the realtor beamed at him from across the room and shuffled his papers in approval. Gitanes smoke drifted across the room.

Chloe's father answered. "She has just left."

"Is she going to be long? I have some good news, that's all."

"I don't know. She said perhaps two hours. She went to the village."

"All right, then. I'll see you later."

"Very well." Chloe's father was no longer gratutitously rude to him, but he never missed an opportunity to make it plain that he disliked and mistrusted him. Chloe's mother rarely spoke to him at all.

Gerry drove back toward Mont St-Michel in an odd, unsettled mood. The sun had been shining all day but now the sky had turned thundery. By the time he reached the water-meadows, the clouds behind the monastery were inky-black, and lightning was flickering in the distance.

The road curved ahead of him, between the nodding trees and the windblown bushes. Just past Beavour, he was overtaken by a large silver Citroën, driving so fast that it slewed from one side of the road to the other. He heard its tires howl as it slewed around the bend just in front of him.

Something was wrong. Something was terribly wrong. For some reason, he felt compelled to accelerate, and to catch up with it, even to overtake it, as if—

As if wherever it was going, he ought to get there first.

He drove faster and faster – much faster than he usually dared. The narrow road unwound in front of him like a firehose. On the sixth or seventh bend, he caught sight of the Citroën's tail-end, and sped breathtakingly fast down the next straightaway. Lightning flashed; thunder grumbled; and huge fat drops of rain began to spatter his windshield.

He swerved around the next bend and the Citroën was in sight. But something else was in sight, too. Along a narrow diagonal pathway, a girl in a primrose-yellow dress was cycling, slow and measured, making her way toward the road. Her head was held high. She could have been singing or cycling with her eyes closed.

God, it was Chloe.

Everything fell into place in front of his eyes. Everything was here – just the same as the day when he had struck the young girl in the yellow dress. The lightning striking the spires of Mont St-Michel. The water-meadows, spangled with light and shadow. Chloe, cycling, his pregnant darling. The Citroën braking, already braking, smoke billowing out of its tires, dark rubber-marks slashing the road.

Then Chloe flying, tumbling. Her bicycle pedalling itself into the ditch. And the Citroën speeding away, not stopping, driving so fast that by the time Gerry had stopped, and stepped out onto the road, even the sound of it had vanished.

She lay face-down and blood ran out of her hair and into the grass. He picked up her skinny-wristed arm and felt for her pulse, but he knew that she was dead. It wasn't just a matter of vital signs – he *knew*. It was fate, it was punishment, it was wheels within wheels.

He turned her over, very gently. Her hair flew in the wind. Half of her face was perfect. The other half had been smashed against the road. One eye lay dangling on her cheek like the eye of a broken doll.

He pressed his hand against her swollen stomach, but of course it was too early to feel anything, or too late. His child was dying, or dead, and there was nothing he could do to save her.

He stood up, and walked a few mechanical steps along the road. Then he knelt on the verge and started to sob. He felt like an empty jug that had been filled to overflowing with pure grief. He couldn't do anything but sob, and sob, until his throat hurt, and he fell face forward into the grass.

He was still lying there when he heard footsteps approach him. He lifted his head, and looked up, but the sun was in his eyes. A man in a grey suit was standing over him. Not far away, a woman was kneeling over Chloe's body. Her primrose-yellow dress billowed in the breeze.

"He killed her," said Gerry, in a swollen voice. "He killed her and he didn't stop."

The man nodded. "They don't realize, do they, that they're not killing just one woman, but many? They're killing a lover, and a wife, and a daughter, and a friend. They're killing a pretty girl that you might glimpse on a bus, and never see again. They're killing a young student who meets her boyfriend outside an art gallery, on the day that it happens to be closed."

He paused, and then he said, "They leave so many lives unlived. They cause so much grief to so many people. Perhaps, if they were to feel that same grief themselves . . .?"

Gerry lay face-down and couldn't move, as if the weight of his grief was greater than gravity; as if a huge stone had been placed on his back. The man in the grey suit walked away and left him to rise as best he could.

He was sitting in the departure lounge at Charles de Gaulle, waiting for his flight back to New York, when he heard the girl laughing.

He lowered his copy of the *Herald Tribune* and looked across at her. She was sitting amongst a group of friends – six or seven girls in their early twenties – but she was obviously the prettiest and the most vivacious. Her blonde hair shone in the sunlight that filled the terminal, her laugh rang like bells.

He sat watching her for a very long time without blinking. He looked very tired and grey, and his eyes were still puffy from nights of hopeless weeping. After a while, she turned her head and caught sight of him watching her. She turned back to her friends, but then she glanced at him again, and then again, and gave him a quick, coquettish smile.

She looked so much like Chloe, and Stephanie, and the girl on the bus in Rouen. She looked so much like Marianne. The same hair, the same cheekbones, the same endearing weakness in her mouth. But this time he didn't feel elated, or excited. This time the feeling of grief pressed down on him harder than ever.

He folded his newspaper and stood up. Leaving his flight bag on the seat, he walked toward the girl and stood right behind her. One of her friends nudged her, and she turned and looked up at him.

"Have we met before?" he asked her.

She laughed, and all her friends laughed, too. "I don't think so," she said. "I think I would have remembered you."

"Your name's not Chloe, or Marianne?"

"No, it isn't. It's Bernice."

"Bernice. Ah. You don't play the cello by any chance?"

"Yes, I do. But I'm only learning. One day—"

"One day you'll be famous. Yes, I know. One day you'll be able to live in a big city in America, where you've always wanted to live."

The girl turned to her friends, perplexed. Then they all giggled again. "You must have met him before!" said one of them. "He knows you better than I do!"

Gerry said, "Your watch. Do you mind if I see your watch?"

The girl protectively covered it with her hand. "It isn't valuable."

"I know. But I just want to look at it."

Cautiously, she lifted her hand toward him, and he took hold of her slender, blue-veined wrist. She was wearing a cheap gold watch with a red strap. On the dial was printed the brand name Hi Tyme, but the second foot of the 'H' had been scratched, so that it looked as if read 'Pi Tyme'.

Pity me.

He took out his billfold, counted out 7,500 F and gave it to her.

"What's this for?" she said. "I can't take this!"

100

"Don't you remember? It's all part of the game."

"But this is so much money!"

Gerry gently touched her shoulder, and gave her a regretful smile. "This time I want you to have it."

"This time?"

There were tears in his eyes. He couldn't tell her. He couldn't tell her anything.

"He's mad!" said one of Bernice's friends. "Look at him, he's crying!"

But Bernice stared up at him and her eyes were as grey as a winter lake.

"I love you," he said. "And I'm sorry."

He walked off, across the departure lounge, and back along the moving walkways that would take him to the terminal exits. He didn't even bother to pick up his flight bag. Bernice watched him go as if she were gradually beginning to remember who he was; or who he might have been.

"You ought to go after him!" urged one of her friends.

But Bernice lifted her hand, and said, "*Un moment*," as if she were expecting something to happen.

Gerry walked out of the airport exit into the first blinding light of a sunny shower. He didn't see the Air France coach that was speeding toward him, and even if he had, he may not have tried to get out of its way. He heard a horrible screeching and then something knocked him so hard that he flew across the concourse and smashed into a glass bus shelter.

He wasn't aware of much else. He lay face-down, his stomach penetrated by a large triangular piece of glass, and he could see blood dripping onto the wet asphalt in front of him.

Somebody said, "What is your name, my son?"

"Gerry," he bubbled.

"*Te absolvo*, Gerry. In the name of the Father, and of the Son, and of the Holy Spirit."

From where he was lying, he couldn't see Bernice, who was standing in the crowd that surrounded him white-faced, her hair blowing in the wind. Unlike everybody else, she looked extraordinarily tranquil, almost satisfied, and after a while she turned and walked away, as if she knew nothing at all about pain, or misfortune, or grief, and never would.

Her parents were waiting for her on the corner, dressed in black.

The Secret Shih-Tan

Los Angeles, California

In a town where lunch is taken even more seriously than death, it is essential for one's image to be seen eating at the right places. Personally I never bothered to eat at the right place. I used to go to the Palm on Santa Monica for steak and lobster because it was good and I used to have salads at Butterfields on Sunset because it meant that I didn't have to use the car. But the standard of cooking in the best restaurants in Los Angeles can rival any cooking in the world, and the only thing that grieves me is that most of the customers are more concerned with where they are than what they're eating.

For the restaurateur, this snobbery can be expensive. When I was researching this story, I heard time and time again of diners who pilfered the ashtrays and cutlery of elite restaurants, just to show their friends that they had been there. In one year, La Scala lost over $5,000 in stolen wine goblets, cappucino cups and cutlery. At La Cave, manager Dean Evans used crystal ashtrays to dress up his tables, and was appalled to see the wife of a judge slipping one of them into her purse. As a counterploy, he gift-wrapped another ashtray and presented it to her as she left, saying, "There – now you have a pair."

The Secret Shih-Tan is another story of predatory diners. But these diners, for once, are not interested in where they dine, or whether they can take home a souvenir. These diners are another face of fear.

THE SECRET SHIH-TAN

'Men eat the flesh of grass-fed and grain-fed animals, deer eat grass, centipedes find snakes tasty, and hawks and falcons relish mice. Of these four, which knows how food ought to taste?' – Wang Ni.

Craig's father had always told him that cooking was just like sex. It aroused you, it empowered you. It enabled you to play God with other people's senses. Afterward it left you feeling sweaty and exhausted, but the first inklings of what you might cook next were already teasing you like a girl who wouldn't stop playing with your softened penis.

Tonight, Craig had cooked over 112 covers since the Burn-the-Tail Restaurant had opened at six o'clock, and now he was sitting on an upturned broccoli box in the back yard, drinking ice-cold Evian water out of the bottle and listening to the clattering and clamouring of dishes being washed.

He smeared his eyes with the back of his hand. He was so tired that he couldn't even think of anything to think. But he knew that there was fresh carp being delivered in the morning, and there were so many amazing things you could do with fresh carp. Carp with dry white wine, horseradish and prunes. Carp with celeriac and leeks, simmered in lager beer and dry white wine. Carp stuffed with scallions and ham and winter bamboo shoots.

Craig didn't look at all like somebody who had been obsessed by cooking ever since he was old enough to stand on a chair and reach the stove-top. He was twenty-eight years old, as gangly as a stork, with a thin, sharply-etched face and short hair that stuck up like Stan Laurel's. But both his parents were brilliant cooks, and had inspired him to play in the kitchen in the same way that the other kids used to take piano lessons.

His father George was French-Canadian, and used to cook for La Bella Fontana at the Beverly Wilshire Hotel. His mother Blossom was half-Chinese, and had taught him everything from the four levels of flame to the eleven shapes by the time he was nine. Between the two of them, they had given him the ability to be able turn the simplest ingredients into dishes about which *Los Angeles* magazine had said, 'there's no other word for Craig Richard's cooking except *erotic*.'

The *Los Angeles Times* had been even more explicit. 'This food is so indecently stimulating that you almost feel embarrassed about eating it in public.'

Craig had opened the Burn-the-Tail on Santa Monica Boulevard a few days after his twenty-third birthday, and now its endlessly surprising juxtaposition of classic French and Oriental cooking meant that it was booked solid almost every night, mainly with movie people and lawyers and record executives. But unlike Ken Hom and Madhur Jaffrey and other celebrity chefs, Craig had shied away from television appearances and recipe book offers. Whenever he was asked to give cooking tips, he always shook his head and said, "Ask me in ten years' time. I'm not good enough yet."

All the same, he had plenty of faith in himself.

106

Almost too much faith. He believed that he was more highly-skilled than almost any other chef in Greater Los Angeles, if not the whole of California. But he had an idea in his mind of food that would arouse such physical and emotional sensations in those who ate it that they would never be able to touch any other kind of food again. He had an idea of food that would literally give men erections when they put it in their mouths, and make women tremble and squeeze their thighs together.

He could cook better than any chef he knew, but until he had cooked food like that, he knew that he wasn't good enough.

He swigged more Evian. On a busy night, he could lose up to three pounds in fluid. He had six assistants working with him, but his style of cooking was furious, fast and highly labour-intensive. It was the Chinese influence: the pride in slicing marinated duck livers so that they looked like chrysanthemum flowers and cutting sea-bass so that it came out in the shape of a bunch of grapes.

Tina, his cocktail waitress, came out into the yard. Tina didn't know Escoffier from Brad Pitt but he liked her. She was very petite, with a shiny blonde bob and a face that was much too pretty. She wore a tight blue velvet dress with a V-shaped décolletage that gave customers a brief but startling view down her cleavage whenever she bent over to serve them a drink. Tina was proud of her cleavage. She had appeared in two episodes of *New Bay-watch* and she had sent pictures of herself to *Playboy*.

"Almond Head's asking to see you," she said.

"Tell him I've been bitten by a rabid dog." Craig hated it when customers asked him to come out of the kitchen so that they could congratulate him. They would kiss their fingertips and say things like, "that *feuillete* of scallops, that was just, *mwuh!*" while all the time Craig knew that the feuillete of scallops was not just "*mwuh!*", it was made from sparkling fresh scallops that he had bought himself from W.R. Merry the exotic fish wholesalers, poached in eggs and cream and served with a cognac-flavoured lobster sauce that had taken him three years to perfect.

"Almond Head seemed kind of insistent. Here."

She handed him a visiting-card. It was slightly larger than the usual type of visiting-card, and printed with severe, dark letters. *Hugo Xawery*. Underneath, the address read The Sanctuary, Stone Canyon Avenue, Bel Air.

Craig turned the card over. On the back were scrawled four words, in fountain pen. The Secret Shih-Tan.

He stared at the words and found that he could hardly breathe, let alone speak. Their effect on him was the same as the words *The Ark of the Covenant* would have been on a devout Christian, if he had known for sure that whoever had written those words had actually found it.

And there was no doubt in Craig's mind that 'Almond Head' had found *The Secret Shih-Tan*, because scarcely anybody knew of its existence.

Craig had never seen a copy. It had been written only for private circulation amongst a privileged number of chefs; and after its publication its author had suffered such deep remorse that he had tried to retrieve every copy and burn them. But two copies had eluded him: and *The Secret Shih-Tan* had been republished in a strictly limited edition in Shanghai in 1898, under the liberal regime of the young emperor Kuang Hsü. Only 100 days later, however, Kuang Hsü had been deposed by the Dowager Empress Tzu Hi, and *The Secret Shih-Tan*, along with hundreds of other books, had been banned and destroyed. It was rumoured that a single copy had been smuggled out of China by the emperor's personal chef, the legendary K'ang Shih-k'ai, but that was the last that anyone had heard of it. As far as Craig knew, it existed only in myth.

Craig first heard about it from one of his Chinese uncles, when he was fourteen. His mother had found a copy of *Penthouse* under his mattress. His uncle Lee had laughed, and said, "At least it wasn't *The Secret Shih-Tan!*" Blossom Richard had been unaccountably disgusted; and George had warned Craig's uncle not to mention it again. But later, Craig had asked his uncle what it was, and his uncle had told him.

Now here was the name again, on this stranger's visiting-card, and Craig was gripped by the same feeling of dread and excitement that had gripped him all those years ago, when his uncle had sat smoking by the window, murmuring all those forbidden and alluring things that *his* uncle had once murmured to him; and his father before that.

"Are you okay?" asked Tina. "You look like you've *really* been bitten by a rabid dog."

Craig swallowed. "I'm fine. Thanks. Tell Mr Xawery I'll be right out.'

"You're going to *see* him?"

"Why not? You have to kow-tow to the customers some of the time. It's *their* money, after all."

When Tina had bounced her way back into the restaurant, he went to the men's room, stripped off his sauce-splashed whites, and vigorously washed his hands. Jean-Pierre, one of his *sous-chefs* came in. He was plump and unshaven, and he mopped sweat from his forehead with a crumpled T-shirt.

"We had idiots tonight, yes?" he asked Craig, in his erratic, up-and-down French accent. "Those people on

109

table five sent back that Columbian River caviar because it was yellow. 'We know caviar,' they said. 'And caviar is black.'"

Craig was trying to comb his hair. He was trembling so much that he had to grip the rim of the washbasin to steady himself.

"Hey, you're not sick, are you?" asked Jean-Pierre.

"No, no," Craig told him.

"You're shaking like jellies."

"Yes. Yes, I'm shaking." He hesitated for a moment, then said, "What's the most terrible thing you've ever done?"

Jean-Pierre blinked at him. "I don't understand the question."

"What I mean is, have you ever deliberately hurt another human being in order to satisfy something that you've always wanted to do?"

"I don't know. I stole quite a lot of money from one of my girlfriends once. Well, I say stole. She kept buying me clothes and presents, thinking that I was going to marry her, but I knew that I never would. She had a what do you call it? A wart. Do you know, I am not fond of warts."

Craig laid a hand on Jean-Pierre's shoulder and said, "Sure. I understand. I don't like warts either."

"Are you certain you're not sick?" frowned Jean-Pierre.

"I don't know. It's hard to diagnose your own sickness, isn't it? What's sick to one person is right as rain to somebody else."

He dressed in jeans, a button-down Oxford shirt and his favourite sand-coloured Armani jacket. Then he walked through the kitchen, turned left, and out through the swing door into the restaurant. It was nearly one o'clock

110

in the morning and almost everybody had left now. The restaurant was decorated in a pale, restrained style, with lots of natural-coloured woods and concealed lighting. The only distinctive decorative motif was a steel and enamel mural of carp leaping across the main wall, with their tails ablaze.

The man whom the waitresses called 'Almond Head' was sitting with a young girl at table nine, the most discreet table in the restaurant, but the table with the best view. He was very tall and swarthy, with a narrow skull and ears that lay flat back against his head. His hair was jet black, and combed in tight oily ripples; his forehead was deeply furrowed, too. His eyes disturbed Craig more than his almond head. They were hooded and withdrawn and as expressionless as two stones. For all that they communicated, he might just as well not have had eyes at all.

He wore an expensive grey suit and his black shoes gleamed as much as his hair. On his hairy wrist hung a huge gold wrist-watch.

However, it was the girl who held Craig's attention most of all. She looked as if she were partly Asian and partly European. She was very slight; all arms and legs; and she wore a short dress of flesh-coloured silk that made her look from a distance as if she were naked. As it was, it concealed very little. Her nipples made little shadowy points, and the silk clung to her thighs as if it was trying to ride up all by itself, and expose her.

Her face was extraordinary. She had black hair cut in a severe cap; and beneath this cap she had the features of a sphinx – slant-eyed, with a narrow nose and lips that looked as if she had just finished fellatio.

She was deeply suntanned. Her skin was so perfect that

111

Craig found it hard to resist the temptation to touch her shoulder, just to see what it felt like.

"I wish to congratulate you on a very exciting meal," said Hugo Xawery. His voice was deep, but it had no trace of a European accent. On the phone, you might have thought he came from Boston.

"You had the beef tendon," said Craig.

"That's right. It takes great skill and patience to make a piece of gristle into one of the finest dishes in the city. 'If one has the art, then a piece of celery or salted cabbage can be made into a marvelous delicacy: whereas if one has not the art, not all the greatest delicacies and rarities of land, sea or sky are of any avail.'

"Wang Hsiao-yu," said Craig. "Quoted by the scholar Yuan Mei."

"You're a very gifted man. I have searched for more than eleven years for a chef as skilful as you. Why don't you sit down? I have a proposition to make."

Craig remained standing, and passed over Hugo Xawery's visiting-card. "Is it this?"

Hugo Xawery's eyes gave away nothing.

Craig said, "I've heard about it, for sure. But I didn't think there were any copies of it still in existence. Besides, it wouldn't exactly be legal to try cooking from it, would it?"

"Some things are so pure in their purpose that they are above illegality."

"You could never say that this book is pure."

Hugo Xawery gave an infinitesimal shrug. "You haven't read it. I myself have read it more than a hundred times. I know it by heart. If I ever lost it, or if it was stolen, I could rewrite it from cover to cover. It is the single greatest recipe book ever compiled. The nature of the recipes takes nothing away from its single-minded purity of purpose."

112

"I don't know whether everybody would see it the same way."

Hugo Xawery leaned forward a little. His watch was a very strange design, with a brand name that Craig had never seen before. "How would you see it?" he asked.

"Academically, I guess."

"How could a chef of your brilliance read a book like *The Secret Shih-Tan* and not have a burning desire to try it out?"

Craig let out a little humourless bark. "Well, you know why. The ingredients are something of a problem, to say the least. And I have my restaurant to think of, my career."

"Ah, yes," said Hugo Xawery. "Your career."

Craig waited but Hugo Xawery said nothing more. He sat with his stone-dead eyes, his watch ticking away the seconds, one of his hands resting on the girl's bare thigh, far higher up than most restaurant-goers would have considered decent.

"I'd certainly like to see it, though," said Craig, after a while.

"You may see it," Hugo Xawery replied. "And that is my proposition."

"Go on."

"You may come to my house and read it. You may read it all the way through, if you so wish. But there is one condition."

"What? That I don't steal any of the recipes and serve them up here? Not very likely! Ha!"

Hugo Xawery turned to the girl. His hand was very high on her thigh now and his little finger had disappeared under the hem of her dress. God, she was alluring, thought Craig. She was so erotic and so vulnerable that he could hardly believe she was real.

113

"Mr Richard here has named his restaurant Burn-The-Tail," Hugo Xawery said to her, almost murmuring. "This comes from the story told in the Tang Dynasty of how the carp used to swim up the Huanghe River to spawn. They did well until they reached the Dragon Gate, which was very narrow and turbulent, and the current was too strong for them to go any further. That is, until one of them learned to leap."

When he said this, he turned back and stared at Craig with such an expression of power and dark intensity that Craig felt a cold shrinking sensation in his spine.

"One of them learned to leap, and so all the others followed, and as they leaped they flew in shimmering arcs through the spray. The gods were so impressed by their beauty and their courage that they burned their tails gold, and changed the carp into scaly dragons who could fly wherever they wanted. In Chinese, if anybody says you have a 'burned tail', it means you have a glittering future."

He almost smiled, and then he said, "Mr Richard could be the first carp to make the leap through the Dragon Gate."

"So what's your condition for reading the book?" asked Craig. He still couldn't bring himself to say its name out loud.

"Very simple, Mr Richard. You may read; but then, having read, you must choose one recipe and cook it for me."

Craig hesitated. "Is this a joke? You're not pulling my leg or anything?"

Hugo Xawery's face made it utterly clear that he found even the word 'joke' to be offensive.

"I'd be using substitute ingredients, right?"

114

"Do you use substitute ingredients here, at the Burn-the-Tail? Do you use small-mouthed bass instead of Mandarin fish? Do you use collard greens instead of Chinese broccoli? Or pig's liver pate instead of foie gras?"

"Of course not."

Hugo Xawery said, "I will provide the ingredients. Whatever you ask."

Craig smiled, and shook his head, and then stopped smiling.

"Very well," Hugo Xawery told him. "If you won't do it, then I will have to continue my search for someone who will. I have to confess that I am gravely disappointed. You are one of the greatest chefs whose creations I have ever had the pleasure to eat."

Tina came up and said, brightly, "Can I bring you some refreshment?"

Hugo Xawery stood up. He was very, very tall – almost six-feet-five. "I do need refreshment, yes. But not wine. I need to have my soul refreshed. I need to taste – I need to taste *God*."

Craig escorted him to the door. The girl silently followed. She brushed past Craig and he felt as if they were both naked.

"Listen, I'm sorry I couldn't help you," he said, as Hugo Xawery buttoned up his coat.

"Don't be sorry, Mr Richard. Only the weak are ever sorry."

When they had gone, Craig went over to the bar and asked Tina to pour him a vodka on the rocks.

"Weird people," she remarked. "That girl looks young enough to be his daughter."

"Maybe she is."

"And do you know what's strange about her? I mean,

apart from the fact that you couldn't stop staring at her with your mouth hanging open?"

"Go on, tell me."

"She wasn't wearing any perfume. None at all. No make-up, either. Don't you think that's strange?"

"Maybe she's allergic."

"I don't know," said Tina. "My grandmother used to say that women can smell fear in other women, even when they're laughing and smiling and trying to show everybody that they're having a great time. That girl wasn't wearing any perfume, but she smelled of fear."

Craig lay alone that night in his pale, sparsely-decorated apartment on Mulholland Drive, unable to sleep. He kept thinking of Uncle Lee, sitting by the window, smoking. He could see him now, his eyes lowered, his voice little more than a dry, crackly whisper.

"*The Secret Shih-Tan* was written by the scholar Yuan Mei during the Ching period. He was a great intellectual, you know, a great philosopher. For him, food was a world in itself. He loved everything about it, and its preparation, and the way in which it was served. He delighted in such tiny nuances as the fact that the word for 'fish' in Chinese sounds exactly like the word for 'more than enough'.

"First of all, he wrote *Shih-Tan*, a very famous book of recipes that was published all over the world. But his fame became so great that he was introduced to a very secretive order of chefs from the province of Shandong, on the east coast of China on the Yellow Sea. They were all master chefs. But they had another interest. Like you, they were interested in the pleasures of a woman's body."

Craig switched on the light and sat up. He kept trying to imagine what *The Secret Shih-Tan* looked like, what

116

it was like to turn the pages of the most forbidden book in the Western world.

His uncle had blown out smoke, and said, "Some meat is traditionally taboo. Ch'en Ts'ang-ch'i said that you should never eat the flesh of a black ox or a goat with a white head, a single-horned goat, any animal that had died facing north, deer spotted like leopards, horse liver, or any meat that a dog had refused to eat."

He could remember staring at his uncle, speechless, waiting for the words that were almost too dreadful to think about.

His uncle said, "Yuan Mei tasted their food and it affected him forever. After the first time, he went to a house in Jinan near the Qianmen and lay face-down on the floor of an empty room for two days and two nights, eating nothing more, because he didn't want his mouth or his body to be affected by the taste of anything else until the food had passed completely through him. Only at the end of the time did he start to write a second *Shih-Tan*, known as *The Secret Shih-Tan*."

Craig had swallowed. "What did he eat?"

And that was when his uncle had put his lips close to Craig's ear, and fired his imagination with *The Secret Shih-Tan* for ever.

The Sanctuary was a large white house set well back from the road on Stone Canyon Avenue; fenced, gated, and almost invisible behind dark, prickly-looking shrubs. Craig drove up to the gate in his red Mercedes and pressed the intercom button.

"*Xawery residence.*" A girl's voice, light and expressionless.

"Hi, this is Craig Richard. I'd like to talk to Mr Xawery."

117

"*Do you have an appointment?*"

"No, I don't. But you can tell Mr Xawery I accept his condition."

"*You'll have to wait.*"

He waited, listening to Beck singing about being screwed up and life's a toilet and why don't you kill me. After a long while, the gates hummed open, and he drove up the steeply-angled driveway to the house.

It was large, but it was also oddly-proportioned and deeply unwelcoming. A rottweiler barked insanely at him as he approached the porch, hurling itself from side to side on its chain. When he rang the doorbell, a small grille opened up, and he was examined for a ridiculously long time by a disembodied pair of glittering eyes.

"You satisfied?" he said, impatiently.

At last he heard bolts being shot back, and the door was opened by an unsmiling Mexican in a black uniform. Inside the house, it was startlingly chilly. The floor was polished marble and there was scarcely any furniture. No flowers, either. Without a word, the Mexican turned and walked off across the hallway, his shoes squeaking. Craig followed him, although he wasn't sure that he was supposed to. They walked all the way down a long gloomy corridor until they eventually reached a sun-room; or what would have been a sun-room if all the drapes hadn't been drawn. Instead, it had a kind of papyrus-coloured light, as if it were an ancient tomb.

Hugo Xawery was sitting in a large armchair, reading. He was dressed in white pants and a white collarless shirt. The girl was kneeling on the floor next to him, one arm on his knee. She was wearing a plain white sleeveless dress, as square as a sack.

"Well," said Hugo Xawery. "It seems that you have changed your mind."

"As a matter of fact, no, I don't think I have. I think I was always going to have to do this, no matter what."

"Of course."

"I'd just like to know how you knew."

"What? That you were interested in seeing *The Secret Shih-Tan*? I met your uncle Lee Chan, the second time I had dinner at the Burn-the-Tail. He's a very educated man, your uncle, even though he shouldn't smoke so much. It ruins the palate, smoking. I like your Uncle Lee, too. I don't like many Chinese. We talked about your talents, you see; and the conversation went around to Paul Bocuse and nouvelle cuisine, and then to some of the great modern chefs in China. I praised your skill with difficult ingredients, and said something like, 'He's probably cooked everything except *The Secret Shih-Tan*.' That was when your uncle said, 'Yes, but he *knows* about it. And that was when I was satisfied that I had found my man. You have only to know about it to want to cook from it."

Craig said, "I want to ask you something. Have you ever – well, have you ever tasted any of the recipes before?"

Hugo Xawery gave him a closed, stony look. "What happens in this house is private, Mr Richard."

Craig hesitated. A moulting white parrot was sitting in a cage, nodding at him with horrible intimacy. Craig knew that what he was about to do was wrong. It was probably the most terrible thing that he would ever do in his life. But he also knew that if he turned around and walked out of Hugo Xawery's house without seeing *The Secret Shih-Tan*, his career as a chef would be finished. He would wonder for the rest of his life what he could have done, what he could have been.

He wanted to cook a meal that made Hugo Xawery want to lie face-down on the floor for forty-eight hours, sobbing because he was digesting it, and that when he had excreted it, it would be gone forever.

"Show me the book," he said, in a throaty voice.

Hugo Xawery put down his book and stood up. "Very well," he said, and extended his hand. "So long as you remember what you have solemnly agreed to do."

"I won't forget."

Hugo Xawery led the way along another dark, echoing corridor until they reached a bare, marble-floored room with nothing in it but a rectangular steel desk, a plain office chair, and a grey-painted safe. A greenish bamboo shade was drawn most of the way down the French windows. Beneath the shade, Craig could see part of a patio, and the feet of a stone cherub, a reminder of the world that he had now decided to leave behind.

Hugo Xawery walked across to the safe, produced two keys, and opened it. Inside there was nothing but the book itself, wrapped in plain white tissue. Hugo Xawery brought it over, laid it on the desk, and unwrapped it.

It wasn't much to look at. A maroon fabric-bound book with a Chinese character stamped into the cover.

"No," said Hugo Xawery. "It isn't very impressive, is it? This edition was published in Paris in 1911. I've only ever seen another one in English, and that was much older, and illustrated. But I don't think you need illustrations in a book of this nature, do you?"

Craig sat down in the chair. Hugo Xawery said, "I'll leave you to it. Tell me when you've had enough. My man will bring you coffee, or wine, or anything else that you'd care for."

He left, and Craig was alone. He sat looking at the book for a long time without opening it. The moment he turned to the first page, he would be committed. He glanced around the room. He wondered if Hugo Xawery

120

were watching him on a closed-circuit camera. Maybe he should stand up, and walk out now. There was always the Burn-the-Tail; there was always business and chatter and laughter, buying produce, inventing new menus, cooking with sauces and sizzling shallots and flames.

But there was nothing like *The Secret Shih-Tan*; and here it was. It was probably the only copy in America. He laid his hand on the cover. Still he didn't open it.

He knew all of the arcane secrets of great French cookery, right down to roast camel's hump, which the Algerians prepare with oil, lemon juice, salt, pepper and spices, roasted like a sirloin of beef and served on a bed of watercress. He knew all of the Chinese recipes that the bravest of his customers couldn't face: like *beche de mer*, the sea-slug, which has no flavour whatsoever and the consistency of a jellyfish; and bird's nest soup, made out of cliff-swallows' nests, a combination of bird spit, sea-moss and feathers.

But this was something else. This was the moment when food, sex, and death came together in the darkest challenge that any chef could face. Food is sex, his father had always told him. But food was death, too. Every time that something was eaten, something had to die.

Craig felt as if he were standing with his toes on the edge of a terrible abyss. It was too late to turn back; and because it was too late to turn back, he opened the book.

The recipes were written with grace and subtle charm, but that only served to make their horror more intense. Craig started with the simplest of them, in the beginning, but he hadn't read more than three before he began to feel as if he were no longer real, as if the room around him were no longer real. What heightened his feeling of

121

unreality was knowing that he had agreed to prepare one of these dishes, and that he would actually be following the instructions in one of the recipes himself.

'*Young Girl's Breast, Braised*: The breast should first be soaked in cold water, blanched, cooled in cold water and carefully flattened under pressure so that its youthful curves are not lost when it is braised. Place the breast in a clay casserole. Cut two thin slices of smoked thigh-meat into 12 inch squares and add to the casserole, with 6 soaked dried black mushrooms. Make horizontal slashes along one side of each of two bamboo shoots, like a fan. These will make decorative 'angel's wings' to surround the breast when it is served. Add salt, sugar, 3 tablespoons of rice wine and 2 slices of peeled fresh ginger. Braise very gently for 3–4 hours. Slice thinly so that each diner receives a full curve, showing the shape of the breast. The most honoured guests will receive a slice with a section of the nipple on it. Serve with braised asparagus and rape hearts. Breast can be eaten fresh, cold or smoked.'

There were over a hundred recipes in all, every one of them using sexual parts, both male and female – sometimes accompanied by other organs, such as liver or pancreas or stomach-lining. Some of the dishes were plain – sexual interpretations of everyday Chinese dishes such as *zha yazhengan*, which was nothing more than duck gizzards deeply fried and served with a dip of 'prickly ash' – a mixture of salt and Szechuan peppercorns. In *The Secret Shih-Tan*, the gizzards were replaced by plates of deep-fried testicles.

There was *Woman In Man*, which was a sausage made from penis-skin and filled with a mixture of finely chopped labia, seasoned with Maotai liquor, salt, sugar and sesame oil, and fat from the pubic mound.

There were elaborate preparations of male and female

organs, marinated, steamed, and served on a dish in the act of disembodied coitus. *Man Takes Many Lovers* was a penis stuffed into rigidity with scores of nipples, and then encircled with six or seven anal sphincters, like quoits. 'These should be cooked in the same way as jellyfish,' the book advised, and in the same way they required 'spirited, vigorous chewing.'

As he turned the pages, Craig didn't notice the room gradually growing darker. He was lost in a world where every meal required the death or mutilation of a human being – sometimes eight or nine people sacrificed for one tantalizing side-dish.

Toward the end of the book, some of the dishes were so perverse that Craig left the table, and stood on the opposite side of the room, almost too horrified to continue reading. But eventually, he returned, and sat down, and read the recipes to the very end.

The last recipe was the most challenging of all. It was called, simply, *Whole Woman Banquet*. A young woman was to be carefully eviscerated, and every organ cleaned, marinated, and cooked in a different way, including her eyes and her brains. Everything would then have to be returned to the body, and her original shape restored, as perfectly as possible. Then she would be steamed.

It was the footnote that riveted Craig more than any of the lengthy descriptions of how to poach lungs in the same way as soft-shelled turtle. The author Yuan Mi had written, 'It is essential for this dish that the woman be as beautiful as can be found; and that the chef should make love to her the evening before the banquet. The making of love endows both the food and its creator with spiritual tenderness, and is a way that a chef can pay homage to his ingredients.'

Craig closed the book. It was dark now, and he hadn't

realized that Hugo Xawery was standing in the doorway, patiently waiting for him.

"What do you think?" he asked, in a voice like brushed velvet.

"I think it's everything I ever imagined it was going to be."

"Did it shock you?"

"I'd be lying if I said it didn't."

"But the technique . . . what do you think of the technique?"

"Very difficult, some of it."

"But not beyond you?"

"No."

Hugo Xawery circled around the table. "Have you decided what you're going to cook?"

"I don't know. You'll have to give me some time to think about it."

"Not too long. I have to find you the ingredients, you understand, and they must be fresh."

Craig stood up. "I'll call you tomorrow."

"Yes. You will," said Hugo Xawery, with an imperative tone in his voice.

"Don't you trust me?" asked Craig.

"I don't know. You could cause me a great deal of embarrassment, as well as disappointment. I've already promised this treat to several very influential people."

"I've given you my word. What more can I do?"

"You don't have to do anything more. Because I've taken one simple precaution, in case you welsh on your agreement. Somewhere in one of your freezers, amongst the rest of your meats, there are human remains – packed, of course, in completely anonymous freezer-bags, just like all of your other meat. I'm sure the police would be interested in having a rummage among your livers and your kidneys and your loin chops."

"You didn't have to do that," said Craig, tersely. "I don't have any intention of welshing on my agreement."

"Let's just call it insurance. And they're very high-quality remains. Even if you cook them and serve them up, they won't harm anybody."

On the way out, Craig saw the girl standing in a half-open doorway at the end of the corridor. She was wearing nothing but the thinnest of silk slips, so short that it scarcely covered her. She was watching him with those slanted, sphinxlike eyes, her skin shining smooth in the lamplight. He stopped, and stared back at her. She made no attempt to turn away, or to close the door.

"You like her?" asked Hugo Xawery.

"She's beautiful."

"I call her Xanthippa. Of course that's not her real name. Her mother and I lived together for a while, in Carmel. One day her mother left and never came back. So I suppose you could call me her guardian."

Craig took one last look at Xanthippa, and then walked across the hallway to the front door, where the Mexican servant was waiting with undisguised displeasure to show him out.

Early next morning, he found his Uncle Lee in his back yard in Westwood, hosing his roses. Uncle Lee was over seventy now, and his face was wrinkled like an aerial view of Death Valley. He wore a coolie hat and a loose blue shift.

"Uncle Lee?"

"Hallo, Craig. I was wondering when you would come."

125

"I've read it, Uncle Lee. *The Secret Shih-Tan*. I read it yesterday evening, from cover to cover."

"Then today you will be different."

"Yes, I'm different." He watched the hosewater splattering into the flowerbed, and then he said, "Why did you tell Hugo Xawery that I knew about it?"

"Because *The Secret Shih-Tan* is as far as any chef can go; and you would never have been satisfied with anything less."

"Hugo Xawery let me look at it on one condition."

Uncle Lee looked up at him, his eyes slitted against the seven o'clock sunlight. "Don't tell me. You have to cook one of the recipes for him."

Craig nodded. "I've been awake all night. I don't know which one to choose."

"Which do you *wish* to choose? The greatest of all the recipes, or the recipe which causes the least human suffering?"

"I don't know. It's not just gastronomy, is it, *The Secret Shih-Tan*? It has so many inner meanings. We kill thousands of people in war, and that's supposed to be moral and glorious, even though war is totally destructive. But if we sacrifice half a dozen human beings to create one of the greatest meals in gastronomic history, that's supposed to be so goddamned evil that we're not even allowed to *talk* about it."

"So which dish are you going to choose?" Uncle Lee repeated.

"I don't know. I'm still trying to work out what it is that *The Secret Shih-Tan* is trying to tell me."

Uncle Lee turned off the faucet, and laid a withered hand on Craig's shoulder. "If you do not see it for yourself, then I cannot tell you."

"You can't even give me a clue?"

"All I can say is that whatever you decide to cook, make sure, above all, that you do it justice."

Craig didn't open the Burn-the-Tail restaurant that day, although he spent a half-hour in thick insulated gloves, sorting through his freezers. He couldn't find any packages of meat that looked human, but how could anyone tell if there was one human kidney amongst thirty lamb's kidneys, or one escalope of human thigh amongst ten escalopes of veal? He would either have to throw away his entire stock, or else he would simply have to wait until he had fulfilled his promise to cook Hugo Xawery's meal.

Later in the afternoon, he drove up to Stone Canyon Avenue. Hugo Xawery was sitting alone in the sun-room, behind tightly-drawn shades. Through the open door, however, Craig could see Xanthippa sitting on the patio under a large green parasol.

"Ah, Mr Richard," said Hugo Xawery. "What a pleasure to see you so soon. Have you come to a decision?"

Craig nodded. "There's no point in playing around with *hors d'ouevres*," he said. "I'm going to cook the Whole Woman Banquet."

Hugo Xawery's face slowly lit up with unholy relish. "The banquet! I knew you would! The greatest challenge that any chef could ever face! The greatest feast that any gastronome could ever imagine!"

"You won't be able to eat it all on your own, will you?"

"I have no intention of eating it on my own. I have – friends."

"Can you get in touch with them? I'd like to start making preparations right away."

"Of course I can get in touch with them. And I can procure your main ingredient, too. In fact, I have it already."

Craig looked out onto the patio. "Xanthippa?"

"Isn't she beautiful? You can't make the banquet of banquets out of inferior raw materials."

"You know what it says at the foot of the recipe?"

"About the chef making love to his uncooked banquet? Of course. And you shall. Xanthippa has been expecting this day for many years."

"You mean she already knows what you're going to do to her?"

Hugo Xawery smiled. "She lives only to serve me; she always has. Her greatest pleasure has always been to know that one day, I shall ingest her. Why do you think she never wears perfume or cosmetics? She doesn't wish to taint the taste of her flesh."

"How about tomorrow evening?" Craig suggested. "Or is that too soon?"

Hugo Xawery wrapped his long arm around Craig's shoulders. "Tomorrow evening will be perfect. Expect six for dinner, including myself. You can stay here tonight, with Xanthippa, and early tomorrow morning you can start your preparations. You will, of course, allow me to watch you at work?"

"You're very welcome, Mr Xawery. In fact I'd be very disappointed if you didn't."

"How about . . . the butchery? Do you need any assistance?"

"I prefer to do my own, thanks."

Hugo Xawery gripped Craig's shoulder, and stared into his eyes with such emotion that Craig thought for a moment that he was going to weep. "You're a great, great chef. Do you know that? After tomorrow, your name will rank with the very finest."

"We'll see," said Craig.

Without taking his eyes off Craig, Hugo Xawery called out, "Xanthippa!"

She turned and frowned at him.

"Xanthippa, I have a surprise for you!"

The bedroom that Hugo Xawery lent him was silent and painted a silky gray. In the centre stood a massive carved-oak bed, heaped with Moorish cushions. It was a warm night, so Craig left the French windows open. The net curtains billowed silently in the breeze, like the ghosts of nuns.

Craig was sitting up in bed reading *The Secret Shih-Tan* when the door quietly opened and Xanthippa came in. She was wearing nothing but a thin shirt of aquamarine linen and small brown beads around her wrists and ankles. She came across the room and climbed onto the bed next to him. She smelled of nothing but the natural biscuity aroma of an aroused young woman.

"You're reading that book," she said, although not accusingly.

Craig closed it, and dropped it down by the side of the bed. "I'm sorry," he said.

"Why should you be?"

"It isn't very good taste, is it, considering what I'm supposed to do to you tomorrow?"

"You don't understand. I'm looking forward to it. Hugo is one of the greatest men in the world. He's intellectual, he's refined, but he doesn't believe in limits. With Hugo, everything is possible. I've already had enough pleasure for five lifetimes. Why should I worry if it ends now?"

Craig gently touched her cheekbones, and then traced the outline of her lips. *Carefully remove the eyes, and set aside on a dish*. Then he leaned forward a little and kissed her.

"You're very beautiful," he told her.

She smiled, and kissed him back. She kissed him like no woman had ever kissed him before, sucking and teasing his lips, and then sliding her tongue into his mouth and stimulating nerve-endings he didn't even think he had. Underneath the blanket, his penis stiffened.

Xanthippa crossed her arms and took off her shirt. She was lean and small-breasted, but her skin was so exquisite that Craig couldn't stop himself from sliding his hands up and down her bare back. Her pubic hair was shiny and black, and she had plaited it tightly and decorated it with small coloured beads, so that the lips of her vulva were exposed.

She said, "Lie back . . . you can taste me first."

He lay back on the pillow and Xanthippa drew aside the blanket. She climbed astride him, with her back to him, and then she lifted her bottom so that he was confronted with her vagina. He kissed all around it, and then he ran the tip of his tongue down the cleft between her buttocks and tasted her tightly wrinkled anus. She sighed, and kissed him all around his penis in return.

The room was so quiet that he heard the moistened lips of her vagina opening, like the softest click in the Xhosa language. He slid his tongue into her wetness and warmth, and tasted saltness and sweetness and something else as well, like highly purified honey. At the same time, she slowly sucked his penis, flicking it and drumming it with her tongue.

They made love for hours, and she showed him all of the tastes of love. He licked her perspiration-beaded armpits, and the soles of her feet. He swallowed her vaginal juices when they were thick with early arousal; and again when they thinned out, just before orgasm. He tasted her saliva when she was excited, and again when she was drowsy. She had eaten a salad for lunch with wildflowers in it, and he could actually taste it.

Eventually, as it began to grow light, she rubbed his penis so that he climaxed into her mouth, and she drank his sperm with long, appreciative swallows. "Did you know that you can *chew* sperm, and that it actually changes texture as you chew it?"

They lay together in silence for a long while. At last Craig sat up and said, "Would you do something for me? Something really special?"

"I'm yours now," she said, her voice husky. "You know that."

"Well, that's the point. I feel like you're not really mine at all. I'm just the chef. I'm a craftsman, not a lover. If you belong to anybody, you belong to Hugo."

She propped herself up on one elbow. "So what do you want me to do?"

"The recipe says that there should be lovemaking before the meal is prepared, to give it spiritual tenderness. But I can't give you anything like the spiritual tenderness that Hugo can give you. I mean, think of it, Hugo's the one who's actually going to— "

"You think I should make love to Hugo?"

"Yes, I do."

She smiled, and kissed him. "If you want me to make love to Hugo, one last time, then I will."

It was nearly six o'clock in the morning. The house was already bright. Craig stood silently outside the door of Hugo Xawery's enormous white-carpeted bedroom. The door was only a half-inch ajar, but that was enough for him to be able to see Hugo Xawery lying on his back on

131

the white silk sheets, while Xanthippa rode up and down on his dark, erect penis as if she were taking part in some dreamlike steeplechase.

He didn't know if either of them knew he was there, but Hugo Xawery looked over Xanthippa's shoulder toward the door, and gave a wide, knowing, lubricious smile.

Craig watched his purple glans disappearing into Xanthippa's stretched open vagina and tried to think of all the spiritual tenderness that was passing between them, one to the other. Hadn't Yuan Mi said that spiritual tenderness flows both ways?

At eight, Craig was woken by a soft knock at the door. Hugo Xawery came in and stood over the bed. "Good-morning, Mr Richard. It's time for the kitchen."

"I'm ready," said Craig.

"Xanthippa . . . was she enjoyable?"

"Oh, she was more than enjoyable. She was a revelation."

Blood hurried down the grooves in the butcher's table and he carefully collected it for blood puddings and gravies. His knives slit open skin and fat, and sliced through connective tissue.

On the stove, pans of stock were already simmering, and the ovens were warming up. The kitchen echoed to the sound of chopping and dicing.

By the middle of the day, the house was already filled with extraordinary fragrances . . . frying liver, poaching lungs, heat-seared filet of human flesh – all of them mingled with the aroma of basil and rosemary and coriander and soy sauce.

Craig worked non-stop, swallowing ice-cold Evian to keep himself going. By six o'clock in the evening he was almost ready, and the Mexican servant knocked at the door and announced that the first two guests had arrived.

They sat at the long mahogany dining-table, none of them speaking. The room was lit only by candles, and the plates and glasses gleamed and sparkled. The cutlery shone like shoals of fish. The sense of drama was immense.

At last, the double doors opened, and Craig appeared, in immaculate whites. Behind him, the Mexican servant was pushing a long trolley, more like a paramedics' gurney than a serving wagon.

Craig recognized at least two of the guests as customers from the Burn-the-Tail, and a famous face from one of the movie studios. They must have recognized him, too, but they gave no hint of it. Their eyes were fastened on the long trolley, with its covering of highly-burnished silver.

Craig said, "I want to welcome you, on behalf of Mr Xawery, who has spent eleven years of his life preparing for this moment, when *The Secret Shih-Tan* becomes more than a book of recipes, but a reality, which you can eat.

"I always thought *The Secret Shih-Tan* was nothing more than the ultimate cookbook. But, you know, it's very much more than that. It's a book of thought, and justice, and devastating truth. Yuan Mei never intended that any of its recipes should ever be cooked. He just wanted us to understand what we are – that we are foodstuffs, too, for anybody or anything who finds us good to eat. He wanted to put us in perspective."

Craig beckoned the manservant to wheel the wagon right up close to the end of the table. Even though the lid was tightly closed, the fragrance of flesh and herbs was overwhelming, and one of the guests was salivating so copiously that he had to cram his linen napkin into his mouth.

Craig said, "I learned about life, cooking this meal. I learned about death. I learned about ambition, too; and vanity. But most of all I learned about love."

The studio director said, "Shouldn't we wait for Hugo? This is Hugo's moment, after all."

Craig took off his chef's hat. "We don't need to wait for Hugo. Hugo's already here."

With that, he rolled back the shining cover on top of the wagon, and there was a human body–glossy, plump, gutted of every organ, braised, fried, steamed and poached, and restored to its original shape. The greatest recipe that man had ever devised. It smelled divine.

Craig laid his hand on the body's belly. "Do you see this? It was my uncle who first told me about *The Secret Shih-Tan*. It was my uncle who gave me the clue to what it meant. Cook your meal, he told me, and do it justice. And this is what this is. Justice."

He turned, and beckoned, and Xanthippa appeared, wearing an impossibly short linen dress, a black bandana tightly braided around her forehead. She stood beside the body but she wouldn't look at it.

"This is my new *sous-chef*," said Craig. "She gave me the inspiration to cook this meal; and help in preparing it; and she also gave it the spiritual meaning that Yuan Mi demanded. Not just an eye for an eye, but a heart for a heart, and a spleen for a spleen, and a liver for a liver. She was the last person to make love to Hugo Xawery, and here she is, to serve him to you. Enjoy."

Three weeks later, he took her to China with him, to Shanxi Province, where the Huanghe roars and froths

134

between two mountainous, cloud-swathed peaks, called the Dragon Gate.

It was a chilly, vaporous day. The skies were the colour of slate. Xanthippa stood a little way away while Craig climbed right to the very edge of the river, carrying the book.

He looked around him, at the mountains, and the clouds. Then he ripped the pages out, six or seven at a time, in clumps, and threw them into the river.

He had almost expected them to catch fire, to burn, to leap in the air. But the Huanghe swallowed them and swamped them and carried them away. He tossed in the book jacket last of all.

"Are you satisfied now?" she asked him. She was wearing a pink ribbed rollneck sweater and tight blue jeans, and she looked almost good enough to eat.

"I don't know," he said. "I don't think I ever will be."

"Aren't you going back to Burn-the-Tail?"

"What's the point? Jean-Pierre is as good as me, he'll keep it going. Once you've cooked from *The Secret Shih- Tan*, how can you cook anything else."

"But what will you do next?"

"Try to understand you."

She touched him, and gave him an enigmatic smile. He could never forget that she had been willing to be eaten.

"What about the human meat that Hugo hid in your freezers?" she asked him. "What are you going to do about that?"

"Well . . . I looked for it, and I couldn't find it, and I think that Hugo was lying. But even if he wasn't lying, it doesn't matter. Human meat is the very best there is. It's one thing to eat an animal. It's another thing to eat an animal which you can talk to, and make love to."

Xanthippa linked arms with him, and kissed him, and together they walked back down the hillside to the waiting tourist bus.

In the Burn-the-Tail restaurant that evening, Morrie Walker, the restaurant critic from *California* magazine, ordered the seared liver with celeriac. He jotted on his notepad that it was 'pungent, strange . . . a variety meat lifted to a spiritual level . . . almost sexual in its sensuality.

'Without being blasphemous. I felt that I was close to God.'

Men of Maes

Ystrad Mynach, Wales

Though Polish by birth, my wife Wiescka was brought up in South Wales, and that was how I first grew to knew the coal-mining valleys of the Rhymney River. By the time I came to know it, the mines were all but abandoned, and the infamous slagheaps were landscaped with trees. These days, the winding-gear has all been demolished, and the valleys are dotted with computer factories and superstores and light engineering facilities.

The Rhymney used to run black with coal dust. Now you can clearly see the stones on the riverbed. The only place where you can see a real mining cottage is in the Welsh Museum near Cardiff.

But toil and suffering always carry an historical resonance. The mines may have gone, but the work that was done has not been forgotten; neither have all the traditions that went with it, not yet. This story presents a different face of fear – the fear of passing time, and the fear of losing everything that we hold dear.

MEN OF MAES

He was approaching the bar in the Butchers Arms to buy himself another pint of lager when he saw Ellis Morgan walking past the window. He felt a split-second's delight. Good old Ellis! But then he dropped his glass onto the floor so that it smashed, and stood totally still, staring at the window with his mouth open.

"Can't even hold a bloody *empty* glass, that one," called out Roger Jones.

"Aye, aye, David, breaking the place up, are we?" said John Snape, from the other side of the bar.

David turned slowly around at stared at his friends. The Butchers was small, low-ceilinged and crowded and filled with cigarette smoke. It had originally been rough and plain, with yellow gloss-painted walls and no carpet, but everything was different these days. The brewery's marketing men had turned it into a bijou mock-Victorian pub, with flowery wallpaper and brass lamps and framed sepia photographs of people whom nobody in the pub had ever known. They even had women in the Butchers these days. They even had women on a Sunday dinnertime, when they should have been home cooking. That's how bloody different things were.

"I saw Ellis," said David, in a voice as transparent as water.

There was a roar of derision. "How many pints

have you had this afternoon then, eh?" shouted Billy Evans.

"No, no! I swear it! Clear as daylight! He just walked past the window!"

"You're bloody daft, mun," said Roger Jones. "What was he doing then, walking past the window? Coming in for a quick half, was he?"

"Ellis Morgan," David repeated. "Clear as daylight. Had to be him. He was even wearing his red scarf."

Through the frosted glass door panels, a dark shadow appeared outside, a man in a cap. The door handle sharply rattled, and for a long moment, all conversation stopped, and all heads turned around. The door opened, hesitated, and then old Glyn Bachelor walked in, the schoolmaster, with his overfed dachshund Nye.

Everybody sucked in their breath, and then burst out laughing.

"Gor, you gave us a turn, then, Glyn," said John Snape.

"Frightened the life out of us, mun."

Old Glyn Bachelor looked around the bar, bewildered by all the amusement. John Snape was already pouring him his usual half of Guinness. He poured the slops into a bowl for Nye. "David thought he saw Ellis Morgan outside."

David was down on his knees, brushing his broken beer-glass into a funneled-up newspaper with a beermat. He was a big man, with dark curly hair and fiery cheeks and intense blue eyes. He wore a cheap grey rollneck sweater that was a size too small for him, and huge jeans. In spite of his size, his voice was high and soft, and anybody in the Butchers could have told you that he wouldn't hurt a fly.

140

"They can laugh. I saw him clear as daylight. Red scarf and all."

Old Glyn Bachelor creaked over to his usual seat and everybody shifted over to let him in, lifting their chairs without taking their bottoms off them, like children. Old Glyn Bachelor always sat in the corner between the fireplace and the window, because he was schoolmaster, and it overlooked the whole bar. Most of these lads had been taught by Old Glyn Bachelor when they were juniors. In those days they had called him Mr Whippy, because of the Mr Whippy ice-cream vans that came around the estates, and because he liked to whip their legs with the thin, thin cane that he used as a board pointer.

He didn't look much different today, like a young, old child, with curly white hair, and a button nose. Starched shirt, county-council tie. He was dressed in layer after layer of green cardigan and brown herringbone tweed, to keep out the damp. The Rhymney Valley could be fatally damp in the winter.

He sipped his Guinness, and brushed the froth from his lips with the back of his hand. "That's the second one, then," he said. He leaned over so that he could dig in his coat pocket for his cigarettes, Players untipped, almost impossible to get hold of these days.

"What do you mean, the second one?" asked Roger Jones. He was another tubby lad, with cropped fair hair and an ear-ring. Brilliant fullback, clumsy car mechanic. Even his thumbs had thumbs.

"Kevin Williams up at the Fleur-de-Lys curry house said he saw his da."

"Never! When was this?"

"Last Friday afternoon, just when it was getting dark. He was crossing the river under the viaduct and he saw his da walking along the road to Ystrad. Just glimpsed

141

him, mind, so he could have been mistaken. But he said he was carrying his old khaki Army bag, the one he always carried his sandwiches in."

"Didn't he go after him?" asked David.

"He said he started to, but then he stopped. He said that if it *weren't* his da, he didn't want to make an idiot of himself by running after him, see? But if he *were* his da, he definitely didn't want to meet him. Not eleven years dead."

David finished sweeping up his glass and gave the newspaper to John Snape so that he could empty it in the bin behind the bar. "Give us another, John," he said.

"What, in a paper cup?" John ribbed him; but David wasn't listening. He went to the front door, and opened it, and stepped out onto the wet grey asphalt of the car-park, and looked around, and listened. The November air was raw and foggy, and there was that smell of damp that never seems to leave the valleys, and coal-fires, and petrol fumes.

Across the street, five or six kids were kicking Tizer cans around the pavement, and one of them was sitting on the steps of the launderette smoking. If that was my boy I'd thrash him, thought David. What's the point of getting out of the pits if you're only going to smoke. David's father suffered from lung disease, and even if he didn't go to chapel any longer, David was evangelical about lungs.

He turned around, looked the other way, across the valley: toward the high, gaunt railway viaduct which spanned the Rhymney. It had once carried coal-trucks and a regular passenger service, but now it was nothing more than a silent monument to Victorian engineering. Deep beneath its arches, its banks overgrown with dripping ferns, the Rhymney river flowed, with a sound like forgotten people whispering. The river had run black once,

142

with coal-dust. Now Markham Colliery was closed, and Pengam, and Aberbargoed, and the men were working in carpet warehouses or electronics companies or (mostly) on the dole, and the only way you could get to see a real Welsh miner's cottage was to visit the Folk Museum just outside Cardiff.

A bird fluttered on the wall.

"Ellis?" David called out. "Ellis Morgan, is that you?"

But the car-park was deserted, and the only voice that replied was Roger Jones, shouting, "Shut that bloody door, mun, it's bloody freezing in here!"

As he went back inside, though, David looked back toward the shops and thought he glimpsed somebody in a grey coat and a red scarf, climbing the steep angled road that led up through Maesy-Cwmmer. Somebody in a grey cloth cap, with a satchel around him, walking fast, the way that Ellis Morgan always used to walk. David had never been able to keep up with him, when he was younger. You had to walk three paces and run the next three, and by the time you reached the colliery gates he had you panting.

"Ellis Morgan," he whispered.

And just as he whispered it, the figure in the grey coat and the red scarf stopped on the corner of Jenkins Street and turned around and lifted one hand in a slight, affectionate wave.

It was too foggy and the figure was too far away for David to be able to distinguish who he really was. His face was nothing but a pale smudge; and before David could focus his eyes any better, he had turned the corner and disappeared. But why had he stopped and waved, if he hadn't been Ellis Morgan?

He went back inside the Butchers and closed the door

very quietly behind him. His pint was waiting for him on the counter. He looked toward Old Glyn Bachelor, sitting in the corner in the photographic daylight. Old Glyn Bachelor looked back at him, and his face was serious, knowing; as if they had just shared a secret.

At half-past two, David left the Butchers and climbed into his pale blue Vauxhall Astra. It whinnied five or six times before it finally started. It didn't like the damp, and it needed a new battery, but there was a fat chance of David being able to afford one, now he was working part-time. He did a bit of van-driving, and the odd bit of carpentry when he could. He used to be a full-time fitter for Glyneth Kitchens, but nobody around here could run to a new gas cooker these days, let alone a fitted kitchen, and Glyneth had gone out of business.

He had liked the kitchen-fitting. Good, clean job and you got to visit some nice houses and they always made you cups of tea. Before that, straight from school, he had followed his father into the Maes-Y-Dderwen Colliery. He had worked at Maes-Y-Dderwen for just five months and one week before the Coal Board closed it down. Job for life, mining, that was what his father always used to say. So long as there's coal, and brave men to dig it out, there'll be jobs.

He hadn't even worn the price label off his sandwich-box before he was standing outside watching them chain the gates and the winding-gear come to a standstill. That had been that. Some job for life.

Of course the Maes-Y-Dderwen disaster had hastened the Coal Board's decision to close. People in the Rhymney Valley could recall that date as well as Christmas, or their own birthdays. Friday morning the 15th of October, 1982. Twenty-seven minutes past ten precisely. A huge blower of firedamp had set off a coal-dust and air explosion in the very lowest and furthest extremity of the mine, the No.7 West tunnel, and eleven men had been buried and never found. They had tried for nearly three weeks to dig them out, but there had been further huge collapses, half a hillside in Hengoed had fallen in, taking three houses with it. In the end the relatives had agreed that the whole west section could be sealed off, and blessed by the Baptist minister and the Roman Catholic priest (for the two Poles among them), and consecrated as a grave.

They had left eleven of their friends down there. Eleven sons, eleven fathers, eleven men of Maes. They had stood in the rain, arm linking arm, and sung *Bread of Heaven*. Not a dry eye in the valley.

David was driving toward Fleur-de-Lys with his windscreen wipers flapping when he overtook Old Glyn Bachelor, walking through the rain with his coat-collar turned up. He pulled into the side of the road, leaned across the passenger seat, and called out, "Want a lift, Mr Bachelor?"

"What about Nye?"

"He's all right mun. There's an old blanket on the back seat."

Old Glyn Bachelor climbed in gratefully and slammed the door. "God. It's raining old women and sticks," he grumbled. He wiped his face with his crumpled-up handkerchief. Nye sniffed the old blanket and opted for the back shelf instead.

They drove off into the rain. Past the stores and the video library and the curry house and the sloping slate-roofed terraces. This was the Wales that Dylan Thomas had never known, a *strange* Wales, he had called it, coal-pitted, mountained, river run, full, as far as he knew, of choirs and sheep and story-book tall hats.

Even stranger now, with the pits mostly closed, and all the traditional shops gone, like Jones & Porter, where they used to cut the cheese with a wire, and wrap it in greaseproof.

"Thought you saw Ellis Morgan, then, did you?" asked Old Glyn Bachelor.

David sniffed and tugged at his bulbous little nose. "Bit scary, isn't it? Could have sworn it was him. He walked past the window and then I saw him again on the corner of Jenkins Street. He even waved to me, waved his hand? But it couldn't have been him, could it"

"It happened before once," said Old Glyn Bachelor.

"What did?"

"Men being seen when they were dead."

"When was that, then?"

"After the Bedwas explosion in 1936. There was seven killed then. I was only five years old so I didn't know any of them, see, but they were fathers and older brothers of some of my friends. It was the same as Maes – far too dangerous to dig them out. They tried, but half the bloody mountain fell down."

"But they were *seen*? I mean, walking about, like?"

"I saw one of them myself, although I didn't know till later. Gareth Evans, my mate William Evans' da. I can remember it now as clear as daylight. It was about six years later, in 1941. I was coming round the corner by the Plas Inn on my bicycle, pretending that I was flying a Spitfire, you know the kind of thing, ah-ah-ah-ah-ah-ah with the pretend machine guns, and there he was walking up the road from Blackwood with his cap and his knapsack and his old coat on, and he sort of *stared* at me like as I went whipping past. I can remember his eyes as if it were yesterday, because they were clear, do you see, they were clear like glass, like looking through windows at a rainy day."

"Come on, now, Mr Bachelor," said David. "You're scaring me now."

"It's true. And it *was* Gareth Evans, too, because I went to William's house about a week later for my tea, and there was his picture on the fireplace. Poor Mrs Evans couldn't understand why I didn't eat my jam sandwiches. She'd saved the jam specially, see, out of her ration. But what was I to say? 'There's a funny thing, Mrs Evans, I saw Mr Evans walking up the hill from Blackwood just a week ago, clear as daylight?' I couldn't have said that, jam ration or not."

They reached Pengam, where Old Glyn Bachelor's sister lived, and David pulled his Astra into the curb. There were narrow terraced houses on either side with shiny picture-windows and elaborately tied-up nets. The curtains in the front room of No. 19 were drawn aside for a moment, and a big beige face peered out.

"You're not late for your dinner, are you?" said David.

Old Glyn Bachelor shook his head. "No, she's nosey, that's all. Saw the car stopping."

"What happened?" asked David.

Old Glyn Bachelor was already half-way out of the car door, and Nye had jumped down from the back shelf to follow him. "What do you mean what happened?"

"Did you ever see Gareth Evans again, or any of the rest of them?"

Old Glyn Bachelor glanced at David quickly, and then looked away. "I heard one or two stories, but I didn't set too much store in them."

"What stories?"

"You're persistent, aren't you? I've got to get in for my dinner."

"Mr Bachelor, I *saw* Ellis Morgan."

Old Glyn Bachelor patted David's arm. "You remember your history lessons, do you? Remember Owen Glyn Dwr?"

David was baffled. But Old Glyn Bachelor wasn't going to tell him any more. He climbed out of the car and slammed the door and he was inside No. 19 even before David could wind down his window and call out *I don't understand what you mean, Mr Bachelor – give us a clue.*

He drove home to his parents' house in Penpedairheol. They lived on a dull, hilly estate, bungalows mostly, although all the houses were neat and tidy and freshly-painted and quite a few of the neighbours had done loft conversions.

His mother was fat and hot and all wrapped up in a flowery pinny. He kissed her sweaty forehead and then looked in on his father. His father was sitting in front of the television watching the football. He was so painfully withered, like a beetroot that's been left for weeks and weeks at the back of the vegetable basket. David wondered if he ought to tell him that he'd seen Ellis Morgan, but then his father coughed and wheezed and he decided against it. Didn't want to start one of those fits, and his father probably wouldn't believe him anyway.

"Where'd you put my old schoolbooks, ma?"

"What do you want them for?"

"Just my old history book, that's all. I want to look something up."

He found his books in an old cardboard box at the far end of the attic, next to the cold water tank. *Mathematics for Modern Schools. Geography Today.*

And here it was, *A History of Wales*, by J.D. Lloyd, green with a red dragon on the cover, and inside the cover the rounded fourth-form writing 'D. Davies, 38 Royce Avenue, Penpedairheol, Mid-Glamorgan, Wales, Europe, the World, the Universe'.

His father called up through the attic door, "How long are you going to be up there, boy? There's a draft like a bloody hurricane!" He then burst into a lengthy and horrendous coughing fit, a pain-wracked extravaganza of breathlessness and torn mucus membranes.

David knelt in the attic with his hand pressed to his forehead in prayer and silent apology. Sorry father, I forgot for just a moment. His father was cantankerous, endlessly ill-tempered, but he was suffocating from anthracosis, his lung-tissues clogged with lesions, so that he felt every minute of every day as if some relentless pest was following him around, pressing a pillow over his face, couldn't breathe, couldn't breathe, and no relief in sight but not to breathe at all.

He quickly thumbed over the soft, thick pages of *A History of Wales*. There they all were, the same pictures he had stared at on summer afternoons, Cadwaladr, King of Gwynedd, wearing the crown of Arthur; Llewelyn ap Iorwerth sitting in his cell at the Cistercian monastery at Aberconway, waiting for death. And here was Owen Glyn Dwr, Owain of Gruffydd, descendant of Llewelyn and the ruling princes of Wales, fighting the English at Knighton, nearly six hundred years ago.

'Owen Glyn Dwr promised his followers that, forever after, any Welshman who died at the hands of the English would return to his native hearth, in order to bid farewell to his loved ones.'

David remembered that paragraph, but he had never understood it at the time, or wanted to understand it, not when he was fourteen years old, and mad on rugby, and the crisp, white, ever-swelling blouse of the girl who sat next to him, Gwen Griffin (Mrs Johnson now, with twin babies as fat as her breasts had once been.) But could it mean what it actually said?

Could it mean that Owen Glyn Dwr had promised that *forever after* any Welshman who had died at the hands of the English would return to his native hearth, back home, even though he were dead – just as Ellis Morgan was dead, and all those other men who had been crushed and lost at Maes-y-Dderwen, they were dead too?

David's skin prickled with the very thought of it, and he felt as if centipedes were running through his hair.

Was this what Old Glyn Bachelor had been trying to tell him? That it was *true*?

His father called up, "Either you shut that bloody door, David, or I'm shutting it myself and you can rot up there for ever."

He drove back along the valley and it was beginning to grow greyly dark. The smell of coal-fires was even sharper and danker, and the curving mountaintops were strung with sodium lamps. It must have been so black and shadowy and wild here once, in the days of Owen Glyn Dwr, with visible stars, instead of this orange-lit valley like a supermarket car-park. He saw two men in flat caps walking along by the side of the road, and he wondered if they had come from Maes-y-Ddwerwen, too, but when he looked in his rear-view mirror they had disappeared, or turned off somewhere perhaps, and he didn't want to go back to find out.

Because what if they were dead? What would he say to them?

Are you dead, boys? And did Owen Glyn Dwr promise that you could say goodbye?

He drove to Maes-y-cwmmer, and across the traffic-lights, and up the curving street to the corner of Jenkins Street. He stopped outside the Morgans' house and switched off the engine. The curtains were drawn tight in the Morgans' front room, orange and brown flowery curtains, but the lights were on, he could see that, and there was no TV flickering, which was unusual at this time of night, most families were having their tea by now, and watching the telly.

At last, he climbed out of the car, opened the wrought-iron gate, and went down the two small concrete steps to the front door. He rang the doorbell and waited. He thought he could hear laughing inside but he couldn't be sure.

After a short while, the door opened and it was Denise Morgan, Ellis's youngest daughter, not so young now, black haired, thick-eyebrowed, her cheeks flushed as if she had been drinking, or laughing, or both.

"David?" she said.

David felt chronically embarrassed. "Listen, Denise . . . I know this sounds stupid, like. But I could have sworn that I saw your father this afternoon. I was having a pint in the Butcher's, see, and he walked right past the window, clear as daylight, I could swear by it. Then he came up the road here, and waved."

Denise stared at him for a long time without saying anything at all. He could hear music in the living-room, somebody playing an old Mel Torme record, and a woman laughing. Then Denise said, "Waved, did he?"

"That's right, waved."

Tears glistened in Denise's eyes. "Come on in and shake his hand, then."

David swallowed; and for the very first time in his life he felt absolute terror. It was like the front step dropping away from under his feet, a lift with no cables, instant vertigo.

"He's *here*?"

Denise reached out and took hold of David's elbow and guided him into the small hallway with its ship's wheel barometer from Barry Island and its pink dyed pampas grass. She opened the door to the front room, and there they all were, the whole Morgan family gathered around, Ivor that David had been to school with, and Janine who was married to a toiletries salesman in Bristol, and the two youngest, Kevin and Brangwyn, and Mrs Morgan, grey-haired, but prettily-dressed in a pink and yellow frock. There was Billy Probert from the hardware shop in Ystrad, too, he used to work at Maes-y-Dderwen, too, on the same shift as Ellis.

And there he was, sitting in his favourite armchair, Ellis Morgan himself. He had been crushed and killed all of eleven years ago, but here he was, sitting in his favourite armchair, with his family and his friends all around him, and they were laughing and talking and drinking rum and black, with Mel Torme on the CD player.

Ellis lifted his eyes when David came into the room. He was whiter, much whiter, as if all the blood had drained out of him, but he hadn't changed since the day that David had last seen him. Thin-faced, hollow-cheeked, with a hawklike nose and an angular chin. His eyes seemed to be paler, so pale that his irises had scarcely any colour at all, although David remembered that they had once been dark.

He smiled at David and his smile was welcoming but strangely detached.

152

"It's David!" said Mrs Morgan. "Look Ellis, it's David, look how much he's grown!"

David crossed the room and held out his hand. His heart was thumping like somebody beating a large cushion with a cricket-bat.

"Hallo, David," said Ellis, taking hold of David's hand and briefly clasping it. "Long time no see."

"You're dead," said David. His whole body was overwhelmed with waves of chilly sickness. It was worse than being on a small boat, on a chilly morning, fishing for mackerel.

Ellis leaned back in his chair and looked up at David with an expression of sadness and regret. "You won't hold that against me, will you, being dead?"

"You're dead, you must be dead."

David turned to Mrs Morgan, but Mrs Morgan quickly lowered her eyes, and so did everybody else. Mel Torme went on groaning but everybody stayed silent and frowned at their drinks.

"He's dead," David appealed. He felt as if the tiny living-room were closing in on him. The cheap varnished sideboard; the 3-D pictures of Christ.

Denise said, "You must have known that. That's why you came, isn't it? So what are you shouting about?"

Ellis smiled. "Don't worry," he said. His voice was oddly echoey, as if he were speaking in another room. "Glenys almost had kittens when I came to the door, didn't you love? It's your children that accept it. They think it's normal, children, when their father comes back, whether he's drunk or missed the bus or simply dead."

"But you're *dead*," David repeated. "For Christ's sake, Ellis, you're dead!"

"Oh, come on, mum, sit down and have a drink. I've only got the one night. Tomorrow it's the graveyard for

153

me. That's what he told us, anyway; and what can I do but believe him?"

Denise brought David a brimming glass of Tennent's Pils, and David tried to drink some, but it was warm, and he was already sweating. Billy Probert budged up and David sat next to him on the very end of the sofa.

"Denise, ask if anybody wants a sausage roll," Mrs Morgan chided.

"Does anybody want a sausage roll?" asked Denise.

There was a universal shaking of heads, but Mrs Morgan said, "Go and get the sausage rolls, Denise, and offer them around. And don't forget the serviettes."

David stared at Ellis and couldn't believe that he was really here. Ellis Morgan, dead all these years, but here to talk to!

"How'd you get out of the mine?" he asked. "We tried to dig you out, but the mountain kept slipping, and in the end they had to leave you underground for safety. No point in risking live men for dead. Not that they didn't try their best, mind."

"Well, right," Ellis shrugged. "But the truth is that I don't remember it very well, only isolated incidents. I heard somebody shouting 'blower!', see; and then a bang, and then a rumble like all the thunder you ever heard in your life, all at once, and the roof come down. I knew I was crushed, David. I could feel it. I couldn't take even one breath. But then it seemed as if I slept, like, and when I opened my eyes there was daylight shining. Not bright daylight, mind, it was raining. But I could see my way out of the gallery, and so I climbed right out of it. I didn't have the time to inspect it close-to, but it looked to me like they'd been excavating down at the smallholdings, right, to do some more building, and they accidentally opened up the gallery where we was trapped into the rain, and here I am."

"But you'd been dead for years," said David.

"I can't answer that one, mun. I feel like I've overslept, that's all."

"Overslept? I can't believe it!"

Ellis nodded soberly. "I know that; and I'm grateful to be here."

"You said you had only one night," said David.

Ellis nodded, and raised his glass. "Better drink to it, hadn't we?"

"But how do you know it's only one night? Couldn't it be more? Couldn't you live out the rest of your life?"

Ellis said, "No. We were told that we had just the one night; one night only; but at least it would give us the chance to say a proper goodbye to the people we loved. You're one of those people, David, and that's why you came now, isn't it?"

"Who told you that you had just the one night?" asked David. He was bewildered, and frightened, but strangely excited, too. It was wonderful to see Ellis Morgan alive again like this, to be able to talk to him, to see him sitting in the middle of his family.

Ellis said, "I saw it when the gallery opened up. It was like a darkness, that's the only way I can describe it. Of course it was dark enough down the pit, but this was even darker. Black as coal. Black as your hat. But it spoke to me, in a way, like somebody speaking very close against my ear. Very old-fashioned sounding, with Cymraeg all mixed up in it."

"*Owen Glyn Dwr,*" David whispered.

"What did you say?" asked Glenys, sharply.

"Owen Glyn Dwr. I read about him in my history book. To his dying day he promised that all Welshmen who were killed at the hands of the English would be able to go back to say goodbye to their families."

Glenys looked at him, wide-eyed, but said nothing at all. Ellis didn't say anything, either, but from the expression on his face David could see that he had struck some kind of chord.

David said, "What about Roger Jones? And Billy Evans? What about John Snape, down at the Butchers? They could come up to say goodbye to you, too, couldn't they? I could call them, they could bring some more beer."

Ellis smiled and nodded. "I'd like that, just for a while. What do you think, Glenys?"

Glenys' eyes suddenly glittered with tears.

"Don't cry, girl," Ellis chided her. "What on earth are you crying for?"

She sniffed and wiped her eyes. "That's the first time you've ever asked me what I thought about anything," she said.

"Bloody chauvinist," laughed David.

So it was that Ellis Morgan's family and Ellis Morgan's friends spent the warmest and strangest of nights together, drinking and talking and clasping hands, too, in the longest farewell that the hours would allow them. They told Ellis all the latest gossip, and all about the new bypass that came up the valley, and which couples had split up, and which shops had closed, even the corner shop in Blackwood where Ellis used to buy his anoraks.

But at five past five the light began to wash weakly through the net curtains, and Ellis looked toward the window with a look on his face of fear and exhaustion and regret.

The eyes that had appeared so animated by artificial

light now seemed dull and haunted. The cheeks were sunken, and the lips were drawn tight across the teeth.

Glenys said, "Better if everybody left now, Ellis," and Ellis said nothing, but nodded in agreement.

"David can stay," he said, huskily. "You'll need a man, when everything's over."

Ellis's friends embraced him and wept openly, without any shame. Then one by one they left the house and walked off into the dawn, their footsteps echoing sharply against the terrace walls.

"Well?" said Ellis, turning to David and smiling. "That was the grandest of nights, wasn't it?"

David said, "Best ever, Ellis. Very best ever."

As the minutes were noisily ticked away by the Westclox on the mantelpiece, and the daylight grew brighter, Ellis grew paler, and his skin began to shrivel, as if it were the finest of silver-leaf, beaten thin and crumpled by the most parsimonious of silversmiths. He clutched the arms of his chair, and David saw that his hands had shrunk into fleshless claws, with stick-like fingerbones and his wriggling veins.

Glenys looked at David in alarm, but David raised one finger to his lips, telling her to shush, and not to be worried.

The front room filled with sunlight, one of the brightest days for weeks. Ellis's chin fell onto his chest, and then his chest collapsed inside his vest, like a rotten bamboo birdcage, and his trouser-legs seemed to empty as if there were nothing inside them but bones.

Right in front of their eyes, Ellis Morgan literally crumbled and fell apart. His face for one moment was beatific, the face of a Celtic saint, smooth and perfect and martyred.

David said, "God bless you and remember you, Ellis,"

157

and then the face was gone, breaking apart like dry clay, and sliding softly into the collar of his shirt. As the sun finally illuminated his chair, there was nothing in it at all but old folded clothes and dust.

Glenys was standing by the door with her hand clasped over her mouth, her eyes sparkling with grief. David went over and put his arm around her.

"We saw him," he said, "he was really here. And I bet all the rest of the lads were home last night, too, every one of them."

Glenys nodded but couldn't speak. The clock on the mantelpiece struck seven.

Next afternoon David and Old Glyn Bachelor walked down through the allotments where it smelled strongly of Brussels sprouts and coal-dust. The clouds hung low like women's washing. Nye ran panting along the rows of overgrown potatoes, and barked at a river rat.

The Rhymney gurgled to itself as it ran over the rocks. It was Nye who found the place where the men of Maes-y-Dderwen had come back to light. It was a soggy, half-collapsed hole by the riverbank, overgrown with dock-leaves and nettles.

"That's your man," said Old Glyn Bachelor.

David peered inside. "Can't see nothing."

"You wouldn't think of going inside?"

"Not me," said David. "I've had enough of going underground, me."

Old Glyn Bachelor shrugged. "Perhaps we all have, when it comes down to it."

David saw something glinting amber-coloured in the weeds. He picked it up and frowned at it. It was a fragment of metal, in a fleur-de-lys shape, pitted with age and deeply discoloured.

He passed it to old Glyn Bachelor without a word. Old Glyn Bachelor examined it closely and then shook his head. "Could be anything. Part of a lamp. Part of a crown."

"Owen Glyn Dwr wore a crown," said David. "There was a picture of it in my history book."

Old Glyn Bachelor clapped him reassuringly on the shoulder. "You can't believe everything you read in history books, boy. Specially the drawings. Artistic licence, see."

They climbed back up through the allotments, just as a fine rain started to fall. Deep in the hole in the riverbank, something dark and shadowy stirred, and a soft noise blew into the mine-workings, a noise that could have been the wind, or the sound of the gentlest of voices.

The rain glistened bright on the slate-roofed terraces, and on the streets of Hengoed and Bargoed and Aberbergoed and Ystrad Mynach.

All across the Rhymney Valley that day there was a huge sense of sadness, and it hung low like the clouds, like women's washing. But as the day faded into evening again, and the sharp tang of coal-fires filled the air, there was a palpable sense of relief, a sense that wives and children and loved ones had at last been allowed to mourn, because the dark proud heart of Wales had at last freed the men of Maes to say goodbye.

Fairy Story

County Kerry, Ireland

The Kerry peninsula is one of my favourite parts of Ireland. The scenery is stunning, with dramatic changes of light and shade that can take place in the blinking of an eye. Kerry is dramatically mountainous, and boasts the highest range in the Republic of Ireland, Mcgillycuddy's Reeks (1041 m).

The rivers in Kerry are short but they boast some very fine fishing. The towns are picturesque; and the villages boast some of the friendliest pubs in the country. My idea of a perfect afternoon is to sit with a pint of Guinness and a fresh-caught lobster salad overlooking Kerry's islands and inlets; and not worrying whether it rains or shines.

But this story isn't concerned with the magic of Kerry's scenery, or the enchantment of its people. It's concerned instead with a different kind of magic, with which nothing is quite what it seems to be. The face of fear in this story is the face of deception.

FAIRY STORY

It was raining hard by the time Raymond left the hotel and hurried over to his rental car. He was already half an hour late, and it would be touch-and-go if he could get to Cork in time to catch the last flight to London. He shook out his umbrella, tossed it onto the back seat, climbed in the car and started up the engine. He shouldn't have stayed so long talking to Dermot Brien; but Dermot knew of some eighteenth-century landscapes that Raymond was very keen to get his hands on, as well as some rare etchings by Conor O'Reilly.

He drove out of the hotel and onto the narrow road that led to Kenmare. The rain was coming down so heavily now that it was almost like being at sea. Raymond's windshield kept steaming up, and he had to keep wiping it with his handkerchief. Mostly, the road was unlit, except for reflective road signs, and the gleaming eyes of startled hares.

He glanced at the clock. He would probably make it to Cork with twenty minutes to spare, but he would have to return his car and check in his suitcase. He put his foot down harder, and the Volvo jolted over the roughly-metalled road and blurted through puddles. He nearly miscalculated a tight left-hand bend, and by the time he had steered his way out of it his heart was beating at twice its normal rate.

He hadn't been driving for more than ten minutes when he saw something light flickering in front of him. He wiped his windshield again, and peered at it hard. At first it looked like a sheet, flapping in the wind; but then he saw that it was a woman, dressed in white, running along by the side of the road. A large dog was running along beside her.

Raymond slowed down. It looked as if the woman was wearing nothing more than a sodden nightdress. He didn't know whether to stop or not, and offer her a lift. But he was late, and she could turn out to be trouble, especially dressed in her night things, on a dark, wet night in the depths of Kerry – and he didn't fancy the look of her dog, either. The woman looked as if she wearing flowers in her hair, which didn't exactly reassure Raymond that she was altogether sane.

He drew out, so that he could pass her. But as he did so, she turned around, and stepped right into the road, with both of her arms lifted. For a split-second he could see her face, white with panic.

He stepped on the brake, but the Volvo hit her head-on. There was dull thumping sound like somebody dropping a sack of flour. Then the Volvo was spinning around, with Raymond scrabbling frantically at the wheel. It slid backward into the ditch, and he heard the crackle of breaking hedge.

He sat behind the wheel for one long moment, quaking with shock. Then he managed to open the door and climb out onto the boggy verge. The rain lashed him in the face as if it wanted to punish him. Turning up his coat-collar, he hurried across the road, praying that the woman wasn't badly hurt, praying that he hadn't killed her.

He found the dog lying on its side. Its front legs were crooked at a peculiar angle and its skull was crushed. One mournful eye stared at him accusingly, while blood was washed and diluted by the rain. There were fresh weals on the dog's smooth-haired flanks, but they looked as if they had come from a fierce and systematic beating, rather than any collision with Raymond's car.

He looked around for the woman, but there was no sign of her. He walked back along the road, looking into the hedgerows and shouting out, "Hallo! Are you there? Is anybody there?"

There was no answer. He trudged back to the dog and wondered what to do. He was frightened that the impact of the collision might have hurled the woman over the hedge and into the fields, and that she was lying in the rain, fatally hurt. There was nothing else he could do: he would have to call the Garda.

He went back to his car and found his mobile phone.

"There's been an accident," he said. "I think I might have killed somebody."

It took more than two hours of searching before the Garda decided that there was no woman anywhere around. Raymond sat miserably in his car with the rain drumming on the roof, drinking a cup of tea that had been brought for him by the landlay of a nearby bed and breakfast.

At last a police sergeant came over and tapped on his window, and he wound it down. "There's no trace whatsoever of a woman, sir."

"I saw her. I'm sure that I hit her."

"Well, sir, if there was a woman, she must have run off, and be well clear by now. Do you think it might have been the dog that caused the impact, rather than her?"

"I don't know. It could have been. It all happened so fast."

"You say the woman was wearing a white nightdress of sorts."

"That's right. And something in her hair, like a garland."

"You mean flowers, sir?"

"Something like that, yes. White flowers, I think, with green leaves."

The sergeant was silent for a long time. The rain dripped off the peak of his cap.

"Is anything wrong?" Raymond asked him.

"Not exactly wrong, sir. But there's more than one kind of individual out here, if you follow my meaning. Some that live with us, and some that live next to us, so to speak."

"I don't know what you mean."

"Well, sir, think of people living in *parallel*, as it were. They're here, but not on the same plane as we are. Except of course if they want to escape from *their* world into ours. Then we see them, now and again."

Raymond was beginning to wonder if the sergeant was drunk.

"You say the woman was running, sir?"

Raymond nodded, and said, "Yes. And she was running quite fast."

"As if somebody were after her, would you say?"

"I suppose so. But I didn't *see* anybody after her."

"No, well, you wouldn't."

"I don't know what you're getting at," Raymond protested. "Are you trying to tell me she wasn't real?"

"Oh, she was real, sir, and I believe you saw her. But let's just say that she wasn't in the same reality as you and me."

"But the dog's real."

"The dog is something else altogether."

The sergeant stood up. "We'll search again in the morning, sir, but I doubt that we'll find anything. Meanwhile, why don't you stay here the night, and I'll talk to you again tomorrow."

"All right," Raymond agreed. He felt exhausted and shivery. "Can you ask one of your men to move the car for me? I don't think I could manage it just yet."

"Oh, sure, no problem."

"There's one thing more."

"Yes, sir?"

"You said that somebody could be after her. Do you have any idea *who?*"

The sergeant gave him a long, expressionless look, and then turned away without answering.

Sarah arrived at Cork Airport just as the clouds began to stain the sky and the wind began to get up. By the time she had crossed the concrete to the terminal building it was already starting to rain. Her friend Shelagh had told her that it always rained in Ireland, every quarter of an hour for fifteen minutes, and now she believed it. She went to the car rental desk with her hair hanging down in long, dark-blonde rat's tails.

"Ah, Mrs Bryce," smiled the carroty-haired man behind the counter. "It's you that were wanting the Corsa."

"Yes, that's right," she said, trying to be composed, with rainwater dripping off the tip of her nose. She looked bedraggled, but she didn't look as bad as she felt: a tall, slim woman in her early thirties, with brown, wide-set eyes and firm bone structure. She could have been a *Vogue* model for sensible country clothes, or the wife of a senior Army officer.

In fact she was neither. She was an antiques dealer, the recently-divorced wife of a lovable but chronically

167

unfaithful artist called Ken who had shown too much appreciation for one of his models just once too often. She missed him; but she relished her freedom. His childish dependence on her had kept her tethered for six years like a sacrificial goat. Now she could travel wherever she liked, whenever she wanted – see who she liked, eat what she liked, and watch whatever television channel she liked, which was one of the greatest new freedoms of all. Like a curiously large number of artists, Ken had been an avid football fan.

The carroty-haired man gave her the car keys. "You'll find the little fellow in space 21. Enjoy your visit."

She hurried through the puddles and found her rental – a tiny Corsa in metallic emerald, very appropriate for Ireland. Gratefully she stowed her bag in the back and climbed inside. She pulled down the sun-vizor and combed her wet hair in the mirror and dabbed her face with her handkerchief. The rain pattered on the roof and ran down the windshield in herringbone patterns.

She was just about to start up the car when she became aware of a man watching her from the other side of the parking-lot. He was very tall and very dark, almost Spanish-looking, although his face was pale. What was strange about him was that he was standing in the pouring rain without a coat and without an umbrella, his hands in his pockets, staring at her unflinchingly, as if he had seen her before and was trying to remember who she was. The runnels of rain distorted her image of him. For a moment he appeared to have a hunched back, and then a twisted torso, and then his face became long and devilish. Sarah started up the Corsa's engine and switched on the windshield wipers, and the man became a normal man again. All the same, she couldn't think why he was staring at her like that.

168

She drove out of the parking-lot and the man turned around to watch her go. She kept checking her rear-view mirror to make sure that he wasn't getting into a car and following her, but he stayed where he was until she had driven round the curve in the airport roadway and he disappeared from view.

The rain continued to lash down as she negotiated Cork's south-western suburbs, past factories and road-works and mean rows of bungalows and semi-detached houses. At last she found the main road westward to Macroom, and began to make her way out into the countryside; although the rain was so torrential now that the windshield wipers couldn't keep up with it, and she could barely see where she was going. She drove for over half an hour along an empty, winding road, before she found herself in a small town with a church and a long stone wall and a sign that announced that she had reached Bandon, miles out of her way south-westward.

She stopped the car by the side of the road, and breathed, "Shit."

She could turn back, and try to find the Macroom road again, but turning back was never in her nature. If she was careful, and followed the map, she could keep going westward, and then follow a convoluted road over the mountains that would take her to Bantry, and then north to Kenmare, which was where she was originally headed. Six or seven haughty London dealers had been on the same plane with her, and if she turned up late she would have to suffer the usual taunts about scatty women amateurs who couldn't empty piss out of a Georgian chamber pot even if the instructions were written on the bottom.

A small boy in a tweed cap and a sodden sleeveless sweater came up to her car and knocked on the window. He was pale and freckled and very earnest-looking.

"Are you lost, miss?" he wanted to know.

"Well, a bit," she admitted. "I'm trying to find the road to Bantry."

"Sure and that's easy," he told her. "You follow the main road till you nearly get to the church. Then you turn right and go up the hill. Then left again, till you reach the main road. The turning for Bantry is half-way up."

"Thanks," she said, and wound up her window, before she realized that he had failed to tell her how far 'half-way up' might be. Oh well, she thought, that's Ireland for you. At least the Irish are mad on purpose.

Although it was still raining. Sarah managed to find the narrow turnoff that would lead her over the hill. Through the frantically-whipping windscreen wipers. She saw a wild, green landscape of mountains and boulders, and valleys veiled with drifting rain, like processions of ghostly brides.

She carried on driving for another half-hour, gradually making her way over the mountains toward Bantry. In all this time she saw only one other vehicle, a speeding farm van, with its windows all steamed up. It overtook her at nearly sixty miles an hour and then went careering off in a plume of spray.

Just before two o'clock she reached a small village, two pubs and a post office, and she pulled up outside the least derelict-looking of the pubs. The Russet Bull, and climbed out of the car. Rain poured down the pub's steeply sloping slate roof and gurgled into its gutters. Inside, there was a long, smoky room with a flagstoned floor and battered old wooden settles. A noisy group of young people were drinking and laughing in one corner. At the far end, two determined-looking men with the tweedy jackets of farmers and the hard faces of terrorists were playing snooker. A

170

tape was playing a Celtic lament, all violin strings and haunted voices.

A plump fair girl behind the bar asked her what she was having.

"A sandwich, if it's not too late."

"Too *late*?" asked the girl, in mild perplexity, as if she couldn't understand what sandwiches had to do with the time of day.

Sarah sat opposite the noisy young people with a huge wholemeal sandwich filled with slices of fresh ham and a half-pint of Guinness. The men with terrorists' faces gave her a good looking over and then went back to their game, although one of them glanced over at her and said something to the other one, who laughed a sharp knowing laugh.

On the creamy-plastered walls of the pub hung pieces of arcane agricultural equipment, with blackened iron prongs and chains and leather straps, like instruments of torture from the Inquisition, alongside framed sepia photographs of downtrodden-looking men in cloth caps and tightly-buttoned up jackets. The rain kept on sprinkling against the windows and the endless laments elegantly wailed of lost loves and times gone by, and Sarah began to feel as if she had been here for ever and would never leave.

She had almost finished her sandwich when she noticed the man sitting in the far corner, in the gloomiest shadows, half-hidden by the trailing cigarette smoke from the snooker table. He was dark, with slashed-back hair, and his cheekbones were knobby as a steer's skull found in the desert. From where Sarah was sitting, his eyes were drowned in shadow, but she could tell that he was watching her. One hand rested on the small table in front of him, a long-fingered hand with a heavy silver ring.

171

He looked so much like the man who had stood watching her at Cork Airport that she felt deeply unsettled. She knew that it couldn't possibly be him. He couldn't have reached this village ahead of her, even if he had taken the Macroom road; and how could he know that she was going to come this way, and stop here?

She finished her sandwich and barely tasted it. The plump fair girl behind the bar said, "God speed, then," and she was embarrassed because she hadn't thought of saying goodbye. "May you find your heart's desire," the girl added, as if it were a perfectly normal thing to say, like 'take care' or 'see you later.' Outside it was raining even more heavily, and she had to run across to her car.

As she drove away from The Russet Bull she glanced several times in the rear-view mirror to see if the man was following her. But the pub door remained closed and soon she was round the bend and well on her way toward Bantry.

It was getting late now, and she made her way through the mountains as fast as she dared. The rain was pelting almost horizontally across the road, and the wind buffeted the car as if it was determined to blow it off the edge of the ridge and send it rolling four hundred feet into the valley below. Water cascaded from the crags on either side, and gushed down cracks and crevices into the heather. Sarah's windscreen wipers could barely cope.

But as she reached the coastal road, and started to drive northward to Kenmare, between caravan-sites and bed and breakfasts, the skies began to clear with almost unnatural swiftness; and by the time she drove into Kenmare itself, the sun was shining and the roads were dry, as if it had never been raining at all.

Kenmare was a small tourist town with two main streets, each of them lined with souvenir shops and pubs and restaurants, all painted in solid reds and greens and yellows. O'Leary's Pub and O'Sullivan's Diner and Shamrock Souvenirs. Sarah drove through it slowly, looking out for antique shops. Even in a town as over-commercialized as Kenmare, it was still possible to discover good quality antiques at reasonable prices – especially chairs and sideboards that had been auctioned off from some of the local country houses. She saw a Regency chiffonier that she liked the look of; and made a note of the shop's telephone number. Then she drove out of Kenmare, heading westward on the narrow road that would take her out onto the Kerry peninsula.

She reached the grand gates of the Parknasilla Hotel and drove into the grounds. The afternoon was brilliant now, and the subtropical palms and bamboo bushes that lined the driveway gave her the feeling that she had driven out of Ireland and into some colonial other-reality, a memory of Mandalay. The hotel itself was a huge Gothic building, looking out over the glittering waters of the Kenmare estuary, with a view of the Caha mountains on the opposite side, still half-concealed by grey pillowy rainclouds.

The light was extraordinary. It was reflected from the ripples of the river in all directions, and gave the whole promontory a spangled, theatrical shine.

Sarah recognized several dealers from London and Brighton, and smiled in particular at Ian Caldecott, a dapper, florid-faced furniture expert from Surrey, who had taught her all about William and Mary chairs and card-tables. He raised his Panama and came over to greet her.

"My dear Sarah, I didn't know you were coming," he said. "We could have traveled together."

"I didn't know I was coming, either, not until the last

moment. Then Fergus told me that they were going to be selling two Daniel Marot chairs."

"Really? They're not in the cataloge."

"Late entries, apparently," said Sarah. "They come from the Ballyclaran estate."

"Well, well. I hope we shan't be bidding too frantically against each other."

"We can always join forces."

Ian tapped the side of his nose with his finger. "Very naughty, Sarah. We don't want to be accused of auction-rigging, now do we?"

"If the chairs are good, I want them," Sarah warned him.

A porter came out to take her bag, and she went into the hallway to register. Inside, the hotel was as Gothic and grand as it was outside, with a wide staircase and sunlit lounges with deep, heavily-upholstered chairs. Sarah was taken to her room by a grinning boy with sticking-out ears.

"Hope you enjoy staying here twice as much as we enjoy having you," he said. She tipped him a punt and he was gone before she understood what he had said; and even then she couldn't be sure that he had understood it himself.

She kicked off her shoes and started to run herself a bath. As she took off her jacket and unbuttoned her blouse she walked toward the window, which looked out over the gardens and the river, and the mountains in the distance. It was odd to think that less than two hours ago, she had been driving through those mountains in devastating rain, and yet here the weather was balmy and bright. She hung up her blouse and she had just reached behind her to unfasten her bra when she saw a man standing in the garden, partially hidden by the

174

shadow of a yucca tree – a man who appeared to be staring up at her window.

He was tall, and dark-haired, and dressed in black. His face was as white as a sheet of notepaper. He didn't move, but there was no way in which Sarah could tell for sure that he was actually watching *her* window. It was just that he looked so much like the man she had seen at the airport, and the man she had seen at The Russet Bull.

She retreated back into the room so that he wouldn't be able to see her. She sat on the end of the bed and she suddenly found that her mouth was dry, and that her heart-rate had quickened. *Come on, Sarah, she thought: dozens of men dress in black; and dozens of men look at you; you're still quite attractive, after all.* It was probably a coincidence: three different men who just happened to look similar. Apart from the sheer logical impossibility of the man in The Russet Bull reaching Parknasilla before her, why on earth would anybody want to follow her? She didn't have very much money. She was attractive but she wasn't a movie star. And as far as she knew – even in the devious world of buying and selling antiques – she hadn't cheated anybody, or trodden on anybody's toes. She had once sold a bureau to a well-known horse trainer on the understanding that it was a Hodson; and when it had turned out to be a fake he had threatened to burn her shop down if she didn't give him his money back, but that was the most alarming thing that had ever happened to her. And she *had* given him his money back.

She bathed and washed her hair and changed into a light grey collarless suit. The first event of the day was a champagne reception for the dealers, to be followed by a viewing of some of the most important lots on sale. She went downstairs into the bar where she found most of the dealers already well into their third glass

175

of Lanson, telling each other jokes and laughing too loudly.

"—and I said, if you want to believe that's a jardinière, my dear, then who am I to say it isn't? But make sure you tell people to take out the potted palm before they piss in it!"

"—squeezed his nose to stop himself from sneezing and found that he'd put in the top bid for two elephant howdahs, parasols, ladders and all!"

Sarah took a glass of champagne from the waiter and circled the room. Although she knew so many of the dealers, very few of them acknowledged her with anything more than a nod, and only one came over to welcome her, Raymond French, an art dealer who specialized in paintings of dogs. Raymond was tall and thin and very intense, with a wonderfully hooked nose and an accent that could have cut diamonds.

"Sarah, you're looking as soignée as ever," he said. "I didn't think this was your kind of thing."

"I'm looking for some chairs," said Sarah.

"Oh, chairs! Well, you were always *very* up on chairs, weren't you? I don't know. There's something about chairs that leaves me cold."

"These are *supposed* to be Daniel Marots," said Sarah, under her breath.

"Sorry, you've lost me. But ask me to find you a Stebbings. He did beautiful cocker spaniels, you have no idea."

"Raymond, you don't understand. These chairs could be really significant. Daniel Marot was a French furniture designer, but he was forced into exile in Holland because he was a Protestant. He designed furniture for William of Orange, and when William of Orange acceded to the English throne, Marot came to England and had a *huge*

176

influence on English furniture. He was totally Baroque. I mean, up until Marot, English chairs had been terribly plain; but Marot gave them high backs, covered in carving, and tasseled seats, and curved legs. His designs had so much *life*."

"Oh, well, I don't know. As far as I'm concerned, Sarah, a chair is a chair. It may have four legs but there isn't much point in throwing a stick for it, is there?"

"You're impossible," laughed Sarah.

It was just at this moment that Sarah became conscious that somebody else was standing very close to her. She could sense his tallness next to her shoulder. She half-turned to the left, and found herself face-to-face with the dark, thin man who had been staring up at her window.

Close up, he appeared much more handsome, in a black-eyebrowed, saturnine way. His skin was very white and pitted, but he had a sharply-cut profile and amber eyes. A white scar ran from the right side of his mouth all the way down his chin. His suit and his shirt were dead black, funeral black, and his necktie was black, too. He smelled of something faintly attractive but very old-fashioned, bay rum and lavender, and the tightly-closed rooms of expensive hotels.

"Excuse me for interrupting," he said. His voice was deep and soft, Irish-accented, like rubbing up the fur of a big black cat in the wrong direction. "I couldn't help overhearing the name of Daniel Marot."

"You're in furniture?" asked Sarah; and again she could feel her heartbeat quickening.

The man slowly smiled. "I'm in . . . finding people what they want."

"And that includes Marots?"

"That includes everything, Mrs Bryce."

Sarah felt herself blushing. "I'm surprised that you know my name."

"You're the only woman dealer . . . it wasn't difficult to guess who you were. But let me introduce myself. Seáth Rider."

"You're a dealer, too?"

"Well, in a sense, yes. But it's a strange business, isn't it, this matter of taking paintings and furniture from people's houses and selling it on, as if you were taking all of their lives to pieces, dismantling their existence so to speak."

"I suppose it is, if you put it like that." Sarah couldn't help but feel conscious of Seáth Rider's aura. He was charged up, almost electrical. She felt that if she touched him, sparks would crackle out of her fingertips. She had never felt like this about a man before, and she didn't know what to make of it. It was partly sexual; but it was partly to do with fear, too. He didn't seem like a man who could be easily disagreed with; or crossed.

"There are two Marot chairs and I've seen them," he said.

"Do you know about furniture? What kind of condition are they in?"

He made a circle with his finger and thumb; and gave her a smile that barely curled his lips. "They're perfect, Mrs Bryce. Seventeen-oh-five or thereabouts. I'd say, soon after Marot published his collection of designs. They were made in London by Shearley, so far as I know, on a special order, and brought out here when Ballyclavan House was first built."

"Are you bidding?" asked Sarah, bluntly.

Seáth Rider shook his head. "I've no interest in them myself, Mrs Bryce; although I know that you have."

"And how do you know that?" She watched him as he lifted his champagne glass and took a small sip. There was a heavy silver ring on his finger, embossed with the design of a beast's face. She couldn't have sworn that it was identical to the ring worn by the man in The Russet Bull, but all the same, it was almost too much of a coincidence to be true.

"I'm always here and there, back and forth," Seáth Rider told her. She liked the delicate Irish way he said 'fort' instead of 'forth'. "I know when people have their heart set upon something, and the lengths to which they'll go to get it."

"Do you have a shop?" Sarah asked him.

"Not a shop as such. But a sort of imaginary market, where you can buy whatever you want. Here," he said, and handed her a business card. *Seáth E. Rider, Acquisitor, Dublin & London.* There was no address, only a mobile telephone number. "For instance, if you had urgent need of an eighteenth-century teapot, I could find you one and bring it to you within the blink of an eye. Or if you had urgent need of anything else for that matter."

"Well, that's very interesting, Mr Rider. Perhaps I can keep you in mind."

Seáth Rider gave her the faintest hint of a smile. "I was hoping that you'd do that, Mrs Bryce."

With that, he gave her a nod, and disappeared into the crowds of dealers, almost sliding rather than walking, like a character in a children's cut-out theatre.

"Well, what do you make of *him*?" asked Raymond. "Rather *louche*, wasn't he? And what's an 'Acquisitor' when it's at home? I don't think there's any such word."

"I don't know," said Sarah, still trying to see where Seáth Rider had gone. "I thought he was quite attractive, in a shifty kind of way."

"That's the trouble with women," Raymond retorted.

"Give them a good, trustworthy man and they won't look twice at him. But give them a rat, and they fall on their backs with their legs in the air."

Sarah looked at him narrowly. "Do you know something, Raymond, I do believe that *you* thought he was attractive, too."

That evening, after dinner, when the sun was sinking over the Kenmare estuary, Sarah went for a walk in the hotel gardens. There was a light breeze blowing from the south-west, but the air was warm and smelled of the sea, and gulls were still circling overhead. She walked through a succession of small, secret gardens, each surrounded by a high hedge. In each there were cast-iron Victorian chairs and tables, all empty now, some tipped over. She felt that she was walking through a garden from *Alice Through The Looking Glass*, or one of Edward Gorey's drawings of Gashlycrumb Hall.

She thought how much her father would have loved this place. He had always adored a bit of grandeur, and she had never forgotten the first time he had taken her for dinner at the Savoy. He hadn't been wealthy: in fact he had run a toyshop in a suburb of South London. But he had always been kind, and smartly-dressed, and gentlemanly, and Sarah had been devastated when he died last year, only sixty-one years old, of a massive heart attack.

As she walked between the dark, enclosed gardens, Sarah was sure that she could hear people talking; but every garden was empty, and growing darker, too, as the sun began to sink even lower. She could hear a girl's voice, persistently arguing, and a man trying to reason with her. Yet she couldn't work out where they were. Perhaps they were somewhere behind the hedges, and their voices were being carried on the breeze.

She came out onto the shoreline, where the tidal waters splashed clear and shallow against the rocks. There were two small islands offshore, which had been connected to the hotel grounds by a causeway built of planks. Each island was overgrown with trees, and was silhouetted now against the sky. There were probably less than twenty minutes of daylight left. The clouds above the mountains were already black, and a huge pillar of cumulus had risen in the west, threatening thundery rain. It looked like a demon, with horns and billowing wings, risen from out of the furnace of the setting sun.

Sarah had thought that she was alone. But as she walked along the causeway, she saw that somebody else was ahead of her, walking in the same direction. It was a tall, white-haired man in a navy-blue blazer and grey pants. He was walking quite quickly, but with an interrupted step, because of the gaps between the planks.

Sarah stopped and shaded her eyes. She was sure she recognized him. There was something so familiar about his slightly-stooped shoulders, and the way he flapped up his hand to beat away the midges. There was something so familiar about his hair. She always remembered her father saying that you can disguise your face but you can never disguise the way you look from the back.

"*Dad?*" she whispered, too frightened to say it out loud. Then, when he kept on walking, "Dad!"

He had reached the end of the first stretch of causeway, and was crossing a small rocky point where the hotel had built bathing huts and benches for guests to sit on while their children swam. Now he was turning toward the woods.

Shocked, thrilled, frightened, Sarah shouted, "Dad! It's me, Sarah! Dad!"

She snatched off her shoes and started to run along

the causeway barefoot. The man had almost reached the shadow of the woods, but she shouted at him again. "Dad! Just wait a minute! Wait for me!"

Even as she ran, she knew that it couldn't be him. He was dead, how could it be him? But it *was* him. It looked so much like him. She couldn't believe that there could be two people on God's earth with the same hair and the same stooping walk and the same irritable way of flapping his hand at insects.

She reached the bathing huts and balanced herself against one of the benches while she put her shoes back on. She could still see the man, walking away from her along the tree-shadowed path that led to the islands. About a hundred feet away, he paused for a moment, and looked around, and although she couldn't see his face clearly she was even more convinced that it was her father.

"Dad! Stop!" she cried out, and ran toward him. Her feet pelted through last autumn's leaves. But whether he heard her or whether he didn't, he turned into the woods and vanished behind the trees.

Sarah came to the turning in the path and stopped. From here, she could see all the way down a narrow, root-entangled path that led to an inlet between the islands. The water gleamed between the trees, but there was no sign of the white-haired man. She listened, but all she could hear was the shushing of the waves on the rocky beach, and the chirping of insects in the woods. Quite close to her, a single leaf quivered excitedly on a branch, making a soft whirring sound, but that was all.

She stayed where she was for almost two minutes, still listening, but it was obvious that there was nobody here. It had all seemed so real, but she must have imagined it. Maybe she was tired, after traveling across the mountains, and spending the whole afternoon talking antiques. She had drunk half a bottle of Chablis with her dinner, and that might have induced an hallucination, or a mirage, or a memory, or whatever it was.

She put her hand up to her face and found that tears were sliding down her cheeks. She had wanted so much to see her father one more time. She had wanted so much for him not to be dead. It had taken her more than six months to come to terms with the fact that he had gone, and even now she found herself unexpectedly crying when she heard one of his favourite songs, or smelled pipe-tobacco, or heard a man tunelessly whistling in the street.

She turned around, and literally jumped. Standing less than ten feet away from her was Seáth Rider, his hands in his pockets, watching her.

"God you scared me."

"I'm sorry. I didn't mean to. I saw you marching off to the islands and wondered if you wanted some company."

"I don't think so, thank you. Besides, I'm going back now. It's getting too late."

"Well, that's a shame. It's a charming walk and it won't take us more than fifteen minutes."

"I'm cold," she said, and tried to push past him; but he took hold of her arm; not roughly; but very insistently.

"You've been piping your eye."

"It's nothing. Hay fever, that's all."

"And you want me to believe that?"

"Quite frankly, I don't care what you believe."

"Oh, come on, now," he said, in that soothing, cat's fur voice. "There's no need to be offish about it, is there? I'm only trying to be sociable. I know what it's like when you've lost somebody dear to you. Everybody thinks that you can get over it, but you never can."

She stared at him, face to face. "How did you know?" she demanded.

"I'm sorry. How did I know what?"

"How did you know why I was crying?"

He gave her a look like no man had ever looked at her before. It was a mixture of desire and teasing and something that was close to greed. She had the disturbing feeling that he had an erection. "I'm always here and there," he said. "You know. Back and forth."

"But you knew why I was crying."

"Well . . . don't think anything of it. It's only intuition. You know what the Irish are like. Tribal, touchy, maudlin, over-sentimental, quick as a flash to take offence and preternaturally slow to forget it. Magical, too; though not in the way that tourists think. None of your little people and your leprechauns' crossings, your Blarney stone and all that tosh. Different magic, that's what."

Sarah waited for a while to see if he was going to explain himself further; but he didn't; and so she drew her arm away. "I'm tired," she said. "I think I'm going back."

"You're missing something, believe me."

"I expect I am. But then we can't always have what we want, can we?"

His eyes glittered in the twilight. He was tall and dark and crowned with midges. "Oh, you're wrong there," he told her. "We can *always* have what we want."

Sarah hesitated for a moment longer, she didn't know why; but then she made her way back toward the bathing huts.

The estuary was lilac when she got there; lilac and grey; and the waters still persistently lapping. She glanced back once, but she couldn't see Seáth Rider at all, because the shadows were so deep, or perhaps he had carried on walking. She didn't understand what had happened. She

184

didn't understand how she could have imagined seeing her father, and how he had vanished so completely. She didn't understand how Seáth Rider could have such an acute sense of what she was feeling. *Here and there, back and forth*, what the hell did that mean?

She walked back through the gardens. This time she heard no voices; only the sound of laughter from the hotel lobby and car doors slamming. She went back inside, where it was noisy and lively, and went to the bar to see if she could have a nightcap with anyone she knew.

On the whole, the auction was disappointing. Some of the best lots had been withdrawn, including paintings by Jack Butler Yeats and Sir John Lavery, and a set of pen-and-ink sketches by William Orpen. A large breakfront bookcase had been taken out, too, much to Ian Caldecott's fury, because he had been specially commissioned to bid for it by a wealthy rock musician who wanted it for his library.

Oddly, Sarah found that she was pleased that so many paintings and so many articles of furniture were staying in Ireland. She kept thinking of what Seáth Rider had said about "taking people's lives to pieces, so to speak." But she still wanted her Daniel Marot chairs. She had inspected them this morning, in daylight, and they were perfect. High-backed, exquisitely carved, with curved legs and curved stretchers; and their original upholstery, in faded rose-pink, with fringes. They had been cared for so well that they could have been nearly new. She had run her hands over the carvings, and they had felt almost as if they were flesh, rather than wood, because they were so warm and smooth.

She was sitting at the back of the conference room

where the auction was being held. There must have been two or three hundred dealers there, illuminated by the sunshine that came through the windows like parishioners in church, a bald head over here shining through it last traces of carefully combed hair; and over there a large pair of ears glowing red. There, some smeary thumbprinted spectacles and here, too close for comfort, a black jacket liberally sprinkled with dandruff.

The auctioneer was bald and pink and smooth as a billiard-ball, with wiry half-glasses and a formal suit. His accent was Kerry-trying-to-be-Posh, and since Kerry is incomprehensible anyway, even to Irishmen from other counties, and Posh meant saying "fornitchewer" and "harty facts", it was difficult for most of the dealers to follow what was going on, and Ian Caldecott became even more enraged when he missed an important Regency writing-table.

At the very end, the Daniel Marot chairs were brought in, and set up on the rostrum. Ian Caldecott glanced back at Sarah and she knew then that she was in trouble. He wanted these badly, almost as badly as she did, and since he still had plenty of money to spend, the chances were that he was going to push her as high as he could.

"Well then lot 167a two upright chairs to the design of Daniel Marot and attributed to Josiah Shearley of London circa 1705. Can we start at three thousand pounds the pair?"

Sarah waved her prospectus and at the same time Ian Caldecott lifted a single finger. This time he didn't look back at her.

"Three thousand five hundred do I hear you now."

Again Sarah waved her prospectus and Ian Caldecott lifted his finger.

"Four thousand is it now."

Sarah had guessed that the two chairs could probably be retailed at £3,750 each, but even that was stretching it. To make any kind of profit, she would have to stop bidding at £6,000. If she went above that, she wouldn't even be able to cover her air fare and her hotel bill and the hire of her emerald-green ear.

But she did want those chairs. They were historic, and they were simply beautiful. They represented the moment when English furniture first came truly alive.

"Four thousand five hundred is that what I'm hearing."

Sarah waved her prospectus. Ian Caldecott lifted his finger.

"Is it five thousand now."

A low murmuring went through the auction-room. It was obvious that the price of the chairs had almost reached their premium trade value, and that the bidding was becoming a personal contest between Sarah and Ian Caldecott, the experienced connoisseur and his assertive young pupil.

"Five thousand five," said the auctioneer. There was a pause, and he raised his gavel. "Any takers at five thousand five,"

Ian Caldecott hesitated for a moment, then bid. Sarah bid too.

"Six is it then. Six thousand pounds."

Ian Caldecott bid, but this time Sarah hesitated. This was the very limit of what she could spend. Then again, she thought, she could always raise the extra money from a few quick sales. She had a Welsh dresser that she had just bought in Lymington which would probably fetch £650, even thought it was unrestored, and she had two Thompson Hobbs paintings that she had been intending to have cleaned but which would raise another £400–£500.

"Going for six thousand," said the auctioneer; but Sarah waved her prospectus again.

For the first time, Ian Caldecott turned around to look at her. She tried to smile at him, but the expression on his face was so furious that her smile died at birth.

"Six thousand five. Seven. Seven thousand five."

Now Sarah knew that she was beyond her budget. If she bid more than £7,500 she would never get her money back, and she wouldn't be able to buy anything else here at Parknasilla in the hope of cutting her losses. All the same, she waved her prospectus one more time.

"Seven thousand five. Is it any more than seven thousand five. Going to Mrs Bryce then for seven thousand five." *They're mine*, thought Sarah, with a surge of triumph. *I've done it!*

Ian Caldecott lifted his finger.

"Eight," said the auctioneer. Everybody turned in their seats to look at Sarah, and right at that moment she could have burst into tears. She had already taken far too much of a risk, and even though she was absolutely desperate to show Ian Caldecott that she could beat him at his own game, she knew that she couldn't commit financial suicide for the sake of two chairs.

"Going for eight thousand to Mr Caldecott; gone."

Sarah got up from her seat and left the auction-room without looking back. She went outside, where the sun was shining on the water and the yuccas were rustling. For the first time in seven years she felt like a cigarette. For the first time in three years she wished that Ken were here, so that she could talk to him. For all of his faults, for all of his tantrums, he had always cheered her up when she was disappointed, and made her laugh.

She leaned against the rail overlooking the estuary, her hair blowing in her face. She heard quiet footsteps, and saw a shadow on the flagstone, and then Seàth Rider came up and leaned on the rail beside her, black-suited as always.

"Another fine day," he remarked. "There's a story that you could see the lost city of Atlantis from here, under certain weather conditions, reflected in the sky."

Sarah said nothing but brushed back her hair with her hand.

"You're looking glum," said Seàth Rider. "You lost the chairs I'll bet."

"Yes, Mr Rider, I lost the bloody chairs. They went for eight thousand and I just couldn't match it."

"That's a terrible pity. They're fine chairs, the both of them."

"God knows how Ian's going to get his money back. They're scarcely worth six."

"Maybe he wasn't looking to get his money back. Maybe he just didn't want you to have them. You know what some of these dealers are like: dogs in the manger. Especially when it comes to women. They're very sensitive about women, and a whole lot of old queens, most of them."

"I'd pack and go home except I haven't bought anything yet."

He smiled at her and shook his head. "You mustn't start thinking like that. No good ever came of giving in."

She didn't reply. She didn't really know what to say. After a while she left him standing by the rail and went back into the hotel. In the lobby she met Ian Caldecott, looking bright-eyed and pleased with himself. "You gave me quite a run for my money, there, Sarah," he effused.

"You must let me buy you a glass of champagne to commiserate."

"You really are a stupid old bastard, aren't you?" Sarah retorted. "You could have agreed not to bid against me and we could have shared the profit. You knew how badly I wanted those chairs. Now neither of us have ended up with anything."

"Just remember who taught you everything you know," said Ian.

"I haven't, and I never will. Because one thing I know now is that a pupil should never trust her teacher. Especially when her teacher grows jealous."

She went upstairs to her room, and threw her prospectus onto the table. Outside her window, the gardens were dappled with sunlight, and even the mountains were clear, for a while. Seáth Rider was still leaning against the rail, but he wasn't watching the water. He was watching her; although he was too far away to see if he was serious or smiling. She stood close to the curtains, so that he wouldn't be able to see her, and she wondered who he really was, and why he took such an interest in her. Perhaps he behaved in the same way with every woman he met. But she had never seen him talking to any other woman the way he talked to her; and she had never seen him staring at any other woman's window.

She began to feel that he was intimately connected with her, in an inexplicable way – that their futures were somehow intertwined. A nemesis, a shadow, a promise of unknown days to come. The kind of man you meet in dreams.

She came back to the window almost an hour later and he was still watching.

The next day was fresher and cooler and so she dressed

in jeans and a white cable-knit sweater. After breakfast, she drove first to the little village of Sneem where she sat in O'Sullivan's Pub with a half of Guinness and wrote postcards to all of her friends. Then she went on to the west, through the fields and the mountains, with bright sandy glimpses of the Kenmare estuary off to her left, and then the Atlantic Ocean, pale and green, listlessly heaping its seaweed onto the beaches.

She drove as far as the little town of Carhicvean and then she parked by the side of the main street and went looking for antique shops. She found a good prie-dieu with a Berlin tapestry seat; and a china display cabinet, a vitrine, which she bought for less than £400; a Sutherland fall-leaf table; and a beautiful papier mâché chair, an original Jennens & Bettridge, inlaid with mother-of-pearl and gilded with flowers.

She was leaving the last antique shop when she thought she saw her ex-husband Ken turning into a pub along the street. He couldn't have been Ken; but he was wearing the same blue linen jacket that Ken always wore when he painted, and he had the same shock of brown hair, and even the same shoes, those awful tan-coloured Hush Puppies that he wore every day of the week.

Sarah turned back to the woman in the antique shop, and said, "Have you ever seen anybody dead?"

"Well, there's a question," said the woman, all pink-cheeked and flustered. "I saw my ma and my da in their caskets, of course; and my Uncle Joe."

"But you've never seen anybody dead walking around the streets? Or anybody who couldn't conceivably be there, dead or alive?"

The woman was wiping her hands on a tea-towel. She gave Sarah a peculiar, bulgy-eyed look. "I can't say that I have. And I think if I did I'd run a mile."

"I'm sorry," said Sarah. "I'll arrange for the shipping and let you know."

She walked cautiously along the street. The afternoon was windy now, and the moving clouds were reflected in every window, like televisions in a television store, with all the same programme playing. The pub was painted liver-red outside, with decorative shamrocks. O'Hagans Pub & Restaurant, Guinness, Murphys and Caffreys, and those were just to quench you thirst before you started on the Bush.

She stepped inside. A single doleful man with grey hedgehog hair and cavernous cheeks was wiping up glasses. He looked like Samuel Beckett's untalented brother.

"Are you open?" she asked. He turned and blinked at her as if he had never expected to have a customer, never, not of any early afternoon.

"Of course we're open. How would you have got in."

Sarah turned back toward the door. "I would have – yes, I see. I see what you mean."

"We're quiet of course. There's not much trade on a Tuesday. Would you care for a drink?"

"Yes, yes please. A Guinness will do."

She turned and there he was, sitting just in front of a strong triangle of sunshine, his hand on the table with its silver ring, a glass of whiskey in front of him catching the light. She left her Guinness on the bar to settle and walked across to him and dragged out a chair.

"Something's going on," she told him, before he could speak. "Something I don't understand. I thought I saw my ex-husband coming in here, but now it's turned out to be you."

"You didn't have to come in here," he said.

"No, I didn't. But I did. I don't know how you managed

192

to look like Ken. I can't begin to imagine how you know what Ken looks like. But it was you, wasn't it? And last night, out on the island, my father was you. You have a knack for it, don't you? Knowing what I want, knowing what I need. What is it, hypnotism, something like that? Or do I make myself so bloody obvious that you don't even need to hypnotise me? Is it a trick? What is it? And what do you want?"

Seáth Rider looked at her ruefully. "Why are you being so vexed with me, Mrs Bryce, when all I want to do is to please you?"

"What? By following me? By making me think that—"

"Please, Mrs Bryce. I'm not making you think anything. Whatever you think, whatever you want, that's up to you."

She said, "Anyway, I'm leaving tomorrow morning, first thing. I didn't get the Daniel Marot chairs; but I think I've made enough to cover my expenses."

Seáth Rider lifted his glass. "I'll drink to that, Mrs Bryce."

And for all that she didn't understand him, and found him so strange and threatening, Sarah lifted her glass, too.

When she returned to her room at the Parknasilla, the chairs were there, waiting for her. She walked in and there they were, side by side, slightly angled, as if two people had been sitting in them, talking, only minutes before. She approached them in disbelief, and touched them, and they were real. Solid, carved, but brilliantly imagined, with tall backs and stretchers that curved as if they were alive. She was always amazed how few people realized that furniture – just as much as paintings, or sculptures, or music – didn't begin to exist until somebody had imagined it, and turned that imagination into something that other people could see and touch. Yes, and even sit on.

She sat on her bed and stared at them. Surely Ian Caldecott couldn't have been so remorseful that he had let her have the chairs. Even if he had, he wouldn't have taken them up to her room, surely? Once they were sold, they were due to be crated and shipped directly back to London.

She had a strange feeling that Seáth Rider was involved in this. She had no proof, of course; but it seemed like his style. She just hoped that he hadn't bullied Ian Caldecott into letting her have them; or something worse. She picked up the phone and asked reception to put her through to Mr Caldecott's room.

"I'm sorry, Mrs Bryce, would you repeat the name?"

"Caldecott, Ian Caldecott. I don't know his room number, but he's one of the antique dealers."

"Caldecott did you say? Well there's no one of that name registered here."

"There must be. I saw him this morning."

"Are you sure he was resident with us, Mrs Bryce, and didn't just come for the auction?"

"Of course I'm sure. He even told me how much he liked his room. Listen – why don't you put me through to the auctioneers? They may know where he is."

She waited for nearly five minutes, listening to an electronic version of *Greensleeves* over and over again. Finally a cultured voice said, "O'Shaughnessy and Drum, Mr Drum speaking."

"Oh hallo, Mr Drum. This is Mrs Bryce."

"Well now, Mrs Bryce. What can I do for you. Congratulations on the chairs, by the way. You got yourself a bargain there, wouldn't you say?"

"But I didn't get the chairs, Ian Caldecott outbid me."

"I'm sorry?"

"I was outbid by Mr Caldecott. But now the chairs have turned up here in my room."

"Where you said you wanted them, Mrs Bryce, so that you could have a chance to admire them for a while before we packed them up for shipping."

Sarah was so confused that she could hardly speak. "Mr Drum – there must be some mistake. I didn't – I didn't even— "

"I'm sorry, Mrs Bryce, did we misunderstand your instructions somehow? If you wish us to pack up the chairs directly, we will be only too happy to oblige."

"But they're not my chairs, Mr Drum! Mr Caldecott bought them!"

There was an embarrassed silence. Then Mr Drum said, "The records show otherwise, Mrs Bryce. There were two principal bidders, yes; and one of them was you. But the other was Mr James McGuinness, and he stopped bidding at £5,500, which is when the chairs were knocked down to you."

"I'm going mad," said Sarah. "Either that, or you're going mad. What about Mr Caldecott?"

Another silence, even longer than the first. Then, "I'm sorry, Mrs Bryce. I hate to contradict a favoured client, such as yourself. But to my knowledge there was no Mr Caldecott present at the auction; and I have never heard of any antique dealer by that name. The only Caldecott I know of is the children's book illustrator, Randolph Caldecott. And of course he died more than a hundred years ago."

"You've never heard of Ian Caldecott?"

"No, Mrs Bryce. Never."

Sarah lowered the receiver. She could hear Mr Drum's tiny voice saying *"Hello? Hello?"* like an insect in a matchbox. She had seen Mr Drum talking to Ian Caldecott; she had seen him shake his hand. How could he possibly say that he had never heard of him?

"*Hello? Hello?*" Mr Drum persisted; so Sarah hung up.

She went back to the chairs and stood between them, with a hand on each one. They were beautiful; they were almost magical; and in some extraordinary way they seemed to be hers. But how? And what had happened to Ian Caldecott? At a stretch, she could imagine that Ian had felt guilty after outbidding her, and had let her have the chairs as a gesture of goodwill. But that sort of spontaneous generosity wasn't really in his nature. She had seen him talk to another woman dealer for almost half an hour, dissuading her from buying a cane-seat Regency chair because it was 'obviously fake', and then buying it himself for less than half what it was really worth.

She was still looking at the chairs when there was a quick, sharp knock at her door. She went to open it, expecting the maid. Instead, it was Seáth Rider, looking pale but excited. He stalked into the room before she could stop him, and walked straight up to the chairs, although he didn't touch them.

"There! They're very fine, aren't they! And are you pleased with them, now?"

"I think they're beautiful. But they still don't belong to me."

Seáth Rider twisted around and stared at her, as if he couldn't believe what he was hearing. "What do you mean, they don't belong to you? You bid for them fair and square, didn't you? You paid for them?"

"Ian Caldecott outbid me."

"Ian Caldecott? Now who would he be?"

"You know exactly who he is. God, you're beginning to sound like all the rest of them now."

Seáth Rider approached her and his face was very serious; almost tragic. "There is no Ian Caldecott, Mrs Bryce. There never was. You bought those chairs. Look at your chequebook if you want the proof."

Sarah went to her purse, opened it up, and took out the Gucci chequebook wallet that Ken had given her for her birthday, after selling two paintings to the Oswald Gallery in Bond Street. That was probably the only time that he had ever had any money of his own. She opened her chequebook, and there it was, the checkstub, in her own handwriting, in her own distinctive violet ink 'O'Shaughnessy & Drum, 4,500, DM Chairs'.

"I didn't write this," she said, her voice wavering. She stepped up to Seáth Rider and shook the chequebook under his nose. "*I didn't write this!*"

Seáth Rider shrugged, and said. "Take it to a hand-writing expert if you wish. You bid for the chairs; you topped the bidding; and you took out your chequebook. Confident as any woman I've ever seen; a queen amongst dealers, I'd say."

"Something's happened, hasn't it?" said Sarah.

"Happened? What would you mean by that?"

"Something's happened to Ian Caldecott . . . you've bribed him, or you've threatened him, or something. He wouldn't have given me those chairs for anything!"

Seath Rider said, "There is no Ian Caldecott. There never was."

"I don't understand you. I don't understand any of this."

"But it's very simple, especially if you know your Irish legends. There was always magic here, of a kind, which people fancified and turned into stories of little people

197

and all that guff. But there's another world here, Mrs Bryce, there always has been; and there was a whole people, Lir's people, the people of the Tuatha, back in ancient times, who disappeared from human view. Vanished!"

"I still don't understand."

"You will if you realize that the portals of the invisible kingdoms were never completely closed, and there were those who could travel with ease from one to the other, having friends and even lovers in both existences.

"The Fianna could do that. They were warriors, trained in every skill. Among them was Iollan, who kept a fairy mistress called Fair Breast. She was his heart's desire, the most beautiful creature that you ever saw, and all Iollan had to do was breathe her name, wherever she was, and she would appear, and she would do anything for him, whatever he wanted. For all of the pleasure she gave him, she asked only one thing in return, and that was his fidelity."

"What the – what the *hell* are you talking about?" Sarah demanded. "I want to know what's happened to Ian Caldecott – not some ridiculous fairy story!"

"But that's what I'm trying to tell you," said Seáth Rider. "Iollan fell in love with a human woman, and married her, and made her pregnant with twin boys. So when Fair Breast found out what had happened, she turned Iollan's wife into a dog, and dragged her off to live with a man who hated dogs, so that she would be starved and whipped. And to Iollan she said: 'I will turn her back into a woman, if you come and live with me forever, in the invisible kingdom.' So what could he do, poor fellow, but agree?

"The only snag was that his sons, who had both been

born as dogs, would have to remain as dogs for the rest of their lives."

"All right," said Sarah. "Tell me what it means. Tell me what you're talking about. And where's Ian Caldecott?"

Seáth Rider went over to the window and looked out over the gardens and the estuary. The mountains were plumed with clouds. "You can always have whatever you desire, Mrs Bryce; just as Iollan of the Fianna had what he desired. But somebody always has to pay the price. It's the magical version of Newton's Law, if you like. No action without a reaction. Maybe the reaction doesn't affect *you*; but it always affects somebody."

Sarah said nothing, but stood waiting for him to say what she knew he was going to say; her fists clenched, her heart beating fast.

Seáth Rider turned away from the window and said, "If there was ever a man called Ian Caldecott, he would have outbid you for these chairs, and taken them away. But now, there never was. Ian Caldecott was never born, and he never grew up, and he never went to university nor started a dealership. You will never find a photograph of him in the South of France; you will never find a school report or a dental record or a social security card. You will never find a tot that knew him, when he was tiny. You will never find a woman who kissed him at his first party. He has evaporated, Mrs Bryce, as if he never existed."

"You've murdered him," said Sarah. She was shaking with shock.

"Of course I haven't. How can you murder somebody who never existed?"

"Then you've – Christ, I don't know what you've done! What have you *done*?"

"I've expunged him, I'd say that's the word. He's not

gone completely, if you get my meaning. Matter can neither be created nor destroyed. But he's certainly not *here*, that's the message, and never was here, ever."

"For two chairs? For two stupid chairs?"

Seáth Rider frowned at her. He looked hurt. "You said those chairs were your heart's desire. What does it matter to you whether Ian Caldecott ever existed or not? *He* doesn't mind: he never existed. His family doesn't mind: they never ever knew him. People get killed every day. Shot, or drowned, or knocked down on pedestrian crossings because they were thinking about what they could eat for their tea, instead of looking. That never worries you does it, so why are you so worried about Ian Caldecott, you have your chairs, and everything's hunky dory."

Sarah had to sit down. "I can't take this in. You erased his entire life, *everything*, just because you wanted me to have these chairs?"

"Oh no, Mrs Bryce. You wanted the chairs, not me. I'm an acquisitor, not a collector. But that was the price, yes. That was the only way to do it."

"But *how*? How do you rub out somebody's whole existence?"

Seàth Rider pointed to the mountains, covered in grey, thunderous clouds; and to the Kenmare estuary, sparking with sunshine. "If you want me to put it simply, Mrs Bryce, there are visible kingdoms and invisible kingdoms; and here in Ireland the doors are still open for those who know how to tread between. And, yes, it was me who watched you at the airport; and it was me sitting at The Russet Bull; and here, too, when you arrived."

"I'm going to have to give the chairs back," said Sarah.

"To whom?" Seàth Rider demanded. "Not to Ian

Caldecott, because there is no Ian Caldecott. Not to his family, because they won't know who he was. They're yours, Mrs Bryce. You bid for them, you paid for them, they're yours."

"And what do *you* get out of this?" asked Sarah.

Seáth Rider smiled; a genuine smile this time. "I will get my commission, Mrs Bryce. Don't you worry about that."

Unexpectedly, he kissed her on the cheek. It was a kiss like no other kiss she had experienced before: soft, yet positive; unusually salacious; a kiss that told her that he wanted more. For some reason she found it incredibly erotic, and when he left the room and closed the door behind him, she stood stiff and wide-eyed, her right hand straight down by her side, her left hand clutching her right elbow, rigid, like a woman who has just witnessed a serious traffic accident.

In the night she dreamed of her father. She was sitting on his lap and he was reading to her. She could smell tobacco and cologne and old tweed coat. Outside the library windows the sky was a bright shade of aniline purple, and the clouds moved as if they were cut out of cardboard. Sarah knew that she was safe for the moment, but she felt a small, nagging anxiety that when her father reached the end of the story that he was telling her, something terrible would happen; and so she kept begging him to read on and on and on.

The story was like no story that she had ever heard before. "The razormen came when the night was darkest and sneaked through the house calling and singing. Everybody knew they were there but nobody dared to open a door. They had razors in their fingers and razors in their backs. They had razors in the palms of their hands. If they once took hold of you, why then you were blood all over before you knew it. They had razors between their teeth and they wanted to kiss you."

She clutched at her father's prickly tweed lapel in fear; and for security, too. Inside his waistcoat his voice was a warm, reassuring rumble. She couldn't think why he was trying to frighten her so much. The razormen! She could see them crawling along the corridor, their backs embedded with two-edged blades, enduring the agony because nobody would dare to touch them when they emptied out your drawers full of jewelry or raped your daughters in a blood-drenched bed. She heard somebody screaming, and she felt somebody jump on the bed.

She woke up, abruptly, and caught herself kicking the mattress with her heels and making a peculiar gargling noise. She lay back, gasping and sweating, and took ten deep breaths.

A dream, she told herself. *That's all it was A ridiculous, terrifying dream.* The moon was high and it shone between the curtains and illuminated the two chairs. She propped herself up on one elbow and stared at them. It was well past three in the morning and she felt exhausted and disoriented. She hadn't bought the chairs, she knew that. Somebody else had bought them. Somebody called—

Somebody called—

At first she couldn't think of his name. She could remember his face, but she simply couldn't think of his name. Ian Somebody. Ian Coldwell. Ian Cottesmore. Something like that. Her memory of him was fading like a photograph left in the sun. But she looked at the chairs and she could remember what Seáth Rider had done for her; giving her just what she wanted.

She climbed out of bed and went into the bathroom to splash her face with cold water. She stared at herself in the mirror and thought that she looked distinctly different. Not older, but different. When you live with somebody, you use your partner's face as a mirror, instead of a real mirror. You see your smiles reflected; you see your anger rising before you even know yourself that you're angry. You see sarcasm, you see affection. But when you live on your own, you have to rely on glass mirror, with silver backs, and there was never a glass mirror with a silver back that ever told the truth.

Sarah's father had once said, "Mirrors are only good for one thing: to hold over a dead man's lips, to make sure that he isn't breathing any longer." And that had scared her, too.

She suddenly thought of seeing her father out on the island; and the more she thought about it, the more convinced she became that she hadn't imagined it, and that Seáth Rider had been involved in conjuring him up. Maybe he had done it to tempt her; to excite her. But then again, maybe he had done it to show her what he was capable of doing. Maybe the chairs were nothing more than a teaser, a way of warming her up.

After all, if he had managed to manipulate history to expunge the man who had originally bought these chairs, this Ian somebody, couldn't he manipulate history to bring her something she wanted even more? Couldn't he alter time and events so that her father hadn't really died?

She realized that the thought was blasphemous. But she had seen her father, alive. Not an illusion, not a trick of the light. And if Seáth Rider could bring him back to her, the way he had brought her these chairs . . .

She went back to bed. It was only 4:00 but she wished it were morning. She was too tired to read but she was too excited to sleep. In the end, however, she *did* sleep, from

5:15 until way past eight. She talked constantly, strange unintelligible sentences, and once or twice she cried, and tears dripped down her cheeks.

She met Seáth Rider outside. The morning was misty; so misty that it was almost raining; but the only concession that Seáth Rider had made to the weather was to turn up his collar.

"Did you sleep well?" he asked her.

"No. I kept worrying about those bloody chairs."

"Ah, you'll get used to them. They're housetrained."

"As a matter of fact I kept worrying about you, what else you could do."

He turned and stared at her in exaggerated surprise. "What *else* I could do? Now what do you mean by that?"

"I was just wondering if you could do other things . . . apart from making that man disappear, so that I could have my chairs."

"Don't they always say that women are never satisfied."

"It's not that . . . it's just that I saw my father, out on the island. I was wondering whether that was anything to do with you."

"Your father's dead."

"The man who bought those chairs was once alive."

Seáth Rider wiped his face with his hand. "You're not trying to suggest that I've got any power over life or death? Because I haven't. All I can do is get you what you want."

She stood beside him, watching him. She was afraid of him and the consequences of knowing him but her need was greater than her fear. "Supposing I want my father."

He looked at her without speaking.

"Supposing *that's* my heart's desire?"

"Well, then," he said, "that would be something of an acquisition now, wouldn't it. But of course it would cost you."

"Is it possible? Is it really possible?"

"I didn't say that it was and I didn't say that it wasn't. All I said was, it would cost you."

"How much?" she demanded.

Seáth Rider shook his head. "More than you could afford, I should say."

"How much? I'll give you anything you want."

"No," he said. "You'd only welsh."

"Mr Rider, if you could bring my father back to me, I swear on my life that I would never go back on my word, no matter what you asked me for."

"I ask only what Fair Breast asked of Iollan. Your fidelity."

"Are you asking me to sleep with you, is that it?"

"Nothing of the kind; unless you wish it. I just want your faithfulness, that's all."

"I don't really understand."

"Your father never taught you what fidelity was? Cleaving to a person through thick and thin; through rain and shine; staying true?"

Sarah was confused. She couldn't think what Seáth Rider wanted her to do. But all the same she said, "Yes, you can have my fidelity; if that's the price of bringing my father back."

"For ever and ever?"

"Yes, for what that's worth."

Seáth Rider shrugged. "Very well, then, if that's what you want."

Sarah waited. "Is that it? Is that all there is to it?"

The rain dripped from the tip of Seáth Rider's nose, and trickled down his cheeks as if he were crying. "What more did you want. A flash of lightning and a rumble of thunder." It still made her shiver when he said "tunder".

"But he's going to come back?"

"You'll just have to wait and see, won't you. You can give me a kiss if you care to."

She stood facing him for a long time and the rain grew steadily heavier. At last she stepped forward, and laid her hands on his shoulders, and kissed him, on the lips.

"You're rare," he said. "You're very rare."

She was about to turn away, but she found that she couldn't resist kissing him again, rain-wet lips touching rain-wet lips, scarcely more than a graze, but enough for the nerve-endings in her lips to tingle, and her eyes to close.

She stared directly into his eyes, but it occurred to her that she didn't even know what she was looking for. "Thank you," she whispered, and then she walked back toward the hotel.

During the afternoon the clouds unraveled and the rain cleared away. Sarah went for a walk around the hotel grounds, and out to the islands. She saw two or three other guests, and exchanged "good-days", but she saw no sign of her father. She began to suspect that Seáth Rider had been deceiving her with all his talk of giving people whatever they wanted, and his 'fidelity'. Irish blarney, that's all it was.

Just after three o'clock she drove into Kenmare to take a look at the shops. She bought two fine linen tablecloths and a set of silver spoons, and was tempted by a small walnut cabinet, but decided that she had probably spent enough on her Daniel Marot chairs. At five she was beginning to feel hungry so she went into O'Leary's Restaurant for a half of Guinness and a prawn sandwich. O'Leary's had a bar on one side and a large, airy restaurant on the other, with gilded mirrors on the walls and old-fashioned fans rotating on the ceiling. Sarah was about to go into the bar, which seemed cosier and jollier, when she noticed a man sitting at one of the tables in the restaurant with his back to her. An elderly man, in a green tweed jacket. Beside him on the tabletop lay a pipe and a tobacco-pouch.

She felt a crawling sensation all the way down her back. It couldn't be him, surely. Not here, in this crowded restaurant, in Kenmare.

She thought: no, it can't be him. She had hoped and prayed that Seáth Rider could give her what she wanted, but at the bottom of her heart she hadn't really believed that it was possible. The dead can't come back – not after a whole year anyway.

All the same, she found herself walking across the restaurant, circling around tables until she was standing close behind him. She closed her eyes for a moment. She didn't know what would upset her the most: if it *were* him, or if it *weren't*. But then she reached out and touched his shoulder, and he turned around. And it was.

Neither of them spoke. Her father pushed back his chair, and stood up, and took her in his arms. For a long, long time the two of them stood in the middle of the restaurant, holding each other, with tears streaming down their faces. A few people looked and a few people smiled, but in Ireland that sort of dearness is never anything to be ashamed of, and that's why they cry when they play their laments.

207

"My dearest Sarah," said her father, at last. "How I've missed you, you've no idea."

"Oh daddy I've missed you too."

They sat down, and held hands across the red-checkered tablecloth. Sarah couldn't believe how young her father looked, and how fit. *He's dead*, she thought, *and I think he looks fit!* It was like one of those awful Jewish jokes about the husband who died after a holiday in Florida, with all the relatives at the funeral home saying how well he looked. She found herself laughing at her own stupidity, but also with pleasure, just to have him back again.

"How have you been keeping?" her father asked her. "You look different. Your hair's different. How's that idle husband of yours?"

"Ken? We're divorced."

"Oh, I'm sorry to hear that. I always rather liked poor old Ken."

"Daddy," she said. "I'm so glad to have you back. Mummy won't know what to say, will she, when I bring you back home?"

Her father lowered his eyes. "How is mummy? Did she take it really badly?"

Sarah nodded, with a lump in her throat. "You'll make her so happy, coming back. We can be a family again, with Sunday lunches and walks and everything."

Her father didn't look up. "I can't do it, Sarah. I can't come back."

"But you're *alive*. You were dead, but now you're alive. Of course you can come back!"

The woman at the next table gave her the oddest of looks, and then went back to her conversation about making jam.

"Perhaps it's physically possible, my darling. But I've got another life now, quite different from the life I had

208

before. I passed from one life into the next; and now I have friends who need me and people who rely on me. I *could* come back, but to tell you the truth . . ."

He squeezed her hands tight, and his eyes filled with tears. "I love you, Sarah, with all my heart. But the life I spent with you and mummy is over now, and no amount of wishing can bring it back. I *could* come back, but I've been living in a very different place – a place of great affection and complete fulfilment – and I simply don't want to."

The waitress brought Sarah's sandwich. She pushed it to one side. She couldn't eat anything now if she tried.

"What are you going to do?" she asked her father. "How long are you going to stay here?"

"Just long enough to tell you that I love you; and goodbye. I didn't have the chance to say goodbye before, did I?"

"You can't go," Sarah begged him. "I've brought you back, daddy. I need you so much; and mummy needs you more."

He gave her the saddest of smiles. "I'm sorry, darling. I really am. But I have to move on. There's so much waiting for me."

He stood up, and the sun came through the restaurant window behind him and dazzled her, so that she couldn't see his face. He said, "I love you, Sarah, and I wish you well," and then he turned and walked out of the restaurant, leaving her sitting alone. She saw him pass by the window, more like a reflection than a real person, but then he was gone. She could have run out after him, and begged him to come back; but she knew that it wasn't any use. *I could come back, but I simply don't want to . . .* and what could be more specific than that?

209

The waitress came over, all concerned. "Is there something wrong with your sandwich?" she asked.

Sarah shook her head and tried to sound bright. "No. Not at all. There's something wrong with me."

"Well, don't worry dear, I won't charge you for it if you didn't like it."

Sarah couldn't speak. Tears flooded out of her eyes, and all she could do was cover her face with her hands and let out a series of deep, muted sobs.

The waitress sat down next to her and put her arm around her. "What's the matter, then? Is it something I can help you with?"

"No," said Sarah. "Nobody can."

The waitress held her and shushed her while she sat on her bentwood chair and let out the longest burst of uncontrollable grief since her father had died.

When she returned from Kenmare it was evening and she found Seáth Rider waiting for her in the bar, with a glass of neat vodka in front of him. He looked darker than ever; edgy and dissatisfied.

"Well?" he said. "What's the matter with you?"

She sat down opposite, on a large loudly-upholstered sofa. Sonny Loony the barman came across and asked her what she wanted to drink. "Dry white wine; very cold."

Sonny gave Seáth Rider a sideways look as if to say, don't you so much as breathe on one hair of this young lady's head, or you'll have me to answer to, Seáth Rider, in return, gave him a black look back.

"You saw your father, is that it?"

"That's it. I went to Kenmare and there he was."

"So where is he now? As if I didn't know."

Sarah clamped her hand over her mouth to prevent

herself from sobbing. She looked around the room and willed her eyes not to fill up with tears.

"You knew, didn't you?" she managed to ask him.

"I didn't know for sure. But it's par for the course. You ask a 20-year-old if he wants to be 16 again, and he won't be having it. You ask a 40-year-old if he wants to be 27 again, and he'll say no, even if he's full of envy. Or you ask a 60-year-old if he wants to be 45, and he'll scoff at you. We *progress*. We change. And after we die, there it is, waiting for us, the invisible kingdom, the same the Fianna could visit, full of light and hope and heavenly charms. I warned you, Mrs Bryce, but you didn't listen to what I saying. The dead will never come back to us. They've gone on, the dead, and they've left us behind."

"I didn't know," said Sarah, with as much dignity as she could summon up.

"Well now you do. You got what you wanted; but what you wanted didn't want you. It happens all the time, believe me."

Sonny brought Sarah's wine, and she sipped it gratefully. She hadn't realized how thirsty she was; and hungry, too.

"You'll have dinner with me?" asked Seáth Rider.

"No, thanks. I'm going to have a bath, and wash my hair. I'm going to make an early start tomorrow."

"I beg your pardon."

"I said, 'I'm going to make an early start.' I'm going to fly back to London tomorrow."

Seáth Rider sat up in his seat, bony and dark, his face as pale as a lantern. "Now look here, you made an agreement with me, now didn't you. You promised me fidelity. On your life, you promised me fidelity. So what's all this talk of going back to London?"

211

Sarah almost laughed. "Fidelity doesn't mean staying in Ireland for the rest of my life!"

"Perhaps not. But it means staying close to me; and since I'm Irish, and choose to live in Ireland, for all of its many faults, this is where you'll be."

"Don't be absurd. I have to be back in London by lunchtime. I'm having a meeting with Sotheby's."

Seáth Rider finished his vodka and lifted his glass for another. "Did you not meet your father?"

"Yes I did."

"So did I not do what I said I was going to do? You had your heart's desire – your chairs, your father."

"Mr Rider," Sarah protested, "I'm very grateful for the chairs; but my father's gone back to wherever dead people go back to; and I'm left with nothing at all."

"You promised me fidelity. I fulfilled my part of the bargain did I not? If your father chose not to stay, well, that was none of my doing, now was it."

"Mr Rider this is absurd."

He snatched hold of her hand and held her tight. "Was it absurd when you were standing in the rain begging me to bring your father back? Was it absurd then?"

Sarah stared at him coldly, and after a while he let go of her hand, and sat back. All the same, her heart was beating like the rain on the rooftops.

"I think I'd better go to my room and pack," she said.

He made a dismissive face, as if she could do whatever she liked, and it would make no difference to him. She left the bar and walked quickly through the lobby. She felt deeply disturbed; not only by what had happened today in the restaurant in Kenmare, but by Seáth Rider's insistence that she keep her promise. She had seen what influence he had, and she was terrified that he was going to *make* her keep it, no matter what.

As she rushed up the staircase, she almost collided with a man coming down, carrying a traveling bag. She looked up at him, and said, "Sorry!" before she saw who it was. Ken, her ex-husband, his hair longer than it was before, in a crumpled blue-linen, jacket. His broad, Celtic face looked well and tanned, and even his eyebrows had gone blonde.

"*Ken*! What on earth are *you* doing here?"

He flushed. "I'm sorry, Sarah. I was trying to leave without you seeing me."

"But what are you *doing* here? I thought you were still in France."

"I was, until last week. Then I decided to do something which I've been wanting to do for a very long time. I came looking for you."

"You followed me all the way here?"

He looked around. "Listen – is there somewhere we can talk?"

They went upstairs to the hotel library, dedicated to George Bernard Shaw. It was huge and gloomy and completely empty. Sarah sat on one of the sofas and Ken pulled up a chair and sat close to her.

"I saw you in Carhiovean, going into a pub," said Sarah. "I thought it was – well, I thought it was somebody else. But it *was* you."

Ken nodded. "I was following you. I wanted to see you, that's all. But then I saw that boyfriend of yours sitting there waiting for you, so I went out the back way."

"You were following me? Why?"

"It was stupid, I suppose. But I wanted to find out if there was any chance of us getting back together again. I've changed, Sarah. I've been thinking about where we

213

went wrong, and how much of it was my fault. I've been working and painting and I've really turned myself around."

"Oh, Ken," she said, and took hold of his hand.

"That's why I followed you here . . . to see if we could give it another try. But then I saw you talking to that boyfriend of yours, and I realized that I'd obviously left it too late. I saw you out on the terrace, too, having a bit of a tête-à-tête, and that's when I decided to pack my bag and leave you to it. I still love you, Sarah; I always will. But I'm not going to stand in your way."

"Ken, why didn't you *try* to talk to me, at least? Seáth Rider isn't my boyfriend! He isn't even my friend! He's just a man I met at the auction. He helped me to buy two Daniel Marot chairs, and we got chatting, but that was all."

"I saw you kissing him."

"Well . . . he promised to do me a favour, that's all; and I was grateful for it."

"Oh, yes? What kind of favour?"

"Listen, you can't start acting jealous. You're my *ex*-husband, remember?"

"I'm sorry."

Sarah glanced at her watch. "Listen, are you leaving right now?"

"I've got to pay first – but, yes."

"Then give me five minutes to stuff my things in my bag, and I'll come with you."

He blinked at her. "You mean it? Back to London?"

"That's right. And on the way you can tell me all about what you've been doing, and how much you've changed."

Ken hesitated for a moment, then nodded, and said, "Right, then! I'll see you downstairs in five minutes!"

He leaned over and kissed her cheek. Neither of them saw the pale face looking in through the library door, or the lean, dark shadow that flitted across the ceiling.

Ken was still waiting in the lobby more than quarter of an hour later. If he waited much longer, they were in danger of missing the last flight to Heathrow. He paced up and down, looking at the pictures on the walls, but in the end he went to the reception desk and asked if he could use the telephone.

"I want Mrs Bryce's number."

The receptionist ran her finger down the guest list. "Mrs Bryce, did you say? We don't have anybody of that name staying here – oh, wait, here's a Bryce, but this is Mr."

"That's me. I've only just checked out. Perhaps she registered under another name."

"Well, why don't you ask the porter, sir. Just describe her to him: he's got a wonderful memory for faces."

Ken went across to the porter's desk, where the porter was arranging copies of the evening's papers. "I'm looking for a woman who registered here two days ago. Blonde, 34 years old. Very smart dresser. She came for the antiques auction."

The porter frowned, and then slowly shook his head. "We've had nobody of that description, sir. Not for a week or two, and certainly not to the auction."

"I'm sorry, but you have. She's my ex-wife. I was talking to her in the library, only twenty minutes ago."

Again the porter shook his head. "You'll have to forgive me, sir. Usually I can remember every single face: but that description has me beat."

Ken went back to the lobby. He waited another half-hour, and then he picked up his bag. The receptionist gave him a sad, sympathetic smile. He should have known that Sarah wouldn't want him back. She had probably gone back up to her room, and started to remember all of the arguments, all of the throwing of pots and pans, all the times that he had left her at parties to chat to younger girls. Well, he couldn't blame her. It was just that she had seemed so keen to come with him.

He left the hotel and walked toward the car-park. The evening was dark and drizzly. He was half-way there before he became aware of a tall, dark man standing by the fence. It was the same man that Sarah had been talking to – and kissing. The man who had promised to do her a favour.

"Leaving us, are you," the man said, as Ken approached. His voice was a soft as cat's fur.

"Yes," said Ken. "I have to be back in London tonight." He paused. "Listen, if you see Mrs Bryce, can you tell her that I don't bear her any ill-will. Tell her that I understand."

"Oh, you think you understand, do you?"

Ken frowned at him. "I beg your pardon. What do you mean by that?"

"I mean that you no more understand than a stone understands calculus."

"I still don't know what you mean."

"I mean that Mrs Bryce has promised to be faithful; and faithful she wasn't; but faithful she'll have to be. She's staying here, in Ireland, but not in Ireland, and they can look for her till their eyes drop out, but they'll never find her."

"What the hell are you talking about? Are you drunk? Where is she?"

"She's here still, like I told you."

Ken put down his bag. "In that case, I want to see her, and I want to see her now."

216

"Oh, you shall," said Seáth Rider. "You shall see her now and always. You shall see her to your heart's desire."

Ken was about to say something else when he felt as if somebody had hit him, very hard, right at the base of his skull. He dropped forward onto his knees; his head bursting with pain. He thought he could hear Seáth Rider talking to him, but his voice seemed to echo, like a man talking down a drain. He put out his hands to stop himself from pitching forward, and crouched on the tarmac on all fours, trying to understand what had happened to him. He felt as if his brain were shrinking, as if his face were being sucked in. He felt his ribcage being pulled in, and his legs tightening. He tried to speak, but his jaws felt as if they been clamped together.

His whole body contracted. It was more painful than anything he had ever experienced in his life, and he screamed as loud as he could, but even his larynx seemed to have contracted into a small, inflexible knot, and all he could manage was a strangled howl.

He found himself naked and shivering in the rain; his faculties dimmed; his feet scratching on the pavement. He had lost all of his perception of who he was and what he was doing here. He looked up at Seáth Rider and all he could feel was fear.

"There now," said Seáth Rider. "There's a good fellow. Let's go and see what Sarah's doing, shall we?"

Sarah came downstairs with her bag packed, but there was no sign of Ken. She went to reception and asked if they had seen him, or if he had left a message, but the receptionist shook her head.

"No, Mrs Bryce; there's been nobody."

"Perhaps he's gone back to his room. Can you tell me what number it is?"

The receptionist looked through the register. "There's Mrs Bryce, but that's you. No record of anybody called *Mr* Bryce."

"Are you sure? He told me he was staying here all weekend."

"You can look for yourself, if you want to."

She was still searching through the register when Seáth Rider came in through the door, with a brindled dog, straining at its leash.

"Ah, then, you're ready," he said.

"Where's Ken?" she asked him, in rising alarm.

"Ken?" he said, with exaggerated innocence.

"My ex-husband. He was here. I saw him, I spoke to him. I want to know what you've done with him."

"Now surely why should I do anything with him. And why should you care. You pledged your fidelity to me remember."

The brindled dog tried to jump up but Seáth Rider briskly smacked it across its muzzle with the back of his hand. "You can't be too strict with these mongrel mutts, now can you." The dog miserably subsided, and circled around the back of Seáth Rider's legs.

"We're off then," said Seáth Rider. "I've taken care of your bill."

"I'm not going off anywhere," said Sarah. "I'm driving to Cork, and then I'm flying back to—" She paused. She knew she was flying somewhere, but where?

"I have to get back to my mother," she said, in desperation. "I have to get back to my business – back to my shop."

Seáth Rider pulled the dog-leash tighter, so that the dog began to breathe in thin, asphyxiated gasps. "You're not going anywhere, Mrs Bryce, except with me. Your mother won't remember you. You never existed, as far as she's concerned. You never went to school, you never grew up. Sarah Thompson, they'll say, I never heard of anybody called Sarah Thompson. Nor Sarah Bryce, neither, when she was married. They won't find a speck of a mention of you anywhere, not in christening notes nor school magazine nor local newspaper. You've gone, vanished, you're invisible, except for here."

Sarah looked around. "I don't understand. This is still the same hotel."

Seáth Rider passed his hand across his face like a camera-shutter. "There isn't any such thing as 'the same hotel', Mrs Bryce. There are thousands of Parknasillas, one for each guest who came here; just as there are millions of Irelands, layer upon layer, depth upon depth. The gates are still open in Ireland, Mrs Bryce, and people still walk through."

"You're trying to tell me that I'm here, but I'm somewhere else?"

Seáth Rider nodded. "You'll be happy here, Mrs Bryce. Happy as Larry. You'll see things that you never imagined possible; and you'll talk to people who'll set your ears ablaze. You'll grow to love me, too. I shouldn't wonder, and you and I will be the best of companions."

He took her hand and led her out into the night. It was still drizzling, but the bright hotel lights made it look as if they were being showered with fairy dust. The dog yapped, and Seáth Rider slapped it again, sharp and short, right across the muzzle. "You behave yourself now you cur."

Raymond French went to her room to say goodbye to her. He found the door open and the chambermaid already stripping the bed. To his surprise, however, the two Daniel Marot chairs were still there. He couldn't imagine that she would have left without seeing them packed up for shipping.

"Have you seen the woman whose room this was?" he asked the chambermaid.

The chambermaid shook her head.

Raymond walked into the room and looked around. The closets were empty; the bathroom had been cleared of cosmetics. The only evidence that anyone had been here was a business card, left in the ashtray, folded in half.

Downstairs, in the lobby, there was no sign of Sarah anywhere. But Raymond was just about to go to the reception desk and ask about her when he ran into Dermot Brien.

"Oh, Dermot – just the man I want to see! You were going to give me the name of that fellow in Dublin who bought those landscapes."

By the time he had finished talking to Dermot, he was running late. It had started to rain much harder, and if he didn't hurry he was going to miss the last flight to London.

Something else had happened, too.

He had completely forgotten about Sarah, as if she had never existed.

By the next morning, the rain had cleared, and the sky was as blue as a baby's eyes. On the Atlantic shore at Ballinskelligs Bay, a man and a woman walked across the beach. He was tall and dark and dressed in black. She wore white, a fine linen gown trimmed with Kerry lace, and there was a garland in wild flowers in her hair. Her gown trailed on the wet reflecting sand but she seemed not to notice; or perhaps she didn't care.

"I love it down here in the morning," the man said,

stopping and looking out to sea, his hand shading his eyes. "It's always so fresh. Like the world born anew."

The woman said nothing but kept on walking. Eventually he caught up with her and took hold of her arm. "You mustn't pine for what was," he told her. "That life is gone now, don't you see? That's what your father was trying to tell you, that it's no good trying to go back. That running away last night, what folly that was; and look what happened to my poor dog. Besides, didn't I keep my part of the bargain? I'm only expecting you to keep yours."

She turned and looked at him. Her face was filled with resentment and bitterness. "You gave me nothing," she said. "You gave me nothing and I owe you nothing."

He gave her a quick frown, as if her words had badly hurt him. But then he cheered up, and said, "This is just the beginning, you know. You'll see what I can give you, given time. It's a strange life, but a fair one. You'll meet all kinds of people just like yourself; rich and beautiful, some of them; and some of them ragged and odder than tinkers. And I'll show you what magic is, too. Real magic. Walking through hillsides and having no concern for time or space. I'll show you how to feed on blood and spiders and baby's breath; and how to win all of the men you could possibly want, and steal them away; the same way that I stole you."

Just then, a man appeared around the rocks, walking his dog. The dog was darting and barking at the sea, but when it caught sight of them it came trotting up and stood a little way away from them, its head cocked to one side, making a high-pitched whining sound.

"Here boy, come on boy," the man called him. "What's got into you?"

The man came nearer and nearer. The woman slowly

221

raised her hand, but the man walked right past her, missing her by only a few inches. He didn't even look at her.

The woman turned around as if to call him; but then she looked at her dark companion in absolute horror. "He couldn't see me," she said, her voice trembling. "*He couldn't see me!*"

Her companion man started to laugh. He walked away, still laughing, and shaking his head.

The woman stayed where she was, mortified, while the sea ebbed slowly away on all sides.

Raymond caught the midday flight to London. The Garda had carried out another intensive search of the ditches and hedges alongside the Kenmare road, but they had found no trace of a woman's body. They called into the bed and breakfast and told Raymond that he was free to go.

It was while he was while he was drinking his first vodka and tonic on the plane that he began to wonder what he had been looking for, just before he left Parknasilla. He remembered searching through somebody's room, but for the life of him he couldn't remember whose it was, or what he had been looking for. There was something about chairs but he couldn't remember that either.

Later, when he was looking for a pen, he discovered the folded business-card out of his jacket pocket. 'Seáth E. Rider, Acquisitor, Dublin & London.'

He regularly tried to solve *The Daily Telegraph* crossword, but it didn't occur to him that 'Seáth E. Rider' was an anagram of 'Heart's Desire'.

Suffer Kate

Sacramento, California

Sacramento is the capital of California – situated on the banks of the Sacramento River in what used to be the state's pivotal point – half-way between the goldfields of the Sierra Nevada and San Francisco, at the point where the first transcontinental wagon and railroads entered the Central Valley.

As times changed, and most of the state's population and wealth gravitated to the south, Sacramento became rather isolated from the life of the people it was built to govern. But it retains an air of historic charm, and it is a strong reminder of California's past and the men and women who crossed the mountains to settle here.

The face of fear that we find in Sacremento is the face of self-destruction – the face of somebody who will risk death time and time again in order to seek pleasure. This story deals with a highly dangerous obsession which, until comparatively recently, was rarely discussed in public. Only a greater openness in the press and the tragic deaths of several well-known men has brought it out into the open.

SUFFER KATE

There are some guys who have to live right on the very edge, the razor's edge, no matter what. I could never understand that; I never wanted the fear. I always used to think there's enough nerve-jingling experience in life, just waking up close to the woman you love, just walking scuffle-footed down some summer street.

Who needs to live right on the very edge? Who needs to test their mortality, time and time again, as if they can never quite believe their luck at being alive?

Maybe it's something to do with the mentality of certain spermatozoa. Maybe some of them don't have too much confidence, and when they penetrate that ovum, they lie there, trembling, with their tail dropped off, thinking, Shit, I can't believe it, I just can't believe it, man, out of all those millions and millions of other spermatozoa, I actually made it. I'm going to be alive, man, while all of those other guys just fade away, just fade away, like a crowd scene in a 1912 silent movie, like unknown soldiers on the Western Front, disappearing through the mustard gas.

But my friend Jamie Ford, he always had to live on the edge. *Beyond* the edge, in fact, so that his toes were way over the abyss, if you understand what I mean, and nothing between him and falling but sheer chance. My friend Jamie Ford had discovered what it is to choke.

That's what he used to call it, a Choke. Like, "I'm going for a Choke, man; I'll see you in physics." And there was nothing I could do. I mean, what could I do? We were both kids, and we were both at Sherman Oaks Senior High. We were friends, we were blood brothers, we'd cut our thumbs and shared our actual life-substance.

I knew everything about him. I knew the scar on the left side of his head, where his spiky blond hair never grew. I knew the grey-blue colour of his eyes. I knew all of the songs that he could remember, and all of his memories. I knew his bedroom as well as he did. I knew where he kept his Superboy comics and where he hid his copies of *Pix* and *Adam*.

I even knew the name of his imaginary friend, the one he'd had when he was three years old.

His imaginary friend whose second name was Kate and whose first name was Suffer.

Suffer Kate.

He used to tell me that it was something to do with his pillow, the pillow in his crib. It had smelled so clean and it had felt so soft, all he ever wanted to do was to plunge his face into it and never breathe, never again. And his mother had leaned over his crib, her face all tight with panic, and said, "No! No, Jamie! No, darling! I don't want you to Suffer Kate!"

She had taken his wonderful pillow away; but he had still found ways to stop himself from breathing. He had wrapped his head in his comforter, round and round, so that it was tight over his nose and mouth. And one day, when he was eleven, his mother had found him naked in the middle of the kitchen floor, with a plastic shopping bag over his head, his features wrinkle-sucked into the lettering of Hallmark cards.

Dr Kennedy had said that he was lucky to survive.

226

Another thirty seconds and he would have Suffer Kated.

His mother could only remember that he had fought her off. Desperately, as if he wanted to die. His mother could only remember that his penis had been totally rigid.

His mother was pretty. I can picture her now. Petite, with the same blue-grey eyes that Jamie had, maybe a little sad-looking. She used to wear a sky-blue checkered cowgirl blouse that I liked a lot, because she had very full breasts, and when she leaned over to butter my corn on the cob I could see her brassiere.

In the sixth grade, one by one, we all grew physically mature enough to ejaculate. At least, most of us did, and the ones who hadn't quite made it yet always pretended that they had. "Oh, sure, I shot about a pint last night. It went right out the window and landed on the cat. He looked like the cat who got the cream, hunh-hunh-hunh!"

It was then that Jamie started to go for his Chokes. Jesus, it makes me go cold and shivery now just to think about it. If I had been an adult then, I would have stopped him, physically stopped him, and insisted that he go for therapy. But when you're a kid, you don't think that way; you're all inexperienced, you're all slightly crazy, believing in myths and legends and all kinds of weird superstitions, living on hormones and fear and expectations and zits and embarrassment.

What was I going to do? Knock on the principal's door and walk up to that dessicated, arroyo-wrinkled face and say, "Please, Mr Marshall, my friend Jamie keeps hanging himself and whacking off"?

But, of course, that was what Jamie was doing. During almost every recess, he was locking himself into one of the heads in the science department, which hardly anybody

227

used during recess. He was taking off all of his clothes. Then he was knotting a damp sports towel into a noose, looping it over the coat peg on the back of the door, and putting his head in it. All he had to do then was twist himself around a quarter-turn and lift his feet clear of the floor. He was literally hanging himself, while his cock rose stiff as a board, and the jism jumped out of him and spattered the walls.

Once he didn't appear in time for class, so I ran to the washrooms and climbed over the partition and found him grey-faced and whining, his fingers caught between his crimson-bruised neck and the tightly wrung towel, unable to pry himself free. He was chilly and white, and his thighs were dripping with sperm. I cut the towel with my Swiss Army penknife and lifted him down. He was like Christ from the cross – thin and tortured, a soul in need of rest and absolution. I'll never forget how he shuddered.

After that, whenever he announced that he was going for a Choke, I used to follow him, as quietly as I could, and wait outside the cubicle while he hanged himself and masturbated. I couldn't bear it. I couldn't bear the choking noises, or the strangulated gasps of pleasure, or the sound of his bare heels knocking against the door. But I was mature enough to understand that if I tried to stop him, he would only do it someplace else, where I wasn't around to take care of him. Maybe he was going to kill himself one day, but I wasn't going to let him do it when *I* was around. I vowed that much.

In a peculiar way, not a homosexual way, I loved him. He was so good-looking, so edgy, so dangerous, a boy's boy. He once asked me if I wanted him to suck my cock, just to see what it was like, but I said no. I had a feeling that all he wanted to do was fill his mouth with penis-flesh, so that he could hardly breathe.

228

He frightened me. I knew that he would have to die. Maybe that was why I loved him so much.

On graduation day, with the school band playing 'Colonel Bogey' and the sun dappling the lawns, I suddenly realized that I couldn't find him. The first students were already lining up beside the rostrum to collect their diplomas, and the principal's voice was echoing, amplified, from the gymnasium wall, and I began to panic. If I wasn't on stage in about a minute and a half, my mom and dad were going to hang me out to dry. But Jamie might have gone for one of his Chokes, and if I did go down to the parade ground, and Jamie died because I wasn't there to save him, then my graduation day was going to be a day of guilt and agony, not only today, but on every anniversary forever.

I ran to the washroom with my gown flapping behind me. I banged open all of the doors, but he wasn't there. I ran to the locker rooms and shouted his name, but he wasn't there, either.

He was dead, I was sure of it. The very last day, the very last minute when I was responsible for him, and he was dead.

I barged into the senior common room, with its blue pastel walls and its carpet tiles and its posters of Jefferson Airplane and the Grateful Dead. And there he was, lying on the floor, stark naked, his head all wrapped up like a science fiction mummy in Saran Wrap. His eyes staring. Sucking for breath. Sucking for breath. The cling film misted with lung moisture and sweat.

And, sitting astride him, Laurel Fay, the cheerleader, with her skirt lifted and her bare breasts bouncing out of her unbuttoned blouse, her arms lifted, her fingers tugging and winding at her golden-red hair. Her eyes were closed, and she was ecstatic, and I wasn't surprised that she was

229

ecstatic, because I'd seen Jamie's boners when he was suffocating – tall and curved and totally hard, like some kind of animal's horn.

She twisted around and stared at me. She started to say, "Get the hell—" when I walked across the room and pushed her off him. She fell awkwardly, and between her plump white thighs I saw a flash of pink sticky flesh and gingery pubic hair. The image of it stuck in my mind the way a Matisse painting sticks in your mind. Clashing colours. Erotic yet tasteless. She swore at me: a curse that was strange and vehement.

"Judas! Judas fucking Iscariot! You don't even understand! You don't even fucking understand! He wants it! He needs it! Damn you and all the rest of you! It's death meets life! It's life meets death!"

I wrenched the Saran Wrap from Jamie's head, twisted it away from his nose and mouth. He gave a terrible, throat-racking gasp, and then he coughed and coughed, bringing up strings of phlegm and half-digested Rice Krispies.

Laurel had sat herself up with her back against the couch. She gave me a quick, venomous, disgusted glance, then looked away.

"He's my friend," I told her, trying to make my voice sound totally cold. "He's my best friend, and you nearly fucking killed him."

"I thought that was the whole point," Laurel retorted. She reached out for her bra, and fastened it up, and lifted her breasts back into it.

I cradled Jamie in my arms. His chest was rising and falling, rising and falling, like an exhausted swimmer who knows that he won't be able to reach the shoreline but can't think of any reason to stop swimming.

His eyes flickered from side to side, and the saliva

230

that slid out of the corner of his mouth was streaked with blood.

"You've been playing with Suffer Kate again," I told him, dabbing his mouth with a Kleenex, and then stroking his sweat-cold forehead.

Jamie tried to smile, but all he could manage was a cough. "Everybody needs somebody to love," he breathed.

I held him in my arms, and I knew that I would miss him. But I was so relieved to be free of his Chokes. I was so relieved that I wouldn't have to take care of him any longer, him and Suffer Kate. If he strangled himself tomorrow, I would feel wretched about it, and miss him like hell, but at least I wouldn't feel responsible for him any longer.

It was almost seven years before I came across Jamie again. I had taken a course in journalism at UCLA and then worked for eleven months as a freelance reporter before landing a job on the city desk at the *Sacramento Bee*. It was a roasting morning in August when Dan Brokerage, my editor, parked himself on the edge of my desk and said, "What do you know about the Golden Horses out on Highway 80?"

I shrugged. "Not much. It's not the kind of place you'd take your sainted mother for an evening out. Why?"

Dan unwound his wire-rimmed glasses. "One of my contacts says that the Golden Horses has been pulling some unusually substantial crowds lately, especially on Friday nights."

"Well, they have strippers, don't they?" I said. "Maybe they've found themselves some girl who's really special."

"That's not what my contact was suggesting. My contact was suggesting that there's something bizarre

231

being staged down there. His exact words were 'There's something real sick going down.'"

I looked at the half-finished story on my VDU screen. 'Mayor Praises Ornamental Gardens'. Unlike most young reporters of my generation, I prided myself on my attention to upbeat civic stories. Most of my contemporaries wanted to be gonzo investigative journalists, exposing bureaucratic corruption and police brutality. But I knew what sold papers like the *Sacramento Bee:* constructive, happy, feel-good stories, with everybody's name included and everybody's name spelled right.

All the same, I was pleased that Dan had chosen me to look into the Golden Horses story. It meant that he trusted me to get my facts straight.

"It's Friday tomorrow," said Dan. "Get yourself along there. It won't be easy to get yourself in. From what my contact says, they're shit-hot on security. But talk to a man on the door called Wolf Bodell, and tell him that Presley sent you. And take at least two and a half bills in cash money. And try to look like a pervert."

"What does a pervert look like?" I asked him.

"I don't know ... but he doesn't look like you. He doesn't have clean-cut hair and an Oxford shirt and Sta-prest pants. I don't know. Just try to look disreputable. Just try to look *shifty.*"

"Shifty," I nodded. "Okay."

The Golden Horses was a low whitewashed building with a shingle roof about a quarter of a mile south of Highway 80, in that flat, heat hazed no-man's-land between West Sacramento and Davis. I arrived just after sunset in my beaten-up metallic-bronze LTD, and I couldn't believe what I saw. The main parking lot was already crowded with hundreds of vehicles of all makes and sizes – Cadillacs

232

and Jeeps and pickups and BMWs and Winnebagos –
some of them dilapidated, some of them gleaming new.
Whatever attraction the Golden Horses was offering, it
obviously appealed to the strangest variety of people,
regardless of age or wealth or social background.

As I drove down the dusty, rutted track, I was flagged
down by a huge man in a white Stetson hat and an ill-fitting
black suit, carrying an r/t.

"Evening, friend. Where d'you think you're going?"
he wanted to know. His eyes were piggy and blood-shot,
and his breath smelled strongly of whiskey and Big Red
chewing gum.

"Presley sent me."

"Presley? You mean *Elvis* Presley?"

"Of course not. I'm supposed to see Wolf Bodell."

The man stared at me for a long, long time, his hand
grasping my car windowsill as if he were quite capable
of tearing off the entire door with one exerted heave.
Then he raised his head and shouted, "Wolf! Guy says
that Presley sent him!"

I didn't hear the answer, but I had to presume that it
was in the affirmative, because the man slapped the roof
of my car and said, "Park yourself as close to that prickly
pear as you can get."

I climbed out. The night was warm. The sky was still
the colour of warm boysenberry jelly. There was a smell
of desert dust and automobile fumes and excitement. A
long line of vehicles was turning off the highway, twenty
or thirty at least, their indicator lights flashing. I could
hear deep, heavy rock 'n' roll on the wind, ZZ Top or
something similar, the kind of music that sounds like
freight trains and people walking, hundreds of people
walking.

On the ridge of the shingled roof, two neon horses

danced. There were flashing lights, too, and smoke, and people yelping in anticipation. I walked across the boarded veranda and up to the doorway, where six or seven muscular-looking men in black suits and dark glasses were vetting everybody who went in.

One of them put out a finger and prodded me right in the centre of my chest. "You got your pass?" he wanted to know.

"Presley sent me. Said I should speak to Wolf Bodell."

A thin man in a blue satin suit emerged from the crimson light and the cigarette smoke. His face was yellowish grey and deeply emaciated. His gums were so eroded that his teeth looked as if they could drop out in front of you. He walked with a slurring limp, and it was obvious that his left arm was wasted or injured, because he kept having to drag it upward with his right arm.

"I'm Wolf Bodell," he said in a distinctive Nebraska accent.

"Presley sent me," I told him, without much confidence.

"Presley, huh? That's okay. How long you known Presley?"

"Longer than I care to admit." I grinned.

Wolf Bodell nodded and said, "That's okay, that's okay. So long as you know Presley. I'm afraid it's still two hundrut 'n' fifty to see the show."

I counted out the cash that Dave Brokerage had given me (and made me sign for). Wolf Bodell watched me dispassionately, not looking at the money even once.

"You seen this show before?" he asked me.

I shook my head.

"You're in for a treat, then. This is the show of shows.

234

What you see tonight, you ain't never going to forget, not for the rest of your born days."

"Seems popular," I remarked, nodding at the crowds who were still arriving.

Wolf Bodell let out a thin, cackling laugh. "What are the two most saleable commodities on this here planet? I ask. And you say sex. And you say vicarious suff'rin'. That's what you say. The fascination of fucking! The fascination of the auto wreck! Death, and sex, and terror, and all of the glee that goes with it, my friend! *Schadenfreude*, to the power of n!"

Wolf Bodell hobble-heaved around me and gripped my elbow. "Let me tell you something," he said, as he guided me into the Golden Horses, through the smoke and the luridly coloured lights and the knee-deep rock 'n' roll. "I stepped on a claymore in Vietnam, and I was blown shitless. I was hanging from a tree by my own intestines. Can you believe that? My buddies unwound me, and they saved me somehow, although I still can't help screaming whenever I shit.

"But, you know, I learned something that day. When I was blown up, my friends were *laughing*. They were laughing, when they saw me hanging from that fucking tree; and the reason they were laughing was their gladness, that it wasn't them; and because they'd seen death, which was me, but it hadn't hurt them.

"If somebody had taken a movie of me, hanging from that fucking tree, I'd of been a fucking millionaire by now. People love to see death. They love it. Which is what makes Jamie Ford so fucking popular."

I stopped, abruptly, causing a big bearded guy in a red-checkered shirt to spill his beer.

"Hey, pencil-neck—" he began to protest. But then he

235

saw Wolf Bodell, and he shrugged and said, "What the fuck, okay? It's only beer."

"Jamie Ford?" I demanded.

Wolf Bodell took off his dark glasses. He had one glass eye, as blue as a summer afternoon, which stared right over my shoulder.

"Jamie Ford, that's right. Presley would've told you. Jamie Ford's been doing this for years. Jamie Ford's the one and only. That's why you came, yes?"

It was then that I turned toward the centre of the Golden Horses saloon, toward the dance floor. On most nights, a country and western band would have been playing; or couples would have been square-dancing or jiving; or drunken truckers would have been breaking chairs over each other's heads. But tonight – through the drifting cigarette smoke, through the red and yellow lights – I saw the tall, gaunt structure of a gallows.

Jamie Ford. I should have known it. *People love to see death. They love it.* And who could show you death more vividly than Jamie?

Wolf Bodell ushered me up to the bar. "What do you want?" he asked me.

"Anything. Coors Lite."

"You can't face the Grim Reaper on Coors Lite," Wolf Bodell cackled. "Leland – give this man a Jack Daniel's, straight up, with a Pabst chaser."

I took out my billfold, but Wolf Bodell shook his hand to show that he didn't want me to pay. "Any friend of Presley's is a friend of mine; and any friend of Presley's is a friend of death. We're all dying, my friend! All of us! So why are we all so bad to each other? What's the point of snatching a woman's purse when both of you are sitting side by side on a bus that's going over a thousand-foot cliff? Die and let die. That's my philosophy."

236

I was handed my drinks by a busty barmaid with a white-powdered pockmarked face and a dusty red velvet basque. She must have been very beautiful once. She winked at me, but I saw nothing in her face except suffering. Eyes unfocused, nose not quite straight. A walking casualty of Smirnoff or crack or a violent husband, who could tell? No joy, for sure. Not even hope. I turned away, and she called out, "Don't be so unsociable, lover!"

Wolf Bodell nudged me with his elbow and grinned. "You know what your trouble is? You're too damned nice. All of Presley's friends are too damned nice. Don't play poker, do you? I relish playing poker with real nice people. Lambs to the slaughter, that's what I call it. *Nasdravye!*"

He tipped back his Jack Daniel's, and I tipped back my Jack Daniel's and coughed. He snapped his fingers for two more, and I was about to say no, not for me, when the lights suddenly dimmed, and there was a rough, blaring fanfare on the amplifiers. A thin gingery man in a scarlet spangly cowboy suit stepped into the spotlight and raised one arm dramatically for silence.

"Maize darmsey maize sewers," he announced. "Tonight, for your sheer excitement, for your outright in-cray-doolity, the Golden Horses presents the act of acts, the laughter in the face of Beelzebub himself, the mocker of mortality! The man who seeks his pleasures on the brink of death.

"Yes, folks . . . one more time, Jamie Ford, the Supremo of the Slipknot, is going to risk oblivion for your entertainment and his own sex-you-ell satisfaction. He will gen-yoo-inely hang himself from this here gallows-tree, as inspected and pronounced authentic, and based on the model used for the hanging of

237

Charles J. Guiteau, the assassin of President Garfield, in 1882.

"What you are about to see is one man facing death for the sheer purr-leasure of it; and he has signed legal documents which hold the Golden Horses blameless should things go awry.

"But be warned . . . the performance you are about to witness is strictly of an adult nature, and more shocking than anything you have ever seen before or will again. So if any of you are having second thoughts, or if any of you wish to have your money refunded, then you'd better do so now.

"Because here he is, maize-darmsey-maize-sewers, the Hero of the Hempen Rope, the Nero of the Noose . . . Ja-a-a-mie Ford!"

We were half deafened by a crackling cornet fanfare on the amplifiers, but scarcely anybody applauded. I looked around the Golden Horses, through the sliding cigarette smoke, and saw that everybody was too tense, everybody had their attention fixed on the gallows. Everybody had that same guilty, mesmerized stare – and I expect I did, too. We were like people driving past a fatal auto accident – horrified, fascinated. The emergency services would have called us ghouls.

"Here," said Wolf Bodell, nudging my elbow and handing me another whiskey. "This is what I call a show. One of the best in the country, though I say so myself."

"You're the *promoter*?" I asked him.

"Well, manager, more like."

"How do you manage a man hanging himself?"

Wolf Bodell tossed back his second drink. "Everything on God's good earth needs managing. You don't think that cows grow by accident? There's always somebody who wants to do something and somebody else who wants to watch them do it. It's as simple as that. But the skill comes in bringing the exhibitionist and the voyeur into the same room, at the same time, and making a profit out of it. That's managing.

"Let me tell you something . . . I was bred and brung up in carny. My grandfather was carny; my father was Henry T. Bodell, the founder of Bodell's Traveling Entertainments and Curiosities. When I was three years old, I was introduced to Prince Randian, the Caterpillar Man, who didn't have no arms and legs, and got about by wriggling. I had nightmares about Prince Randian for years later, but, boy, I never forgot him. Never.

"Of course, those days are gone now, the days of freaks and bearded ladies. Very long gone. But every now and then, you still come across people like Jamie Ford, whose need for attention doesn't fit into any of your usual molds. They're still carny entertainers, even if the carnies are dead and gone. They still have the devil in them. They still have the *need*. What's more, people still have the need to watch them. Deplorable, ain't it? But there's nothing in this whole world more fascinating than watching a human being die, except if it's watching a human being die by *choice*. It's like watching those Booh-dist monks, who set fire to themselves. I saw one or two of those out in Nam. Can you imagine doing that by *choice?* Because I sure fucking can't."

He sniffed and wiped his nose with the back of his hand. "It's just like I can't imagine why Jamie keeps on hanging himself. Don't tell me the high is *that* fucking great. But he wants to do it, and people want to watch him do it, and it's a pity to let a good psychosis go to waste."

At that moment, out of the smoke, Jamie appeared, my old school friend Jamie Ford. He was much thinner and greyer, and his eyes seemed to have lost all of that bright, vicious sparkle. Now they were dead men's eyes.

His blond hair was greasy and lank and almost shoulder-length now, and he wore a black and yellow bandanna tightly tied around his head. He was wrapped up in a faded black cloak that trailed on the floor, but as he stepped forward it parted a little and I saw his thin bare leg, and realized that – underneath the cloak – he was chicken-naked.

"And now!" cried the man in the sparkly cowboy suit. "For your extra delight . . . for your unmatched excitement . . . Mr Ford's dee-lectable assistant . . . Ms Suffer Kate!"

There was another scratchy fanfare, followed by a desultory assortment of "yahoos" and wolf-whistles. A tall girl came prancing onto the stage, white-skinned, naked except for black stiletto shoes, a tiny black-sequined thong, and a headdress of nodding black ostrich feathers.

She twirled around, and the spotlights gleamed on her chubby, luminous flesh. Her breasts were enormous and wallowed on her chest like two white whales dipping and rolling in a slow flood tide. Her stomach was rounded, but she had no stretch marks. She had the figure of a girl who drinks too much and eats too many hamburgers and too many taco chips and spends too much of her life watching too much TV in too many Howard Johnson's.

She lifted her arms and blew kisses all around the crowd, and it was then that I recognized her. 'Ms Suffer Kate' was none other than Laurel Fay, the cheerleader from Sherman Oaks Senior High. A raddled, puffy, corrupted version of a once-beautiful 'most-likely-to.' I could have shed tears, believe me.

But I remembered that curse that Laurel had cursed,

on graduation day, the day that I had caught her riding up and down on him while he slowly suffocated in Saran Wrap.

"Judas! Judas fucking Iscariot! He wants it! He needs it! It's death meets life! It's life meets death!"

Now Jamie was circling the gallows, eyeing it up and down, gripping it and shaking it to make sure that it was firm. The hi-fi played 'Tie a Yellow Ribbon 'Round the Old Oak Tree'.

It wasn't a proper executioner's gallows, for all that the master of ceremonies had described it as an authentic copy of the gallows on which Charles J. Guiteau had been executed. The drop on a proper executioner's gallows is more than twice the height of the man to be hanged. When the trap opens, and the man falls through, the chances are high that he will instantaneously break his neck. But this wasn't a gallows designed for the quick judicial extinction of life. This was a gallows designed for long, slow strangulation.

Watching Jamie shaking that gallows gave me a spasm of utter dread, like nothing I had ever experienced before. I turned to Wolf Bodell and said, "Is there a phone in this place?"

"Sure, next to the jakes. But don't take too long . . . he's just about to do the business."

I pushed my way through the murmuring, mesmerized crowd. As I did so, I think Jamie must have caught sight of me, because he stopped shaking the gallows and peered into the darkness which enveloped the audience, his hand raised over his eyes to cut out the glare from the spotlight. I dodged behind a large red-faced man in a crumpled business suit and continued my journey to the telephone with my face turned away from the gallows and my shoulders hunched.

241

I reached the booth, closed the folding door, and thumbed in a dime. The phone rang for a long, long time before anybody answered.

"Bryce."

"Deputy Bryce? It's Gerry, from the *Bee*. If I were you, I'd come on out to the Golden Horses with your foot flat to the floor. And bring some backup."

"I just started supper. Can't it wait?"

"Not unless you want a man to die."

Deputy Bryce said something unintelligible, but I didn't wait to hear what it was. I pushed my way back to the bar, where Wolf Bodell had already lined up another Jack Daniel's for me. I was half drunk already, but he wouldn't take no for an answer. "You can't face the Grim Reaper sober," he told me.

With Ms Suffer Kate prancing and pirouetting around him, Jamie mounted the low grey-painted trestle which stood directly below the noose. The trestle was arranged so that when Jamie himself tugged on a lanyard, the legs would collapse flat and he would be left hanging six or seven inches above the floor. He took hold of the noose and gently tugged it, to test that the rope was running free. The hi-fi music changed to 'Stand By Your Man'. Jamie loosened the collar of his cloak – and it was then that I saw for the first time the terrible blue and red bruises and rope burns that disfigured his neck. His carotid artery bulged in several purplish lumps, and his Adam's apple was crisscrossed with deep shiny weals.

He lifted the noose over his head with all the solemnity of a king crowning himself. I thought I caught the faintest trace of a smile on his lips, but I couldn't be sure.

Ms Suffer Kate made an exaggerated Betty Boop O with her red-lipsticked mouth, her breasts bounce-delay-bouncing with every step she took.

Wolf Bodell grinned at me and said, "Heart-stopping stuff, ain't it? The odds against him surviving are about three to one. So you see *my* livelihood's going to be hanging by a thread, too."

'Stand By Your Man' was abruptly interrupted by a long, thunderous drumroll. Jamie was standing straight-backed amidst the eddying cigarette smoke, the noose around his neck, staring at someplace far in the distance. I looked for sweat on his face, but he appeared dry and pale and almost saintly. I wondered what he was thinking; but maybe he wasn't thinking anything at all. Did he really want to die? Or was he mortally afraid?

"Maize darmsey maize sewers, burr-ace yourselves!" screamed the master of ceremonies.

Jamie took a tighter grip on the lanyard. The drumroll went on and on. In fact, it went on for so long that I began to think that he wasn't going to do it. Maybe he had lost his nerve. Maybe he had stood on this trestle and faced his Maker just once too often.

But then, with his left hand, he pushed back his cloak, so that it slid off his shoulders and revealed his nakedness. More red-lipsticked O's from Ms Suffer Kate. She perched on the edge of the trestle and caressed Jamie's scarred and bony legs, smiling up at him and O-ing the audience alternately.

Jamie's penis hung heavy and dark between his thighs, not yet aroused. Ms Suffer Kate ran her hands up and weighed his hairy scrotum in her hand. Then she squeezed and rubbed his penis until it began to swell up a little. The drumroll continued, but they didn't really need a drumroll. Everybody in the Golden Horses was staring at Jamie transfixed, their mouths open, their eyes wide, daring him actually to do it, begging him not to do it, fearful and fascinated at the same time.

243

I found myself pushing my way forward.

"Jamie!" I shouted. "Jamie, it's Gerry! *Jamie!*"

Wolf Bodell snatched at my elbow. "Hey, come on, man, don't break his concentration!"

"*Jamie!*" I yelled.

I forced my way right to the front and stood in front of the gallows. Ms Suffer Kate stared at me – crossly at first, but then with growing recognition.

"*You?*" she said, in a blurry voice.

She looked up at Jamie, and I did, too. He was smiling down at me with a wounded, beatific smile. The Hero of the Hempen Rope. The Nero of the Noose.

"Jamie," I said, as loudly as I could, so that he would hear me over the drumroll, and over the impatient whistling of the crowd, and over his own dreamlike trance. "Jamie, it's over. It's time to come down now. You don't have to do this anymore."

"Hey, mister, mind your own fucking business and get out of the fucking way!" somebody roared at me; and there was a roar of approval and a locomotive-like stamping of feet.

Jamie looked down at me, and I don't know whether he recognized me or not. I like to think that he didn't. Because the next thing that happened was – without warning – he pulled the lanyard, and the trestle table collapsed with an ear-splitting bang. Jamie dropped three feet and then jolted to a stop as the noose tightened. He swung around, spun around, his feet bicycling wildly in the air, his hands clawing at his throat. He made the most terrible cackling sound; and when he spun around again and I saw his face I felt a surge of warm sick in the back of my mouth. His eyes were almost bursting out of his head. He was purple – a dark, eggplant purple – and he kept opening and closing his mouth in a desperate attempt to breathe.

244

I tried to push my way forward, but I felt Wolf Bodell gripping my arm. "You can't help him, my friend. You can't help him. It's something he has to do. If you save him today, he'll do it again tomorrow."

Jamie was twisting around and around, and the crowd was baying in horror. A woman was screaming, "*No! No! No! No!*" and a man was roaring, "Cut him down, for Christ's sake! Cut him down!"

The whole of the Golden Horses was surging with fear and disgust and a hideous unbalancing fascination. It was like wading through a warm, heavy swell with ice-cold undercurrents.

Jamie kept on gargling and kicking. Whenever he stopped twisting, Ms Suffer Kate gave him another push, so that he spun round yet again, and again. His eyes were bulging so much now that I could see the swollen scarlet flesh behind the eyeball, and he had clawed at the noose around his neck so furiously that one of his fingernails was flapping loose.

Now, however, came the climax. As Jamie spun around again, Ms Suffer Kate stopped him, and steadied him, and we could see that his penis had stiffened into a hugely distended erection. His testicles were scrunched up tight, and the shaft rose thick and veiny and hard as an antler.

Ms Suffer Kate stood up in front of him and kissed him, leaving lipstick imprints all over his heaving white stomach.

Then she stepped back, so that she was at least six inches away from his rigid penis, and stretched her mouth open wide.

"Holy Mother of God," I heard a man say; and his words weren't a blasphemy; not even here; not even while we were witnessing a slow and deliberate self-suffocation.

245

There was a second's agonized pause. Jamie's entire body was arched like a bow. He had stopped scrabbling at his noose, and his hands were held up in front of him, his fingers skeletal with tension. He let out one gargling, strangulated breath, and then another. He was so taut, he was straining so hard, that his right eyeball at last squeezed right out of its socket and bobbled on top of his cheek, staring downward without expression at Ms Suffer Kate.

Then – with a sickening convulsion – he climaxed. His penis seemed to swell even more, the head swelled, and then a thick spurt of sperm flew out of it, right into Ms Suffer Kate's stretched open mouth. It spurted again, and again, and again – more sperm than I had ever seen a man ejaculate in my life – and it covered Ms Suffer Kate's lips and cheeks and eyelashes and clung in her black funereal ostrich plumes.

Throughout the whole ejaculation, she hadn't touched him once. He had climaxed from lack of oxygen, from agony, from dancing with death.

Ms Suffer Kate turned around, and raised her arms, and nodded her plumes, her face still glistening with sperm. Then, with no more hesitation, she stepped up onto one of the trestles and released the locking catch that had prevented Jamie (when the table had collapsed beneath him) from reaching the floor.

Jamie was lowered swiftly down; and Wolf Bodell was right beside him; and so was a man with thinning greased-back hair and a cigarette between his lips and a worn-out medical bag. Ms Suffer Kate meanwhile was standing a little way back, wrapped in a grubby baby-pink toweling robe, wiping her face with Kleenex. She looked no more concerned about what she had just done than a runner who has just completed the 500 meters in a fairly unspectacular time.

For some reason I looked at my watch. Then I walked stiffly to the bar and said, in a kaleidoscopic voice, "Jack Daniel's, straight up."

I was still trying to lift the shot glass without spilling the whiskey when I heard the double doors crashing open and a familiar voice shouting, "Police! This is a raid! Everybody stay where you are!"

I turned and looked down at Wolf Bodell, and Wolf Bodell looked back up at me. I don't know whether he suspected me of tipping off the sheriff or not, but right at that particular moment I didn't care. Somebody had just said, "He's breathing . . . he'll make it," and that was all I cared about. That, and making sure that Jamie never tried to hang himself again.

I went up to Ms Suffer Kate and said, "Hallo, Laurel."

She slowly turned her eyes toward me, still dabbing her right cheek with a crumpled-up tissue.

"Hallo, you rat," she replied.

The case never went to trial, of course. The Golden Horses was closed down by county ordinance and reopened eleven months later as the Old Placer Rib Shack, and promptly closed down again after an outbreak of food poisoning.

In lieu of prosecution, Jamie agreed to undergo a minimum of three years' analysis and rehabilitation at the appropriately named Fruitridge Psychiatric Centre in Sacramento, a secure institution for the gravely whacko.

Laurel Fay's parents stood bail for her and produced an oleaginous San Francisco lawyer who looked like

Jabba the Hutt in a seersucker suit, and who promised such a long and expensive and complicated trial that the district attorney decided that it would be against the public interest for the case to proceed any further. Laurel sent me thirty dimes in the mail, along with a postcard of the Last Supper and a ballpoint arrow pointing to Judas Iscariot.

I went to visit Jamie in the first week of September. The Fruitridge Psychiatric Centre had cool white corridors, and a courtyard with terra cotta pots and fan palms, and yellow-uniformed nurses who came and went with pleasant, proprietary smiles.

Jamie was sitting in his plain white room on a plain wooden chair, staring at the wall. He was wearing what looked like judo robes, without the belt. His hair had turned white and was cropped very short. His eye was back in its socket, but it had an odd cast to it now, so that I never quite knew if he was looking at me or not. His skin was peculiarly pale and smooth, but I suppose it was the drugs they were giving him.

He talked for a long time about backgammon. He said he was trying to play it in his head. His voice had no colour, no expression, no substance. It was like listening to water running. He didn't talk once about school, or the old days, or Chokes. He didn't ask what had happened to Suffer Kate. I came away sad because of what he had become; but also glad that I had saved him at last.

Two years later, the telephone rang at 2:30 in the morning, when my metabolism was almost at zero and I was dreaming of death. I scrabbled around for the receiver, found it, dropped it, then picked it up again.

"Did I wake you?" asked a hoarse, scarcely audible voice.

"Who is this?" I wanted to know.

"Did I wake you? I didn't mean to wake you."

I switched on the bedside lamp. On the nightstand there was my wrist-watch, a framed photograph of my parents, a glass of water, and a dog-eared copy of *Specimen Days in America*.

"Gerry, is that you?"

A silence. A cough.

"Gerry?"

"I need your help. I badly need your help."

"You need my help *now?*"

"There's been an accident, Gerry. I really need you."

"What kind of an accident?" I asked. A cold feeling started to crawl down my back.

"You have to help me. You really have to help me."

I parked outside the Fort Hotel and climbed out of my car. The streets of Sacramento were deserted. The Fort was an old six-storey building with a flaking brown-painted facade and an epileptic neon sign that kept flickering out the words ORT HOT. Next door there was a Chinese restaurant with a painting of a glaring dragon in the window.

Inside, the hotel smelled strongly of Black Flag, with an undertone of disinfected vomit. A surprisingly neat and good-looking young man was sitting at the desk, short-sleeved shirt and cropped blond hair, reading *Europe on $60 a Day*. When I asked him for Jamie's room, he said, "Six-oh-three," without even looking up at me.

I walked toward the elevator.

"Out of commission," he said, still without raising his eyes.

249

I walked up five flights of stairs. It was like climbing the five flights of Purgatory. From behind closed doors, I heard muttering televisions, heard blurted conversations, smelled pungent cooking smells. At last I reached the sixth floor and walked along a dark, narrow, linoleum-floored corridor until I found 603. I listened for a while at the door. I thought I could faintly hear marching music. I knocked.

"Jamie? Are you there, Jamie? It's me."

He took a long, long time to open the door. Security chains, locks, bolts. At last the door swung ajar, and I heard him say, "You'd better come along in."

I hesitated for a moment and then stepped inside. The room was lit by a single desk lamp, without a shade, so that the shadows it cast were coarse and uncompromising. There was a terrible smell in the room – a sweet smell of urine and decay. On the far side, there was a sofa bed, heaped with dirty red blankets. On my left, a tipped-over armchair, revealing its torn-out innards.

Jamie was naked. His body was so scarred and emaciated that I wouldn't have recognized him. His eyes were red-rimmed, and his hair was sticking up in wild, mad tufts. Around his neck, tied in a hangman's noose, was a long, thin nylon cord. It was so long that he had loosely coiled it, and had looped the coil over his left forearm, like a waiter holding a napkin.

"I thought you were cured of all this," I told him.

He gave me a furtive, erratic smile. "You're never cured. It's the way you are."

"You said there'd been an accident. What accident?"

He limped over to the sofa bed. He glanced at me once, and then he dragged back the filthy blankets. At first I couldn't understand what I was looking at. A white, curved shape. Then – when I stepped closer

250

– I saw that it was Ms Suffer Kate. She was wearing black lacy split-crotch panties, and the butt of a huge blue plastic vibrator protruded from her hairy vulva. Her stomach sagged sideways. Her breasts were bruised, and her nipples were purple, like prunes. She was staring unblinkingly at the fold in the blanket only an inch in front of her nose, as if she found it totally absorbing. Her face was so white. So white that it was almost blue. Around her neck was a thin cord, which had been twisted around and around with a broken pencil until it had throttled her.

"She's dead," said Jamie.

I covered her up with the blanket. "You know I can't save you now," I told him. "Christ knows, I've tried to save you. But I really can't save you now."

"It was what she wanted," said Jamie, in a matter-of-fact voice. "We talked about it for weeks beforehand. And when I twisted that pencil, and twisted that pencil, she came and she came and she came." He paused. "I wish it could have been me, instead of that . . . dildo thing. But these days, there's only one way that *I* can get it up."

"I'm calling the cops now."

Jamie fingered the noose around his neck. "Sure you are. You have to."

"Do you have a phone in here?"

"Unh-unh. But there's a pay phone at the end of the hall."

I was shuddering, as if I were freezing cold, but I knew that it was only shock. "You'll have to come with me," I told him. "I can't leave you here alone."

"That's okay." He nodded. He thought for a moment, and then he handed me the end of his rope. "You can hold onto this. Stop me from running away."

We stepped out into the corridor, Jamie limping a little way in front of me.

"Are you okay?" I asked him.

He lifted one hand. "Okay as I'll ever be."

I was trying to think what I was going to say to the police when we turned the corner in the corridor. Directly in front of us was the elevator shaft – and it was open. A dark, drafty doorway to noplace at all. Somebody had wedged the trellis gates with a paint-spotted pickax handle. No wonder the porter had thought it was out of commission.

There was an instant when I knew what Jamie was going to do – a stroboscopic split-second when I might have been able to stop him. But you and I and most of the rest of the world are doing their darndest to survive – so when somebody is determined to do the opposite, we have a fatal tendency not to believe it.

And Jamie ran – *sprinted* – right to the open elevator gate and threw himself into it, without a scream, without any sound at all. Tumbled, fell, disappeared like a conjuring trick.

The rope that I was holding wriggled and snaked, and then abruptly thumped tight. It almost took my arms out of my sockets. I shuffle-staggered to the elevator gates, straining at it, pulling at it, until I reached the very brink.

With my shoulder pressed against the folded trellis gates to give myself support, I leaned over the edge of the elevator shaft and cautiously looked down. I was panting and sweating and whispering under my breath, "God help me, please, God help me."

Thirty feet below me, in the windy echoing half darkness of the elevator shaft, Jamie was hanging with the noose tight around his neck. His arms were spread wide, his toes were pointed, like a ballet dancer. His head was thrown back in ecstasy. The rope creaked, and paused, and creaked, and paused.

252

He opened his eyes and looked up at me, and his face was triumphant and grey with oxygen starvation. He had done it. He had done it to me, after all these years. I had worried about him and cared for him and promised to save him, and he had made me the instrument of his own terminal hanging.

Jamie tried to speak, tried to mock me, but the noose was clutching his larynx too tight. He twisted around and around, and as he twisted, I could see his penis rising, pulsing with every heartbeat. His eyes bulged. His tongue suddenly slopped out from between his lips, fat and grey.

I had a simple choice: I could hold on to my end of the rope, hanging him, or else I could let go. In which case, he would drop four stories down the elevator shaft.

I waited, and clung on to the rope, and as I clung on to the rope, it all became clear to me. What is any saviour, in the long run? What is any devoted friend? We do nothing except delay the inevitable, for our own selfish ends. We are nothing less than executioners-in-waiting.

I had been so unctuous. I had cared so much. In fact, I had prolonged Jamie's agony.

I should have let him hang himself in high school. Better still, his mother should have let him smother himself in his own pillow.

Thirty feet below me, he twisted and twisted; and then he let out a high, thin cry that was like nothing I have ever heard, before or since. It was pitiful, saintly, ecstatic, sad. Sperm jumped from his penis, two, three, four times, and dropped down the elevator shaft.

I leaned over. I said, "God damn you, Jamie." I don't know if he heard me.

Then I let him go.

Spirit-Jump

New York City

My very first horror novel, *The Manitou*, told the story of Misquamacus, the legendary Native American medicine-man, and how he tried to return from the dead to wreak his revenge on the white man. He was reborn as a hideous lump on the neck of a young girl called Karen Tandy – an experience which she only just managed to survive.

Misquamacus reappeared in *The Revenge of the Manitou* and *Burial*, in which he attempted to revive the Ghost Dance, a religious ritual with which the desperate North American Indians tried to beat back the encroaching settlers.

Now he tries to return one more time, using an arcane spell which was devised by Cheyenne wonder-workers in order to bring back the spirits of those who were unable to reach the Happy Hunting Ground.

It takes place in the New York of today, but also in the New York of many years ago, when the island was a rocky wilderness. This face of fear has many sides to it; but more than anything else, it is the face of hatred and the face of unbridled revenge.

SPIRIT-JUMP

I was waiting in the hallway to collect Lucy from nursery school when her teacher came up to me and said, "Mr Erskine? Do you think we could have a private word?"

Immediately, I felt guilty. It was ridiculous, but teachers still have that effect on me, even today. Especially this one, Ms Eisenheim, a thin domineering hawklike woman in a grey two-piece suit. She was young and she was actually quite attractive, if you're into thin domineering hawklike women. I could imagine her in black stockings and a black basque, whipping me soundly for forgetting to scour the bathtub.

All of the other parents gave me sympathetic smiles as I followed Ms Eisenheim to her office. All of the other parents were women. Their husbands were doctors or lawyers or Wall Street analysts, which meant that I was the only man who had the time to come to Lennox Nursery School every lunchtime to collect his child. At first the mothers had treated me with deep suspicion, especially since I find it difficult to dress really smart. I mean my tan leather jacket coat is just about as soigne as it gets. But after a while they began to realize that I wasn't a down and out or a potential child-molester, and they began to include me into their gossip. After the first term I was almost an honorary mother.

Ms Eisenheim led me along the echoing, wax-polished

corridor until we reached a small stuffy office, its walls pinned with maps and graphs and a reproduction of George Washington crossing the Potomac. Through the window I could see the asphalt play-yard, its wire-mesh fencing snagged with curled-up yellow and grey leaves.

"Please close the door," said Ms Eisenheim.

"Is there a problem?" I asked her.

"I'm afraid there is. I tried to call you earlier, but you weren't in. There was an incident during recess today and I'm afraid we were obliged to separate Lucy from the rest of her class."

"An incident? What kind of an incident?" (Instantly shirty and defensive reaction of overprotective father toward his special little sugar plum fairy.) "She's only four years old, for God's sake."

"There was a scuffle, of sorts, in the play-yard. Two little children were badly hurt."

"How badly?"

"One of them suffered a sprained ankle and the other had a deeply-grazed knee."

"So what are you trying to tell me? That *Lucy* did it?"

Ms Eisenheim pursed his lips. "I'm afraid there were witnesses, Mr Erskine, and not just children. Ms Woolcott saw what happened, too."

"And what *did* happen? Come on, Ms Eisenheim, this is very hard for me to believe. Lucy has the sweetest nature of any child I ever knew. We're talking about a little girl who walks around *ants*."

"Well, I have to say, Mr Erskine, that up until now, that was our experience of Lucy, too. Today's outburst was quite uncharacteristic, but you can understand that we had to take steps."

"You had to lock her up? What is this, Attica?"

258

"Please don't get upset, Mr Erskine. Lucy wasn't locked up. She was simply made to stay in a room away from the other children. One of our young teaching assistants has been reading to her."

"What's she been reading? 'You have the right to remain silent, but anything you say can and will be used against you in a court of law?' Listen, Ms Eisenheim, I want to see Lucy now, if you don't mind. I can't believe that you're treating a four-year-old girl like a hardened criminal just because two kids couldn't manage to keep their balance in the schoolyard."

Ms Eisenheim slapped her hand on her desk. "Mr Erskine! This wasn't a case of anybody losing their balance! This wasn't even a scuffle! Lucy threw Janice Mulgrew right across the yard and into the fencing, and she pushed Laurence Cullen face-first into a brick wall. She knocked down seven other children and then it was all that Ms Woolcott could do to restrain her."

I stared at her; and for the first time I couldn't think what to say.

"This was nothing to do with *balance*, Mr Erskine! This was a wild and deliberate attack of extraordinary ferocity. I'm going to have to ask you for a psychiatic evaluation before we can allow Lucy to spend another day here."

"She *threw* Janice Mulgrew right across the yard?" I repeated. "Am I right, and is Janice Mulgrew that big, fat kid with the ginger braids?"

"Janice does have russet hair, yes. And, yes, she is a little challenged by her weight."

"A little challenged? Have you seen the size of her? I couldn't even lift her feet off the ground, let alone throw her anywhere. And you expect me to believe that *Lucy* threw her?"

"Five or six feet, yes. There were witnesses."

"Witnesses saw a skinny little kid like Lucy throw a barrel of lard like Janice Mulgrew five or six feet? What are you putting in their milk, Ms Eisenheim?"

"You can say what you like, Mr Erskine. Lucy will still have to undergo psychiatric tests before we can think of allowing her back."

I found Lucy sitting alone in a small classroom at the back of the building. The grey fall light made her look very small and pale and vulnerable, and her eyes were still red from crying. A young blonde-haired assistant teacher was sitting at the next desk, reading a story about a girl who fell in love with a bear, and gradually changed into a bear herself.

"Look, Lucy," said the teacher, closing her book. "Daddy's here."

Lucy climbed of her chair and came slowly toward me. She tried not to cry at first, but then her face collapsed into painful sobbing. I picked her up and held her tight. "Come on, now, sweetheart; Daddy's here. Everything's going to be fine."

"I didn't mean to," she wept. "I didn't mean to."

"Sure, sweetheart, I know you didn't. Come on, hush now. We'll go home to see mommy now, shall we?"

The teacher said, "She's very upset. I did what I could to cheer her up."

"What's that story you've been reading her?"

"Oh, that. It's an old Navaho legend. We do try to raise the children's awareness of Native American culture."

"Well, I'd rather you didn't try it on *my* kid, okay?"

The teacher looked taken aback. "I'm sorry you feel that way," she said. "We like to think that it's enriching."

I didn't bother to argue with her. My own encounters

with Native American culture had been dangerous frightening, and often tragic; but it would have taken too long to tell her about them, and I doubt if she would have believed me anyway. She looked like one of those bright young college girls with plenty of moralistic opinions and no experience whatever. I just wondered how she would have reacted if *she* had been faced with the Lizard-of-the-Trees, or the hunched and shadowy shape of Aktunowihio, the dark presence that drags people down to the so-called Happy Hunting Grounds.

I left the school with Lucy huddled in my arms and by now word about the play-yard incident must have gotten around, so when I walked through the hallway all of my women friends somehow contrived to be looking the other way, or rummaging in their purses, or having some trouble with their contact lens. When your kids get into trouble, you soon find out who your friends aren't.

My new white Caprice was parked under a tree and a flock of starlings had spattered it. By the look of it, they'd been lunching at Lutece. I let Lucy into the back seat, made sure she was buckled up, and then drove back home. It was only nine blocks but owning a car was still a novelty as far as I was concerned, and I was prepared to put up with any kind of traffic snarl-up just for the joy of my own air-conditioned environment, with soul music on the CD, and my sugar plum fairy sitting in back, jabbering on about what she was doing at nursery school.

Except that today my sugar plum fairy didn't jabber. She didn't say a word. She sat staring out of the window, her head sadly inclined to one side, and nothing I said to her made any difference. For some reason, I kept thinking of the story that her teacher had been reading her. "Gradually, the maiden underwent a change. Her

261

teeth grew long, her nails became claws, and soon her whole body was covered in thick, black hair."

I glanced in the rear-view mirror. I had never been a father before, but up until now it had all been pretty straightforward. A stomach was empty, you filled it. A diaper was filled up, you changed it. You taught her not to say "horsey" and "baa-lamb" and you tried to teach her a little basic math, like daddy + mommy + sugar plum fairy = great contentment. I don't mean to sound too gooey about it, but marrying Karen and having Lucy had fulfilled me more than anything I had ever done before. It was just as if I had been sitting in a gloomy room, right up until the age of 43, and then suddenly God had opened up the door and let the sunlight come flooding in, and said, "What have you been doing in that gloomy room all of these years, Harry? Your life has been waiting for you out here."

We reached our apartment on E 86 and I managed to park in a space that was just big enough for a bagel cart. No wonder I used to call myself the Incredible Erskine. I carried Lucy out of the car, and up the steps, but when we reached the door she said, "I want to get down, please, daddy. I don't want you to carry me any more."

I put her down. "Okay, fine, whatever you want."

She looked at me with big, dark, serious eyes. She wasn't what you'd call a pretty little girl. She wasn't a Shirley Temple or anything like that. She had straight, dark hair, cut in a bob, and the same delicate bone structure as Karen, elfin almost. I always thought she looked too pale, but then most city children do. She had such skinny arms and legs, you felt you had to be careful when you held her, in case you broke her wrist or something.

"Listen," I said, "mommy's going to ask what you happened. What are you going to say to her?"

A single tear slid down her left cheek, and dripped onto the collar of her little blue-checkered blouse. "I didn't mean to," she wept. "I told them they were all bad, which was true, and then they got angry and I had to make them go away."

"You told them they were bad? Why did you do that, sweetheart?"

"Muldrews, Cullens, they're all bad. They kill people. They kill babies."

I stroked the tear away from her cheek. "They kill *babies*? Who told you they kill babies?"

She sniffled for a moment, but then she raised her head and looked me directly in the eye. "The *mistai* told me. The *mistai* never tell lies."

I felt a feeling go through me like swallowing a large lump of ice, painful and very cold. "The *mistai*?" I asked her. "The *mistai* told you? What do you know about the *mistai*?"

But immediately, Lucy burst into tears, and clung to me; and there was nothing I could do but open up the door and take her inside. The lobby was clad in marble, with a compass-rose pattern on the floor. There were mirrors and fresh flowers everywhere, and a reassuring smell of 'expensive'. Soon after Karen and I were married, her aunt had died, Aunt Millie who doted on her, and she had left this fine three-bedroomed apartment on E 86, fully furnished in a style you could have described as 'Walt Disney goes to Versailles', with gilded chairs and rococo dressers and brocade drapes that you could have cut into 500 new uniforms for the Vatican Guard. In other words, quantity and tastelessness, in equal proportions. But I never complained. Don't look a gift apartment in the mouth, that's what I always say, even if it does look like Marie Antoinette's second-best boudoir. And

263

especially don't look in the mouth the $2.1 million that came with it.

I carried Lucy into the apartment and set her down on the wide yellow-striped couch. Karen was sitting at the small walnut desk in the corner, breathlessly preparing her accounts on a laptop computer.

"Hey . . . you're home!" said Karen. "I won't be a moment . . . I just have to download the Foggia case."

I came up and laid my hand on her shoulder. We had been together for five years now, and she was still just as pretty and fragile as the day she first came to see me. There are some women you love because they're best friends, and they're sexy and supportive. But I loved Karen because I *had* to love her. She was my destiny. If the Lord God had put me on earth to do anything, he had put me on earth to take care of her, and I did.

"Listen . . . Lucy's been in trouble at nursery school."

"What? What kind of trouble? Lucy! Are you all right?"

Lucy turned her head away and wouldn't look at her. I took hold of Karen's arm and gently restrained her. "This might be serious," I said. "There's more to this than meets the eye."

"Harry, stop being all mysterious and just tell me what's happened!"

I went over to Lucy and sat down next to her. "Come on, kiddo. Why don't you tell mommy what happened?"

But Lucy shook her head, and buried her face even more deeply in the cushions.

"Okay," I said. "According to the school – and before you blow your top, I'm only reporting what they said to me, and I don't believe it either – *according* to the school, Lucy threw Janice Muldrew five or six feet across the play-yard, so that she sustained multiple bruises and a

264

sprained ankle. She then smashed Laurence Cullen into a wall, so that he damn near broke his nose. Then she did a Bruce Lee job on seven other kids, knocking them over, scratching them, biting them, and kicking the boys in the heritage department."

Karen stared at Lucy and her face was bloodless. "That's *insane*! Look at her, she's the second-smallest kid in her class! She *threw* Janice Muldrew? I never heard anything so ridiculous in my entire life!"

She stalked over to the eighteenth-century-style telephone table, and picked up the phone.

"What are you doing?" I demanded.

"I'm phoning the school, of course. Nobody, but *nobody*, accuses my daughter of violence! She's only a baby, for God's sake!"

I walked over and pushed my finger down on the cradle. "Don't call anybody, not just yet. There's something else."

"Harry, what are you talking about, this is our *daughter*!"

"Exactly. And we both know how and when we conceived her, don't we? Which makes her something of a special case."

Karen slowly raised her hand and touched my sleeve as if to reassure herself that I was real. "I hoped we'd forgotten all that. God, Harry, I never even *dream* about it!"

"All the same, when Lucy was talking to me downstairs, she mentioned the word 'mistai'. Not just once, but twice."

"*Mistai*? Where have I heard that before?"

It wasn't easy to tell her. Karen had suffered more than anybody, and the last thing she wanted to hear about was Native American ritual. I had first met her

265

in the mid-1970s when the Algonquin wonder-worker Misquamacus had tried to use her body to return to New York, for the sole and dedicated purpose of taking his revenge on the white men who had decimated his people. He had used his immense magical powers to impregnate himself into her body, and it was only with the help of a modern medicine-man, Singing Rock, that we had managed to save her. Only four years ago, Misquamacus had tried to possess her for a second time – and it was then, under the shadow of his influence, that Karen and I had first had sex together, and Lucy had been conceived.

It had been up to me to save her that time; Misquamacus had killed Singing Rock by beheading him, just to make sure that his spirit could never find peace.

Karen and I would always have that bond between us. We had both faced the same hideous danger, and survived. But even for survivors, time moves on. These days, Karen was spending more and more time away from home – business meetings, conventions, foreign travel – and as much as I loved her, as much as our lives were intertwined, we had grown more distant in the past eighteen months. But for Lucy's sake, and maybe for our own sake, too, this was a time when we needed to be close.

I took hold of Karen's hand. "*Mistai* are what the Pawnee Indians used to call ghosts. Lucy said that the *mistai* told her that Janice Muldrew and Laurence Cullen were bad people. They killed babies."

"How on earth could Lucy know about Pawnee ghosts?"

"I don't know. They teach Native American mythology at Lennox. Maybe she picked it up from there. For Christ's sake, she's only four. You know what imaginations they have at that age."

Karen took hold of my other hand, and gripped it tight. "Did she really throw Janice across the play-yard?"

"I don't know. Ms Eisenheim says they've got witnesses – but, well. You know how unreliable witnesses can be, especially kids."

"Do *you* believe that Lucy threw Janice across the play-yard?" asked Karen, intently.

I shook my head. "Of course not. Janice is twice Lucy's size."

Karen released my hands and turned away. "I've been afraid of this," she said, her face silhouetted against the window. "I've been afraid of this ever since I first found out that I was pregnant."

I didn't say anything, but came up and laid my hand on her shoulder.

"It's too much of a coincidence, isn't it, her talking about *mistai* on the same day that she attacks all of those children."

"Come on, Karen, you're not trying to suggest—"

"I'm not trying to suggest anything. Lucy is a gentle, loving, sweet-natured little girl, and the only way that she could have done what she did today was if somebody took hold of her. Somebody stronger – somebody strong enough to throw Janice Muldrew six feet in the air and hit all of those other kids. Somebody that nobody could see, because he wasn't standing behind her, he was right inside her, the way he was right inside me!"

"Karen—"

"I knew this would happen! I knew it! I knew that he would never leave us alone! He wants a way to get back and the only way he can do it now is through Lucy; the same way that he tried to get back through me."

"You really believe that? Come on, Karen, it's been years."

Her eyes were bright with fear, but they were determined, too. "When he was right inside me, I could feel what it was like to be him. It was like a raging fire. I felt that I could do anything, and nobody could stop me. I could have killed people then, I could have smashed their heads and cracked their bones, and relished it. I'll never forget it, Harry, and I don't want it to happen again. Not to Lucy, please."

Neither of us dared to say the name *Misquamacus*. For nearly five years, we had liked to believe that his spirit had been sent back to the skies, or the underworld, or the Hanging Road, which is what the Indians used to call the Milky Way, the sparkling highway of dead souls.

We didn't want to think that he had somehow managed to influence the one person we both cherished more than life itself: our own daughter, Lucy.

"Hey . . . maybe we're being oversensitive," I suggested. "Maybe it was just a tantrum. Kids get tantrums. Their adrenaline builds up . . . you know what people are capable of doing, when their adrenaline builds up. There was that woman in Indiana who lifted a two-ton Pontiac station-wagon, because it was crushing her son. I mean they proved scientifically that she couldn't have done, but she did. Maybe that was what happened to Lucy."

"I'm going to have to call Janice's parents," said Karen. "Laurence's, too."

"She hurt seven other kids besides," I told her. "And if I were you, I wouldn't start admitting any liability just yet, in case they start thinking about lawsuits and compensation. For the first time in my life, I've got a little money. I don't want to lose it all because of some rumpus in the romper room.

"Besides," I added, very uncomfortably, "Ms Eisenheim won't let her back until she's had a psychiatric evaluation."

"*What?*" Karen demanded. "Is she trying to suggest that my daughter's mentally unbalanced? Don't talk to me about lawsuits and compensation! That woman! I'll hang her ass out to dry!"

I tried to calm her down. "Karen . . . this is crazy. We don't exactly know what happened. There's no point in getting hysterical about it."

"Our daughter's accused of being a psychopath and I can't get hysterical about it?"

I held her close against me. She was warm, and she smelled, as always, of Chanel. I loved her so much you couldn't believe it. But I was beginning to feel that so long as she and I stayed together, the shadow of Misquamacus would dog us, the way that Indian hunters had dogged their prey over miles and miles of empty prairie, so that in the very end, they could cast their shadows over their enemies' graves.

The next morning was sharp and sunny. Lucy was sitting in her room playing with her dolls house. Barbie had been trying to climb out of the upstairs window, and had got her bust stuck on the windowledge. I sat crosslegged on the floor watching Lucy while she played; and then at last I said, "These *mistai.*"

She turned and stared at me with those coal-hole eyes. "What *mistai?*"

"Those mistai who told you that Janice and Laurence were bad. I mean – how did you know that they were called *mistai?*"

"Because they were."

"You saw them? What did they look like?"

Lucy thought for a moment, and then covered her face with her fingers, so that only her eyes looked out. If you hadn't known what she was doing, you wouldn't have thought anything of it. But I remembered what the old texts had said, the old texts about Misquamacus. *'On being ask'd whay ye Daemon look'd like, the antient Wonder-Worker Misquamacus covered his face so that onlie ye Eyes look'd out, and then gave a very curious and Circumstantiall Relation, saying it was sometimes small and solid, like a Great Toad ye Bigness of many Ground-Hogs, but sometimes big and cloudy, with no Shape, though with a face which had Serpents grown from it.'*

"They had their hands over their faces?" I asked her.

She shook her head. "They had *no* faces. They were *mistai.*"

"They came to the schoolyard and spoke to you?"

"Sure. They were all grey and I couldn't hardly see them but they said that Janice Muldrew was bad and Laurence Cullen was bad and some of the other kids. And all I did was say that they were bad; because they were."

"Then what?" I asked her.

She looked away. "Then Janice tried to hit me and I told her to fly through the air."

"You *told* her? You didn't pick her up?"

"Janice is too fat. I couldn't pick her up."

"Then what? You told Laurence to push his face into a wall?"

"Unh-huh. I never touched him."

"You told them and they did it? Just like that?"

"Uh-huh."

"And what about the other kids? The same thing with them?"

"That's right. They wanted to hit me but I told them all to fall over, and they did."

I took off my glasses and rubbed my eyes. This was serious. This was even more serious than I had imagined. If Lucy had told Janice to fly through the air and hurt herself; and forced Laurence to run into a wall; then she could be using a hugely powerful form of Indian magic known as Enemy-Hurts-Himself, a form of supernatural judo, in which all of your opponents' hate and aggression is turned against him.

I could feel Misquamacus. I could feel his influence, like a huge dark sea-creature resting hundreds of feet below the surface of human consciousness. In his day, in the 1600s, he had been the most startling medicine-man of his age – the only medicine-man who had dared to make direct contact with the ancient gods of North America, the Great Old Ones. His magic had been legendary. He had changed the course of rivers, caused it to rain, and been seen by reliable witnesses on both sides of the American continent in the space of a few hours – at a time when it had taken months to cross from the eastern seaboard to the west.

I could almost *smell* him, he was so close. He had been there when Lucy was conceived, with his black, glittering headdress of living beetles, and his hard-hewn face, and his eyes that were filled with all the rage and malevolence of a man whose people had been systematically wiped out, and whose world of natural magic had been overwhelmed by money and guns and the principle of manifest destiny.

"Have you had your breakfast?" I asked Lucy.

She nodded. "Lucky Charms."

"Oh, sure. And I bet you ate all the mallow bits and left all the plain bits."

She laughed. She seemed perfectly normal now. But Misquamacus had always proved himself to be fiercely unpredictable, and there was no telling how or when he would choose to make his presence felt. I closed Lucy's door and went back to the living-room, where Karen was reading *Architectural Digest* and drinking espresso.

271

"I'm going to call Norman Vogel," I told her. "Maybe he could see Lucy this afternoon."

"Harry, you know that there's nothing wrong with her, not psychiatrically."

"Of course. But she's still going to need a clean bill of health from a psychiatrist before they'll let her back into school. And if I can take her today, she'll get one. She's calm, she's rested. She's going to be fine."

"And what if she goes back to school and the same thing happens again?"

"It won't. I'm going to find out if it *was* Misquamacus who made her behave like that; and if it was, I'm going to make sure that he leaves her alone. And leaves her alone permanent."

"-ly," added Karen. She was always correcting me.

I poured myself a cup of coffee, sat back on the sofa and picked up the phone. However, I had hardly finished dialing Dr Vogel's number when we heard a piercing screaming coming from Lucy's room. I banged down the phone, jumped up, and knocked espresso all over the lemon-yellow carpet. Together, Karen and I ran along the corridor and opened Lucy's door.

Lucy's dolls house was in flames. Its roof was alight and already the sides were burning. Lucy had her hand caught in one of the windows, and was screaming wildly as she tried to pull it out. Without a second's hesitation I pulled out the whole plastic window-frame and freed her, but all the same I burned the back of my hand. I said, "Here!" and handed her to Karen, while I went over to Lucy's bed, pulled off the quilt, and dropped it over the dolls house to smother the flames.

It was all over in seconds, but the bedroom was filled with smoke and Lucy was totally hysterical, screaming and coughing and kicking her legs. Karen carried her over

272

to the washbasin and we ran cold water over her fingers. They didn't look too badly burned, but I thought we ought to call the doctor to make sure they were bandaged properly, and to give Lucy something for shock. After we had kept her hands under running water for a while, she began to calm down, but she was deathly pale and she was shivering all over.

While Karen wrapped her up in a blanket and carried her into the living-room, I cautiously lifted the quilt off the dolls house to make sure that the fire was out. The plastic roof had been reduced to stringy, rancid loops, and the wooden sides were badly charred. Inside, Barbie had half melted. Her hair was nothing but a blackened brush and one side of her face was distorted. What made her look even more grotesque was the way she was still smiling at me, as if she had enjoyed her immolation.

I carried the dolls house out of the apartment and into the elevator. Mick the doorman opened the door to the back yard for me. He peered inside at Barbie's remains, and said, "That'll teach her for smoking in bed."

Dr Van Steen came around a half-hour later. He didn't usually make housecalls, but he had known the Tandys even before Karen was born, and he was a close family friend as well as a physician. He was white-haired, immaculately dressed in black and grey, with shining steel-rimmed spectacles and shining patent-leather shoes.

"Well, now," he said, sitting next to Lucy on the sofa. "I understand your dolls house burned down. How did that happen?"

Lucy said nothing, and turned away.

"There were no matches anyplace around," I said. "I can't understand how it happened."

"Let's take a look at those fingers," said Dr Van Steen, and took hold of Lucy's hands. "They're a little blistered, aren't they, but they'll heal up all right. Little girls of your age, they heal so quick they're usually better before I can get around to see them."

Lucy turned back and stared at him. "I wanted Barbie to die," she said, very clearly, and with great emphasis on the word '*die*'.

Dr Van Steen looked over at me with his eyebrows lifted. "That wasn't a very nice thing to do, was it? Why did you want her to die?"

"Because she's a yellow-hair."

"A yellow-hair? Don't you like yellow-hairs?"

"All yellow-hairs have to die. And all white faces." At that, she covered her face with her bandaged hands, so that only her eyes looked out.

"Just a little joke of hers," I put in. I didn't want Dr Van Steen to push her any further.

"Oh, I see," said Dr Van Steen. "Well . . . no accounting for humour, is there?"

After he was finished bandaging Lucy's fingers, however, I took him into the hallway and closed the living-room door behind us.

"Between you and me, doctor, Lucy's been acting real strange. She had a fight in the schoolyard today and hurt some of her classmates. The school won't let her back until she's undergone a psychiatric evaluation. Now this."

"Is there anything worrying her?"

"Not that I know of. What does a four-year-old have to worry about? Too many repeats of *Sesame Street*? The rising price of M&Ms?"

"You'll forgive my being personal, but are you and Karen getting along okay? There aren't any domestic upsets?"

"Well, Karen's been working pretty hard lately, and we've had one or two contretemps about that. But nothing else."

"She's not being teased or bullied at her nursery-school?"

"No . . . no indication of that."

Dr Van Steen said, "What's all this about yellow-hair? Do you know what that means?"

"Yellow-hair used to be the Native American name for a blonde. Like General Custer, for example."

"Why should a four-year-old Caucasian child say that all yellow-hairs must die?"

I shrugged, I had my own theory about that, but I wasn't going to tell Dr Van Steen. Before I stirred up any old and unwelcome influences, I wanted to make absolutely sure that Lucy wasn't simply suffering from some conventional psychiatric glitch.

"I'm taking her to see Dr Vogel," I said. "Maybe *he* can work out what's wrong."

"Let me know how things go," said Dr Van Steen. "And – oh – if you find out, let me know how Lucy could start a fire without matches."

He gave me an odd, knowing look, as if he suspected that I was holding something back. I was; but even if I had told him what it was, he wouldn't have believed me. I didn't want to believe it myself.

The following afternoon we took Lucy to Dr Vogel's clinic on Park Avenue. The city was covered in low, grey cloud, and it was raining. Lucy wore her red hooded raincoat and her little red rubbers, and carried her favourite doll with her, a grubby, floppy thing with the highly original name of Doll.

Inside Dr Vogel's office it was all dark oak paneling

275

and gloom. Dr Vogel looked more like a bear hunter than a psychiatrist. He was broad-shouldered, with a huge brown beard and bright blue eyes, and hands as big as snow-shovels. He wore a blue-checkered backwoods shirt and stonewashed jeans, and he laughed a lot. He had been recommended to me by Dr Hughes, the tumour specialist who had helped Karen during the days when Misquamacus had attempted his first reincarnation. Dr Hughes had lost part of his hand to the ancient demon that Misquamacus had summoned to help him, the Lizard-of-the-Trees, and it had taken him years of surgery and years of psychiatric counseling before he had recovered. Even so, he had lost all of his hair and all of his spirit; and I had never seen a man so broken.

"Well, then, little lady," said Dr Vogel. "It sounds like you've been having some pretty good fun at school."

Lucy clutched Doll, and swung her head from side to side.

"So . . . not so much fun, huh?" asked Dr Vogel.

"Muldrews and Cullens kill babies," she said.

"They kill *babies*? What babies?"

"All the babies at Sand Creek. All the babies at Washita River."

Dr Vogel looked at me in perplexity. "Sand Creek? Washita River?"

"Indian massacres," I told him. "Worse than Wounded Knee."

"Indian massacres? What the hell have you been teaching her, Harry? She's four."

"I never taught her that. They've been teaching her all about Native Americans at nursery school . . . but not about Sand Creek, for Christ's sake. Leastways, they'd better not."

276

"So how does she know about Sand Creek and Washita River?"

I shook my head. "I don't have any idea. I just want to know if she's sane."

Dr Vogel was silent for a moment. I liked him; I trusted him; but I didn't have any alternative. I had to lie to him because I wanted him to tell me that Lucy was suffering from juvenile depression or playschool psychosis or neurotic aversion to the alphabet.

I wanted him to tell me anything except that Lucy was possessed.

Karen and I sat in the waiting-room pretending to read last month's copies of *The New Yorker* and *Schizophrenic News* while Dr Vogel ran a series of tests on Lucy's intelligence, sensitivity, audio-visual responses, and what she thought an ink-blot in the shape of Cookie Monster looked like (Cookie Monster.) On the wall of the waiting-room was a brass plaque which read 'Anybody who goes to see a psychiatrist needs their head examined.'

Eventually we were called back in. Dr Vogel unwrapped a strawberry sucker and gave it to Lucy, and then sat back with his legs crossed, looking serious. "I have to tell you, Harry, I never came across anything like this before. Lucy appears to be highly intelligent, *highly* motivated, with perceptual and analytical skills that are way above her age group. She also has extraordinary gifts of intuition."

"But?" I asked him.

"But she persists in this aggressive delusion that her classmates were responsible for killing babies, and that they not only deserved the whupping she gave them, they actually deserve to die. And she's full of all this Native American mumbo-jumbo. For instance—" he frowned down at his notepad "—do you have any idea what a *mistai* is?"

"Sure. It's an Indian ghost. It frightens people by tugging at their blankets at night. It's kind of a messenger, too, and it whispers in people's ears and tells them what the spirits want them to do."

"Lucy said that the *mistai* told her to kill her classmates."

"I was afraid of that."

"She also said that the *mistai* told her to kill any yellow-hairs . . . though why she should have started by burning her Barbie doll, I really couldn't say."

"The Indians set great store by doll-figures," I said. "The Crow used to have a sun-dance doll made of beads and animal skin. If you danced with it, and stared it in the face, it would tell you where to find your enemy, so that you could kill him. To an Indian mystic, a doll-figure like Barbie wouldn't be a toy . . . it would represent everything that white people had done to destroy his culture and his religion."

"You're something of an expert, then?" said Dr Vogel.

"There was a time when I had to be."

"Meaning?"

"Meaning that Karen and I have had encounters with Native American mysticism a couple of times in the past."

"And you think that Lucy's present condition might have something to do with these encounters?"

Karen nodded. "Since you say that she's sane and intelligent, we can't think of anything else that could be making her behave this way."

"I see," said Dr Vogel, although he looked deeply troubled. "You don't think that Lucy's behaviour could have been affected by your talking about this Native American mysticism in front of her, or when you might have thought that she couldn't hear you?"

"We *never* talk about it," said Karen, emphatically.

"Well . . . I wouldn't mind running some more detailed tests," said Dr Vogel. "Maybe you could see how Lucy gets along and then bring her back in a couple of days."

"If you think it'll do any good."

"I don't know . . . do you have any better ideas?"

"Not really. Except that I'm going to try to find out what it is that's making Lucy behave this way, and once I know what it is, I might have a chance of getting rid of it."

"Well, be careful," Dr Vogel warned me. "Lucy's very impressionable. Whatever you do, you shouldn't give her the impression that you believe in any of this mysticism. You'll run the risk of reinforcing her delusion, and make it doubly difficult for me to readjust her."

I didn't say anything. I was used to scepticism. Before Misquamacus first reared his head, I used to be a card-carrying member of the National Society of Sceptics myself. I used to pay the rent by telling fortunes to rich old ladies, under the name of the Incredible Erskine, and you need to be a sceptic to make a living like that. If you really believed what the Tarot cards foretold, you'd go right out, put bricks in your pockets, and drown yourself in the East River. You really want to know when you're going to lose your loved ones, and how? You really want to know when you're going to die? Not for me, *gracias*. Since Karen had come into money, I had hung up my spangled cloak and put the Tarot out to grass, which was just as well, because I had seen things that still gave me nightmares, and I believed in 'Native American mumbo-jumbo' because it was just as real as I was.

"I'll give you a call," I told Dr Vogel, and stood up. "Thanks for taking a look at Lucy, anyhow."

"There's just one more thing I wanted to ask her," said Dr Vogel. "How did she manage to set her dolls house alight? You said there was no sign that she was playing with matches."

"I just burned it," said Lucy.

Dr Vogel leaned forward and gave her an encouraging smile. "Yes, honey, we know you burned it. But *how* did you burn it?"

Lucy blinked at him as if he were totally stupid.

"I burned it," she repeated. "Like this."

She looked over at his desk, and pointed her finger at it. There was a moment's pause, and then a wisp of smoke started to rise from the papers on the blotter. Then there was the softest of flaring noises, and every paper on the desk burst into flame.

Dr Vogel jumped up. "For God's sake! What the hell are you doing? Harry – there's a fire extinguisher in the waiting-room – quick!"

But flames were already leaping upward, and the desk's leather top was beginning to shrivel like human skin. Dr Vogel picked up a folder and tried to beat the flames down, but all he succeeded in doing was fanning them even higher, and sending showers of sparks all over the carpets and the furniture.

I managed to wrestle the fire-extinguisher free from its bracket on the waiting-room wall. I hurried back in and sprayed powder all over Dr Vogel's desk, and onto the seat of his leather chair, which was already starting to smolder.

Dr Vogel picked up a half-charred report. "What the hell have you done?" he bellowed at Lucy. "Do you know how long it took to – For God's sake, Harry! What the hell has she done?"

Karen put her hands protectively on Lucy's shoulders. "Dr Vogel – please don't shout. It was just an accident."

"Accident? That was no accident! She deliberately put out her finger and – and – look at this mess! This is going to take me days to sort out! Weeks!"

"Come on Michael, quiet down," I told him. "There's no way Lucy could have started it."

"Then what?" he shouted. "A cigarette? I don't smoke. A short-circuit? All I have is a battery-operated calculator. An Act of God? Or a Goddamned act of vandalism? Get her out of here, go on. I don't want to see her again. Think yourself lucky if I don't sue your for criminal damage."

I was trying to think of something to say that would calm Dr Vogel down when Lucy pointed her finger at his face. Again, there was a moment's pause; but then Dr Vogel suddenly clamped his hands to his face and let out a terrible shout. His beard had burst into flame, hundreds of pinpricks of orange fire, like a burning brush. His hair suddenly caught fire, too, and then his shirt-collar and his cuffs. He screamed and beat at his face, stumbling from side to side in agony, but in only a few seconds he was blazing from the shoulders upward.

I stripped off my leather jacket, bundled it over his head, and pushed him heavily to the floor, jarring my knee against the side of his desk. He writhed and struggled and kept on screaming, and I turned to Karen and said, "Get Lucy out of here, fast! And call an ambulance!"

Dr Vogel stopped screaming and began to whimper and shiver, I carefully lifted up my leather jacket, and the smoke that rose from underneath it smelled as if somebody had accidently barbecued a cat. Dr Vogel's face was unrecognizable – not just as Dr Vogel, but as a human being. His beard had burned down to fine black ash, his nose and his lips were swollen and raw, and as he breathed out, smoke poured out of his nostrils.

"Hurts," he mumbled, quaking as if he were cold.

"Hold on," I told him, I was shivering almost as much as he was. "The medics won't be long."

"Hurts, Harry," he repeated. "Hurts like all hell."

"Don't worry, Michael, they'll soon give you something for the pain."

He tried to open his eyes, but the skin around his eyelids had fused together, so that his eyes looked like two roughly-peeled plums.

"Did she really do this?" he asked me.

"You mean Lucy? I don't know. Maybe not Lucy, but whatever's taken control of her."

"I'm going to die," said Dr Vogel. "This hurts too much. I'm going to die."

He didn't say anything else. I stayed beside him until the paramedics arrived, and then I took one last look at him and left the office. Karen and Lucy were waiting for me in the reception area, talking to two police officers.

"You're this lady's husband?" asked one of them. "Can you tell us what exactly happened in there?"

"Dr Vogel caught fire," I told him. "I don't know how it happened. He just spontaneously combusted, right in front of us."

"Do you have any idea how that could have happened?" the policeman asked me.

I shook my head. But Lucy took hold of my hand, and looked up at the officers, and said, "He was a yellow-hair."

The officers grinned at each other. But if only they had understood the significance of what Lucy had told them, they wouldn't have been grinning. They would have been putting as much distance between themselves and Lucy as they possibly could.

*   *   *

"You realize how dangerous this could be?" said Karen, as I drew the drapes and blocked out the daylight.

"I can't think of any other way," I told her. "Who's going to believe that a four-year-old girl has been misbehaving at school because she's possessed by an Indian medicine-man? Who's going to believe that she can start fires just by pointing her finger?"

"Wouldn't Amelia help?" she asked me. Amelia was the spirit medium who had first contacted Misquamacus. She and I had later become lovers, on and off, and usually more off than on. I hadn't seen her in a long while and I couldn't ask her to risk her life again.

"It has to be me," I told her. "The whole reason this is happening is because of me. It's like an unwritten law. If an enemy defeats you, you can't just turn your back and go on to other things. You have to return to his lodge and seek to defeat him in return. There's no way that Misquamacus can regain his honour until he's had his revenge."

"Why didn't he try to possess you, or me, instead of Lucy?"

"Maybe he isn't strong enough. Remember that the last time we beat him, he literally *dispersed*, like electrical energy. And what Lucy can do – pushing her schoolmates around, starting spontaneous fires – that might be frightening, but it isn't exactly the stuff of great tribal magic, is it? In his heyday, this guy could literally move mountains."

Karen pressed her hand against her forehead as if she had an incipient migraine. "I'm so frightened," she said. "What if anything happens to Lucy? I couldn't bear it, Harry. I think I'd die."

"Karen," I said, "we have to. Otherwise, who knows how many people are going to be hurt?"

I had moved a circular card-table right into the middle of the living-room, and covered it with a maroon blanket. There was a small bronze Japanese nightlight in the centre of the table, and I lit it. Then I went around and switched off all the table-lamps. The nightlight cast flickering shadows of Japanese ideograms on the walls all around.

"Why don't you go get Lucy?" I asked Karen. "Tell her this is just a new game we're going to play. Kind of like hide-and-seek."

I sat down at the table. In front of me was a long bundle of old, uncured leather, tied with cords made of tightly-twisted hair. I hadn't opened this bundle since it was first given to me, over twenty years ago, by the son of Singing Rock. It had been intended as nothing more than a sentimental reminder of a man who had given everything in order to prevent the forces of the past from destroying the equilibrium of the future. Singing Rock had sympathized in many ways with Misquamacus, but he hadn't shared his thirst for revenge. Singing Rock had believed that what is past is past, and that all you can do is wipe away your tears so that you can look more clearly to the future.

I picked open the knots with my thumbnails and loosened the strings. Then I unrolled the bundle and revealed its contents: two human thigh-bones, decorated at each end with red and white beads and hanks of human hair, dyed blue. They had been taken from the body of White Bull, the medicine-man who had made a magical war-bonnet for the legendary chief Roman Nose. It was said that when they were beaten together, up and down, White Bull was running into the world of the spirits, and whoever was holding the bones would be carried into the world of the spirits behind him.

Karen came back into the room, holding Lucy's hand. It had been two days now since the burning incident in Dr Vogel's office, and Lucy was beginning to get over the shock. Although she had been used to channel the power that had started the fires, she was still a little girl, she was still my little sugar plum fairy, and afterward she had been just as distressed about what had happened as we were.

Karen and Lucy sat at the table.

"Why is it so dark in here?" asked Lucy, looking around.

"It's dark because we're going to play a game."

"What game?" she wanted to know. She peered at the two thighbones lying on the table in front of me. "Knick-knack-paddywhack-give-a-dog-a-bone?"

"Unh-hunh. We're yoing to play a game of imaginary friends."

"What's that?"

"That's when we call pretend people to come and play with us; and we see whether they really do."

"That's silly. There's no pretend people."

"What about Miss Ellie? She was pretend." Miss Ellie had been Lucy's invisible companion for over a year, and a goddamned nuisance she had been, too. She always had to have a place laid for her at the table, and we could never drive anywhere until Miss Ellie had buckled up.

"Miss Ellie's gone now," said Lucy. "She's gone away and she's never coming back."

"Well, let's see if we can find another pretend friend. If Miss Ellie's gone, how about finding Miss Quamacus?"

Lucy put her hand to her mouth and gave an affected titter. "*That's* a silly name!"

"All the same, let's give it a try. What we have to do is think very, very hard, and keep on saying, Miss

Quamacus, I want to see you. Miss Quamacus, I want to hear your voice, Miss Quamacus, I want to feel your hand. Do you think you can do that?"

Karen was staring at me in apprehension. I didn't say anything, but I gave her a look which meant that we had to go through it. There was no other choice.

"Right," I said. "We tap these bones together and we think very hard and then we start chanting. Miss Quamacus, I want to see you. Miss Quamacus, I want to hear your voice."

I held the thighbones, one in each hand, and began to tap them rhythmically together as if they belonged to a man who was walking across a prairie. Imagine the grass, Singing Rock had told me, as deep as your knees. Imagine the tiny white flowers. Then imagine the prairie growing darker and darker as evening falls, and the shadow of Aktunowihio falling across the land, Aktunowihio the spirit of the night. Imagine that the tiny white flowers have become stars, sparkling in the heavens, and that you are walking through the world of the spirits now, accompanied on all sides by *tasooms*, the souls of the dead who are rising into the sky like the smoke from the lodges in which they once lived."

I closed my eyes, I kept on knocking the bones together at a slow walking pace. The three of us kept on reciting the words that Singing Rock had taught me. "*Misquamacus, I want to see you. Misquamacus, I want to hear your voice. Misquamacus, I want to touch your hand.*

We went on like this for almost five minutes, and I began to think that it wasn't going to work. I might have White Bull's thighbones, and I might be reciting the right words, but I was a white man, out of touch with the spirits of the earth and the sky, the manitous of rocks and trees and running water. *Singing Rock*, I thought, *help me. I'm not getting anywhere here, I just can't do what you used to do.*

I was still crossing that grassy, flower-speckled prairie, to the clacking rhythm of White Bull's bones. But I distinctly felt a shiver in the grass, as if a cold wind had blown across it. In my mind's eye I felt a stormcloud moving in, as dark as slate, and the feeling that somebody was walking close beside me. I could hear the rustling of his feet, and the closeness of his breathing. It wasn't frightening. It was a good feeling: a feeling of companionship.

"*Misquamacus, I want to see you,*" I chanted, and this time I could hear another voice joining in; a deeper voice; a voice right inside of my head. "*Misquamacus I want to touch your hand.*"

In my mind's eye, I turned my head, and for one instant I saw Singing Rock walking close beside me, dressed in all the feathers and beads and finery of a fully-fledged wonder-worker. But the second I looked, he vanished; and when I turned back, I wasn't walking through the prairie grass any longer, I was walking knee-deep in stars – high in the sky, in the Hanging Road, where the spirits walked beside me.

I heard a sharp electrical crackling. I opened my eyes. Both Karen and Lucy had their eyes closed now, and they were still chanting, soft and monotonous, as if they were hypnotized. The shadows from the Japanese nightlight dipped and flickered like dancing ghosts. I heard the crackling again, louder this time, and I smelled the raw ozone aroma of a powerful electrical short-circuit. The area around Lucy began to ripple and distort, the way that heat ripples on a midsummer sidewalk.

Karen's eyes suddenly opened. She looked toward Lucy and saw what I could see, too. A huge, hunched shape, formed of shadows and refracted light, almost invisible to the naked eye, shifting and changing, but so intense in its presence that neither of us could mistake it for what it was.

It was a man, wearing an immense head-dress that appeared to have feathers and beads and even small skulls dangling from it. It was impossible to make out his face. It shifted and changed like the surface of a shallow pool. I was sure that I could see clouds reflected in it, and smoke, and fog that hung heavy over winter reservations.

The crackling of static grew louder, sparks jumped around Lucy's head in a crown of electrical thorns. Karen half stood up, and reached out toward her, but I shouted, "*No!* Don't touch her! He's all around her!"

The crackling was suddenly filled out with a heavy rushing noise, like a badly-tuned radio turned up to full volume. Through the noise, I could just hear somebody speaking – a slow, cold, emotionless voice – a voice that should have been silenced for ever more than three hundred years ago.

"*The spirits . . . will bring me justice . . . my weak white brother . . . the spirits . . . will reward me for what I have done . . . and will fill you with . . . all the arrows of sacrifice . . .*"

"Misquamacus," I said. I was trying to sound challenging, but my voice was wobbling all over the place. "What kind of a warrior are you, that you have to take the spirit of a four-year-old child; and a girl-child, at that? I thought you were brave! I thought you could work amazing wonders!"

"*You speak to me of bravery . . . you that used nothing but cunning and trickery? Now you shall know what cunning and trickery are.*"

"Leave my daughter alone," I told him. "I don't

care what you do to me. But you leave my daughter alone."

"*Don't you remember . . . your daughter was mine? I possessed your woman when she was conceived. This child is heiress to my heritage, not yours. She is my way back . . . into your world . . . and when I am returned . . . she will be my princess, and a worker of wonders, too . . . and her name will be Nepauz-had, which means Moon Goddess.*"

"You won't have her!" Karen screamed at him. "She's our daughter, not yours! You couldn't have me and you're not having her, either!"

The shifting shape turned toward her, with a harsh spitting of static. I could *almost* make out Misquamacus' flint-like profile. I could *almost* see the folds of his deerskin robes. But then the vision melted and changed again, and all I could see were thin red flickers of electricity, like graveworms crawling over a body that had already been devoured.

"*Remember that fate chose you to be my vessel,*" Misquamacus told Karen. "*When I was nothing but the smallest spark of life, carried over three thousand moons to find justice for my people, you were waiting for me. When I lost all physical existence, you and this man created a new way for me to walk once again in the world of men. I was reborn in your daughter; and now that I am strong enough, I shall take human shape, and finish the task that the gods appointed me to do.*"

"Bullshit," I told him. "If you so much as pluck one hair out of my daughter's head, I'll take your medicine bundle and shove it so far up your ass you won't be able to sit down until the drying-grass moon."

"*You were always a man of no respect,*" said Misquamacus. "*But now is your chance to be the greatest living wonder worker. I will leave this child alone if you allow me to*

289

take your substance . . . if you surrender your flesh and your blood and your bones so that I may once again live not only as a spirit but as a man."

"What the hell are you talking about?" I snarled at him; although I had mostly got the picture already. He had used Lucy's spirit as a way of returning to the material world, but now he needed real sinew and real muscle. In other word, I may have been thinning on top and seriously unfit, but he needed *me.*

As Misquamacus spoke, Lucy's eyes glowed an eerie phosphorescent blue, and her skin turned as white as plaster. I felt like snatching her away, but I knew enough about Misquamacus to realize how dangerous that could be. He was only able to make himself visible by externalizing some of Lucy's spirit, and to try to tear her away could easily kill her.

"We must go to the sacred place where I was born; and on that spot I must invoke the spirit of Ka-tua-la-hu. You will become nothing more than a spirit, a tasoom, *as I am now, while I will regain the form in which I was in the great and magical days before the white devils came."*

"You're going to *kill* him?" asked Karen, desperately.

"I am going to send his spirit on a journey to the Hanging Road."

"You can't do that!" Karen insisted.

"Then I will have to take the child; and bring her up as Nepauz-had; and teach her the ways of magic, until she has the power to release me."

When he said that, Lucy's eyes blazed like two blowtorches, and she stretched open her mouth in a terrible grimace. Misquamacus was showing us that he could do anything he wanted with her.

I'm not a brave person, never was. I dodged the draft and I would always rather conciliate than start slugging.

But I knew then that I had to do something brave. If the price of Lucy's survival was for me to take an early journey along the Hanging Road; then that was the price that I would have to pay. I was her father, it was my responsibility.

I took hold of Karen's hand and I felt calmer than I ever had before. "Okay, then," I said. "Where's this sacred place of yours?"

"*You will have to search for it in your maps and writings. Its name was Natukko, and it was here on this island.*"

"But supposing I can't find it?"

"*You will have to find it; and you will have to be there tomorrow, when the moon rises. Otherwise, I will take Nepauz-had and you will never see her again.*"

Karen's cheeks were stained with tears. "That's impossible!" she shouted. "That's impossible!"

But there was a deep, sucking sound like an ocean breaker sliding back over a pebbled shore; and then the tiniest sparkle of static, and Misquamacus had vanished. The air in the room was cold that our breath smoked.

Karen and I looked at each other; and then at Lucy. At that moment, Lucy's eyes rolled up into her head and she collapsed onto the floor like a broken doll.

I spent a bad night, and I was already standing on the steps of the New York Public Library when it opened at ten. I hurried directly to the Main Reading Room, and logged myself onto a computer. I needn't have rushed. By mid-afternoon I was still frowning and tapping away at the keyboard, while the fall sun moved around the room and lit up one section of grandiose paneling after another.

I was almost ready to give up when I located a book entitled *Native Locations* by Professor Harvey Fischer, from the Bentley College in Waltham, Massachusetts. It was an extensive list of Native American place names in New York and New England, what they meant, and where they used to be. I surreptitiously ate torn-off pieces of a KFC chicken burger which I had smuggled into the library in my pocket, and searched with finger-lickin' greasy keypads for *Natukko*.

I found Pontanipo (meaning 'cold water'); and Cowissewaschook ('proud peak'); as well as Ammanoosuc ('small fishing river'); and Uncanoonucks ('hills that look like a woman's breasts'). At last I located Natukko. It meant 'clearing' or 'cleared ground'. A few more punches on the keyboard, and I found its exact location, from a map of Manhattan Island dating from 1624, when it was owned by the Dutch West India Company. The map was signed 'Pieter van Huiven fecit'. I superimposed a modern streetmap of Manhattan on top of the old map, and apart from some minor distortions along the coastline, they matched surprisingly closely. There was only one problem that I could see. The clearing called Natukko was positioned on the Conrail tracks just where they came out of the tunnels at 96th Street.

I sat back and stared at the screen in total despondency. When would the gods *ever* give me an even break? Here I was, trying to make the ultimate sacrifice to save Lucy's life, and they couldn't even give me a nice piece of lawn to be sacrificed on. I had to make my grand gesture on a goddamned railroad track.

I was still sitting there with my chin in my hands when a pretty girl student came up to me. Her hair was long and braided, and she wore a navy-blue duffel coat.

"Are you through with that terminal yet?" she asked me. "I have some really important work to do."

"Oh, sure. Sorry."

"There's one thing you ought to remember about computers," she said, putting down her bag of books.

"What's that?"

She smiled. "Don't tell me you've forgotten."

"I'm sorry. I seem to be out of the loop here. Don't you tell I've forgotten *what*?"

"The one thing you ought to remember about computers."

I stood up, and brushed chicken burger crumbs from the chair. We seemed to be having one of those conversations that goes around and around in circles until it disappears up its own medicine-case holder.

The girl said, "Computers are *your* friends." She emphasized '*your*' as if to imply that they weren't *her* friends.

I still didn't understand it. I shrugged and said, "Well . . . sure, it's all technology these days. Even reading a book." But as I turned to leave she sat down, and lifted her left arm so that the sleeve of her duffel coat dropped back a little way. Around her wrist was a bracelet of bones and beads, entwined with hair. An Alqonquin charm bracelet.

She had already started to work, so I didn't disturb her. Besides, I now had some inkling of what she had been trying to tell me. Computers are *your* friends. Meaning you, as a white man; because she was obviously Native American. As my old friend Singing Rock told me, everything in the natural world has its own spirit, its manitou, from the humblest stone by the side of the road to the greatest redwood in the north-western forests. In the great days before the white invasion of North America, Indian wonder-workers were able to summon almost every spirit, living, inanimate or dead, and use it to make their own magic. Water, fire, wind and earth,

293

they all had tumultuous natural power – and this power could be harnessed to strange and devastating effect.

But the white men had brought their own brand of magic with them; and what Singing Rock had taught me was that every object made by whites had a spirit, too: a manitou of its own. A clock has a manitou, a typewriter has a manitou. And computers have manitous too. We had used a computer to beat Misquamacus when he had first appeared – not its calculating-power, but its *spirit*, the essential meaning of what it was, and the creativity of the men who had made it.

In his oblique way, Singing Rock had found a way of reminding me that I was a white man living in a white man's world, and that I was surrounded by influences and artefacts that could help me.

I arrived back home a little after five. Karen was looking drawn and worried, but Lucy was playing quite contentedly in her bedroom.

"Well?" said Karen.

"Well, I've found out where we're supposed to go."

"You have?" She touched my sleeve. It was obvious that she didn't know whether to sound pleased or sad.

"I checked it with an old map. It couldn't be more convenient, believe me. Right on the Conrail tracks at East 96th."

"You're not serious?"

"Unless some seventeenth-century Dutch mapmaker called Pieter van Huiven didn't know his ass from his astrolabe, that's exactly where Natukko was located. Didn't I always say that Misquamacus was born on the wrong side of the tracks?"

"Harry, do you have to make a joke of it?"

"Goddamn it, Karen, I'm as scared as you are. Scareder. But I think there's a chance."

"What do you mean?"

I told her about the girl in the library; and the feeling that she had given me that she was passing on a message from Singing Rock.

"So what do you have to do?" Karen wanted to know.

"I have to use my head, that's what I have to do. I have to remember who I am, and who my people are; the same way that Misquamacus is always aware of what he is. I have to have a sense of *tribe*. I have to have a sense of *belonging*, Karen, that's all. It's something that most of us white people have long forgotten."

I went into the small, cluttered room that I liked to call my study. There was some pretty nostalgic stuff in there, from the days when I was still the Incredible Erskine, Fortunes Foretold, Futures Fixed, Destinies Dealt Out. Astrological charts, Tarot cards, mah-jongg tiles. A crystal ball that I had bought from an exquisitely beautiful hippie girl in the Cafe Reggio, in the Village, longer ago than I cared to recall (and was she so beautiful now?) On the top shelf of the bookcase, however, were more than a dozen well-thumbed books on Native American magic and mythology. I took down *Spirit Transference And Soul Stealing* by Louis Sola. It was book I had turned to more than once. The last time I had put it back on the shelf, I had hoped that I would never have to turn to it, ever again.

I sat down and started to read through it. Karen brought me a cup of coffee and stood beside me for a while, her hand on my shoulder.

"How long before the moon comes up?" she asked me.

I checked my watch. "Two-and-a-half hours."

"What are you looking for?"

"I'm not sure. Anything that could give me an edge."

"Harry . . . are you sure this is the right way? Misquamacus can't be all that strong. Maybe you should try talking to Amelia . . . anybody. Maybe Lucy could be exorcized."

"Believe me, Karen, he's serious. If I don't do what he tells me, he'll take her away. You couldn't bear that, any more than me."

I reached up and squeezed her hand. "Listen," I said, "thanks for the coffee; thanks for all of your caring. I love you. But right now I have to find some way of beating this son-of-a-bitch."

She left me in peace, God bless her, and I went back to *Spirit Transference And Soul Stealing*. There were pages of dry discussion about the realities of Indian magic, and whether it was really possible for a spirit to return to the material world by possessing a live human being. 'After a death that has been brought about by the breaking of a tribal taboo it may often be so weakened that it is unable to make its journey to the Happy Hunting Ground. This happened to the Cheyenne warrior Roman Nose at Beecher's Island in Colorado in 1868, after he had unwittingly eaten food with a metal fork.'

Aha. This sounded like it. The last time we had managed to dismiss Misquamacus we had literally grounded his spirit like a lightning strike, using two metal forks. He had escaped, but his spirit had been discharged into the sky. I thought then that his life-force had been dispersed for ever. It just goes to show you, doesn't it, that even a genius can make mistakes.

I read more about poor old Roman Nose. 'For years afterward, his voice was heard in the dead of the night begging for his spirit to be made whole again. It wasn't until 1924 that the wonder-worker George Eagle Claw was able to give Roman Nose the peace that he so desperately wanted, in a very obscure Cheyenne ceremony known as *spirit-jumping*.

'In the ceremony of *spirit-jumping* a wonder-worker will invoke the spirit of the moon, which is the mistress of time. He can alter time so that his spirit can jump out of his body for a few brief minutes and into an animal such as buffalo or an elk or even an inanimate object such as a tree or a rock. This leaves his body empty of spirit – thus allowing the weakened spirit to occupy it, and to bring back together all of its different aspects – its voice, its memory, its sense of duty, its wisdom and its pride.

'In the wonder-worker's body, the newly-restored spirit atones for breaking a taboo by making offerings to the Great One. He makes offerings of sacred objects and he sings a song of remorse. He is then allowed to leave the wonder-worker's body and make his journey to eternal peace.

'After the spirit has left, the wonder-worker leaves his temporary host and returns to his own body.

'However, if the weakened spirit is *himself* a wonder-worker, he may find his own way back into the material world by occupying the body of an animal or someone who is much weaker than himself, such as a newborn infant. This accounts for several interesting cases over the past century of very young children speaking in strange languages and exhibiting uncharacteristic behaviour patterns, such as sudden bouts of violence.

'In May, 1915, Nathan Toomey, a five-year-old from Casper, Wyoming, killed his six-year-old playmate with a heavy stone. When restrained, he began to shout in a

297

language that the local doctor recognized as Kiowa. He transcribed it, and translated it, and it turned out that the boy (or whoever was possessing the boy) was promising to return to the world of men and seek his revenge on those who had murdered him.

'He appeared to be possessed by the notorious Kiowa wonder-worker Black Crow, the chief magical adviser to the rebellious chief Satanta. Black Crow had been captured by the military and imprisoned in Texas. The military reported that he had committed suicide by leaping out of his cell window.

'Once such spirits have possessed a human or an animal shape, they will attempt to increase their strength by 'jumping' to the body of an older and stronger person, until, in essence, they are 'real' again. They can only achieve this, however, by using the influence of the moon to force somebody's spirit out of their body, leaving it free for occupation. There are only two known cases of this happening, although there are rumours of many more. In each case, it was claimed that the invading spirit forced the spirit of his victim to 'jump' into an inanimate object – in one case, a large rock; in another, a tree.

'Some Native Americans say that this accounts for so-called 'haunted trees' and for poltergeist phenomena, such as chairs that move by themselves or gates that will never stay shut.'

I read the passage on spirit-jumping a second time and then closed the book. It looked as if Misquamacus was going to evict my spirit out of my body and set up home there himself. And what would happen to me? I'd wind up as fence-post or a block of concrete, imprisoned for ever, with no hope of remission for good behaviour. It sounded ludicrous, but I had seen enough of Misquamacus' magic to know that there was nothing amusing about it, and

298

that he was capable of turning the most ordinary day in your life into a nightmare from which you would never wake up.

At 96th Street, the tunnels underneath Park Avenue come to an end, and – as the ground-level falls away, the trains continue on elevated tracks all the way to the Bronx. When I was a snotty-nosed kid with holes in the seats of his jeans, my friends and I used to climb up onto the tracks and walk along them. We had a fantasy about making our way through the tunnels as far as Grand Central Station, fifty-four blocks underground, so that we could exit by way of the platforms.

We tried twice, but we never managed to get any further than two or three hundred feet before we lost our nerve and made our way back again. The first time we were almost turned into puree of boy by a northbound commuter train and the second time we were caught by a railroad linesman, and we had to run for our lives, panting in panic as he came lumbering after us with a ten-pound hammer.

We climbed out of the cab and crossed Park Avenue, each of us holding Lucy's hand. The traffic booped and echoed all around us. Karen said, "I hope you know what you're doing, Harry. I really do."

I suppose I should have said "trust me", but I didn't even trust myself. I just gave her my famous seasick grin, and said, "So do I."

I found the place where – all of those years ago – I used to climb onto the tracks. There was still a narrow gap in the fencing. I checked my watch. There were only six or seven minutes to go before the moon came up. I knelt down beside Lucy and said, "Listen, sugar plum fairy, we have to climb through this gap and over this wall onto the railroad. I know it's going to be frightening, but we have to do it."

She looked back at me with those big dark eyes and I thought for a moment she was going to say that she was too frightened, that she wouldn't do it. But then she gave me a wide, eerie smile, and nodded; and I knew then that even if I failed, and Misquamacus took my body, I couldn't let him take Lucy. She said something, but just then a train went rattling and clashing past, and I couldn't hear what it was. Only the last two words, " – *white face.*"

I checked around to see if there were any police in sight. Then I pushed myself through the gap, and started to climb over the barrier. It was filthy – thickly coated in soot and grime. But once I was at the top I reached down for Lucy's hand and said, "Come on up, sweetheart, I've got you."

Lucy looked up at me, and she still had that creepy smile on her face. Somewhere inside of her, Misquamacus must have been relishing this moment – the night when he regained an earthly body, and the night when he finally revenged himself on Karen and me. Another train clattered past, and I ducked my head and kept myself low against the barrier, in case anybody was looking in my direction. The lighted windows passed me by like all the days in my life, one after the other, and then they were gone.

I helped Lucy to climb up, and then Karen followed her, her trainers scuffling against the rusted steel. Then we dropped down onto the aggregate, and brushed ourselves down. Karen was shivering and her white cable-knit sweater was smudged with dirt. "Where to now?" she asked me.

Lucy took hold of my hand. "I know the way," she said. She stepped over the tracks and began to walk toward the tunnel, hopping from one greasy sleeper to the next.

"Lucy, get off the track!" I shouted at her. But all she did was turn and laugh, and start to run. I went running after her, and caught hold of her hand.

"Get off the track, Lucy. There'll be trains coming."

Lucy kept on smiling at me. "We're almost here," she said; and suddenly her voice became overlaid with the harsh, echoing tones of Misquamacus. "This is my birthplace, Nakkro, where I first saw light of day."

I thought I heard a train approaching, and I quickly looked around, but all I could see was the blackness of the tunnel.

"Come on," said Lucy, and carried on walking toward the tunnel. As we entered it, I could hear the late rush hour bustling and beeping of traffic, and the faraway wailing of sirens. Normal, everyday noises. I kept hearing clattering sounds behind me, and glancing around, but they say that railroad workers never hear the train that hits them.

Only a few feet into the tunnel entrance Lucy stopped, and pointed to the ground. "*It's here,*" she announced triumphantly. "*This is the sacred place where I was born.*" She looked up to the sky. According to my watch, the moon must have risen, although it was impossible to see it behind all the buildings. "*This is the place, and the time has come.*"

Together, Lucy and I stood between the tracks, facing each other.

"What do we do now?" I asked her.

She closed her eyes for a moment. When she opened them they were glowing incandescent blue. Her shadow appeared to rise from the railroad tracks, like somebody climbing out of bed, and stand up right behind her, a dark and threatening outline of somebody tall, unnaturally tall, with a head-dress of skulls and tails.

Lucy clapped her hands. *"Let the spirit of the moon descend to help me! Let the moment be moved, let the night hold its breath! Spirit of the* winds, *blow away this man's spirit out of his body and find a lodge for it in this woman's body, along with hers, so they might live together for the rest of their days.'*

"What?" I demanded. "What the hell are you trying to do? You can't lodge my spirit in Karen's body!"

"Would you rather be a cockroach, or a piece of wood? I am giving you what you always wanted. A closeness that other lovers can only dream of!"

"Two spirits in one body? We'll go insane in five minutes flat!"

"It is my final act of mercy."

"You don't have a merciful bone in your body. You're going to take your revenge on all of us, that's all. On me and Karen, by wrapping both of us up in the same body, and on Lucy, too, because Lucy won't have a mommy and a daddy. Lucy will have nothing less than some screaming lunatic who has to be locked up."

Lucy closed her glowing blue eyes, as if to indicate that she wasn't going to discuss it any more.

"Spirit of moon, I worship you and serve you. Hold back the night for me, for the space of five long heartbeats. Spirit of wind, blow this man's *spirit out of his body, leave him empty. Find him a home in the woman's body, two spirits in one earthly lodge."*

Behind us, the night began to darken, and the wind began to rise. Scraps of newspaper and gum wrappers blew around the tracks, along with a fine stinging grit. I had to shield my eyes with my upraised arm. Above the blustering of the wind, Lucy was starting to scream – a harsh, high-pitched scream that was filled with unbridled fury.

"Spirit of wind, blow this man's spirit out of his body! Leave him empty! Spirit of moon! Command the night to hold its breath!"

At first, I didn't think that anything was going to happen. After all, Misquamacus was a seriously weakened spirit, and his only physical presence was that of a four-year-old girl. But then suddenly everything grew darker still. It was that darkness that closes in on you when you're just about to faint – except that I didn't faint. I was aware of everything that was going on.

Lucy's voice grew slow and slurred. *"Spppirrriittt offff wiiiinnnndddd."* Soon it grew so slow that I couldn't even understand it, and then it stopped In fact, everything stopped. There was total silence, and nobody moved. Newspapers that had been blown into mid-air over the railroad tracks remained where they were, in mid-air.

Misquamacus had done it. For me, at least, he had temporarily arrested time.

It was then that two things happened almost at once. I began to feel a *tugging* sensation inside of my head, almost as if somebody were trying to pull out my brain by the roots. I began to feel everything that I ever was being dragged out of me. My boyhood, my school days, my first pet dog. My mother, my father, my Uncle Jim, looning and laughing on my fifteenth birthday. Bicycle rides – baseball games – girls in starched petticoats and girls in pink-checkered swimsuits – trips to Coney Island and Brighton Beach – sunshine, cotton candy, electric storms – they were all being drawn out of me like brightly-coloured picture-cards being sucked into a Hoover. My soul was going; my spirit was going. Dear God, I was dying.

But the other thing was: a train was approaching, its lights reflecting from the tracks. It was momentarily frozen in time, but in the next few seconds, when Misquamacus had taken over my body, it would come out of the tunnel and bear down on Lucy and *that* was going to be the bastard's real revenge, to wrap us together in the same body, and to kill our daughter, too.

At that moment, with my spirit being forcibly wrenched out of my body, I could have tried anything, with no guarantee of whether it would work. I could have run to Lucy and pushed her off the railroad tracks, but then I would have been saving Misquamacus, too. I could have accepted my fate, and let Misquamacus transfer my spirit into Karen's body, and faced a life of complete madness.

Or – I could have remembered what Singing Rock had been trying to tell me – through the dark-haired girl in the library. Computers are your friends. Computers are *your* friends.

My spirit was being twisted out of my body like the guts out of a cod. It was like dying, only it was worse than dying, because I knew that I was still alive. I rose up, floating, and I could see my body standing on the railroad tracks. I could see Lucy, with her arms outstretched, her eyes ablaze, and the dark shadow of Misquamacus hovering over her.

I had left my own body now. It was the weirdest experience of my whole life. I was conscious, I was wide awake, and yet I had been pulled right out of myself, so that I was weightless, floating, with no substance at all.

I felt a wind catching me; like a kite being tugged, I spun, and turned, and I knew that Misquamacus had directed the wind manitou to take me to Karen. I could see her, motionless, her back against the wall, frozen in time like the whole of Park Avenue was frozen in time. I was blown nearer and nearer, and I tried to twist and spin myself away. If I ever entered Karen's body, she and I would both go mad, and die the kind of death that even schizophrenics couldn't understand.

Computers are your friends.

I twisted around just once more, and there was the train, pausing in time. A Metro North commuter service, on its way out to Westchester. A train with computers. A train with a soul. A train with its very own manitou, its white manitou, composed of every design that has ever been drawn for it, and every inch of engineering that had ever gone into it. A modest but direct descendant of the trains that had howled their way across the Great Plains, and had helped to bring abut the final downfall of the Native American Indian.

And I prayed to that train. I *prayed* to it. "*Help me, take me, I want to be part of you, rather than anything else. I want to meld in your metal and sparkle in your kilobytes. You have a spirit; you have a manitou. Help me.*"

But the wind was blowing more fiercely now, and I felt myself being buffeted across the tracks to the place where Karen was standing. She was still motionless, and her face was rigid with fright. I didn't know how long Misquamacus had managed to hold back the night, but there couldn't be very much time left, only seconds. If I didn't find a host by then, my spirit would probably scatter and disperse, the same way that Misquamacus' spirit had scattered and dispersed.

I felt myself tilting. Karen was even closer. I tried to twist myself around, and all the time I prayed to that train, I *prayed* to that train, take me, you son-of-a-bitch, a train is stronger than wind and stronger than water and stronger than all of the wonder-workers ever assembled together, from Ute to Iroquois, so give me a break, will you, and *take me.*

Karen suddenly turned and looked up at me. I didn't know whether she could see me or not, but her mouth was open and she looked surprised. At the same moment the train started rolling towards us, and the traffic started honking and the sky started moving, and everything was back to normal. Except that I was jolted away from Karen and found myself plunging into aluminium and plastics. I was literally yanked into that train's conscious mind; and instead of finding myself shoulder-to-shoulder with Karen, two spirits jostling each other in the same body till death do us part, I found myself

Cool and clean and calculating; full of switching information and speed limits and braking distances. I was the train and the train was me, and we were rocking and swaying along the track past 97th Street, and there was *Jesus!* a child on the track, and a man, too; and it was Lucy and it was me.

I saw Karen run across the track, snatch up Lucy in her arms, and tumble sideways in the aggregate. I saw my own body, standing in front of the train, which was me. Behind me, I saw the blackest of boiling shadows, which was Misquamacus. *His arms were uplifted, and his face was boiling with serpents. This was what he was, the servant of the Great Old Ones, no longer a tribal wonder-worker but a way through which the ancient and evil spirits of America could find their way back to reality; and destroy us all.*

He began to billow toward my abandoned body, like a black silk cover thrown over a bed. But I thought to myself: I'd rather kill him than let him do that. And because I had the mind of a train and the weight of a train, I short-circuited the speed controls and the train began to pick up speed, pick up speed,

306

until it was clattering toward my teetering body at 65 mph.

The black shadow of Misquamacus' spirit funneled itself into my body like smoke down a drain. I staggered once, and then turned toward the accelerating train.

But it was too late. Inside the train's computers, my spirit was running like liquid fire through every speed control, through every braking check, and there was nothing on earth that could have stopped that mother from hitting me directly in the chest, so that I went spinning and cartwheeling off the track, with blood spraying like a pinwheel, until I came to rest on the opposite side of the tracks.

I closed my (metaphorical) eyes and shut the train down. Its brakes squealed and howled like a herd of protesting pigs, and showers of orange sparks cascaded from its wheels. Even as it slid past my crumpled body, however, I felt something change. A victory won; a burden lifted. From out of my body, a shadow now, a shadow as dark and as vengeful as anything you could ever imagine. Inside the train's computer, I could only perceive it through the black and white video system, but this is what I saw:

A creature that was half-man and half-reptile. A man who had bargained so often with the gods that they had recreated him, in their own image.

The image rose out of my body and stood for a long time looking down at me. Then, quite nonchalantly, it took hold of the left rail and the right rail, and clutched them both.

"*Weejoo-suk,*" it whispered in Alqonquian. The wind is blowing. There was a sharp scurrying burst of paper and grit, and then the black shadow was lifted away, flying out of the tunnel entrance and high over the streets of Manhattan like a bat or a bird or a memory of times

307

that can never be redeemed. Way up in the sky, it caught the light of the rising moon, and the spirit of the moon was not in a forgiving mood. Misquamacus had promised her an offering, a sacrifice, and now he could offer her nothing but his own shadow.

The shadow flared like a loose-woven shawl that has trailed accidentally in the fire; and blazed for a moment; and fell from the sky as a shower of light grey ashes. They sifted across the railroad tracks, and you would have been forgiven for thinking that snow was early this year.

I opened my eyes. Karen was standing next to me, and Lucy, too. Blue and red lights were flashing. A paramedic was kneeling next to me, fixing an intravenous drip. I looked down and saw that my left leg was sticking out at right-angles. I felt totally unreal. I didn't know whether I was a man or a train. But I could see the train twenty feet away, standing stationary, with six or seven cops and railroad personnel standing around it.

"You're going to be fine," the paramedic told me. "Broken leg, fractured wrist, possible ruptured spleen, multiple bruising. Otherwise you're great for somebody who got hit by a train."

Lucy bent over and gave me a wet kiss. I looked up into those big dark eyes of hers and I'm sure that she understood something about what had happened; although I shall never know what.

"I love you, daddy," she said, and this time she meant it.

"I love you too, sugar plum fairy."

Karen bent over me and kissed me, too. "What happened?" she whispered. "What did you *do*?"

"I didn't let the wind take me where it wanted to, that's all. The train was stronger than the wind."

"You mean— ?"

"For those few seconds, *I* was part of the train. The thinking part. Misquamacus should have known better than to mess with modern technology."

Karen turned away for a moment. I didn't mind. She had a beautiful profile. But then she turned back and said, "Will he *ever* leave us alone?" And there were tears in her eyes.

Lucy was holding a police officer's hand. She was swinging one leg and chanting. "*Weksit-paktesk, weksit-paktesk, nayew neechnw, weksit-paktesk.*"

I squeezed Karen's hand. I simply didn't know what to say.